Dane Thorburn
and the
CITY OF LOST SOULS

By Matt Galanos

Publisher:
ASPG (Australian Self Publishing Group)
P.O. Box 159, Calwell, ACT Australia 2905
Email: publishaspg@gmail.com
http://www.inspiringpublishers.com

National Library of Australia Cataloguing-in-Publication entry

Author: Galanos, Matt

Title: **Dane Thorburn and the City of Lost Souls/***Matt Galanos*

978-1-922618-07-8 Matt Galinos (Print)
978-1-922618-08-5 Matt Galinos (eBook)
978-1-922618-09-2 Matt Galinos (Hardcover)

*For Caroline, Melissa
and Michael*

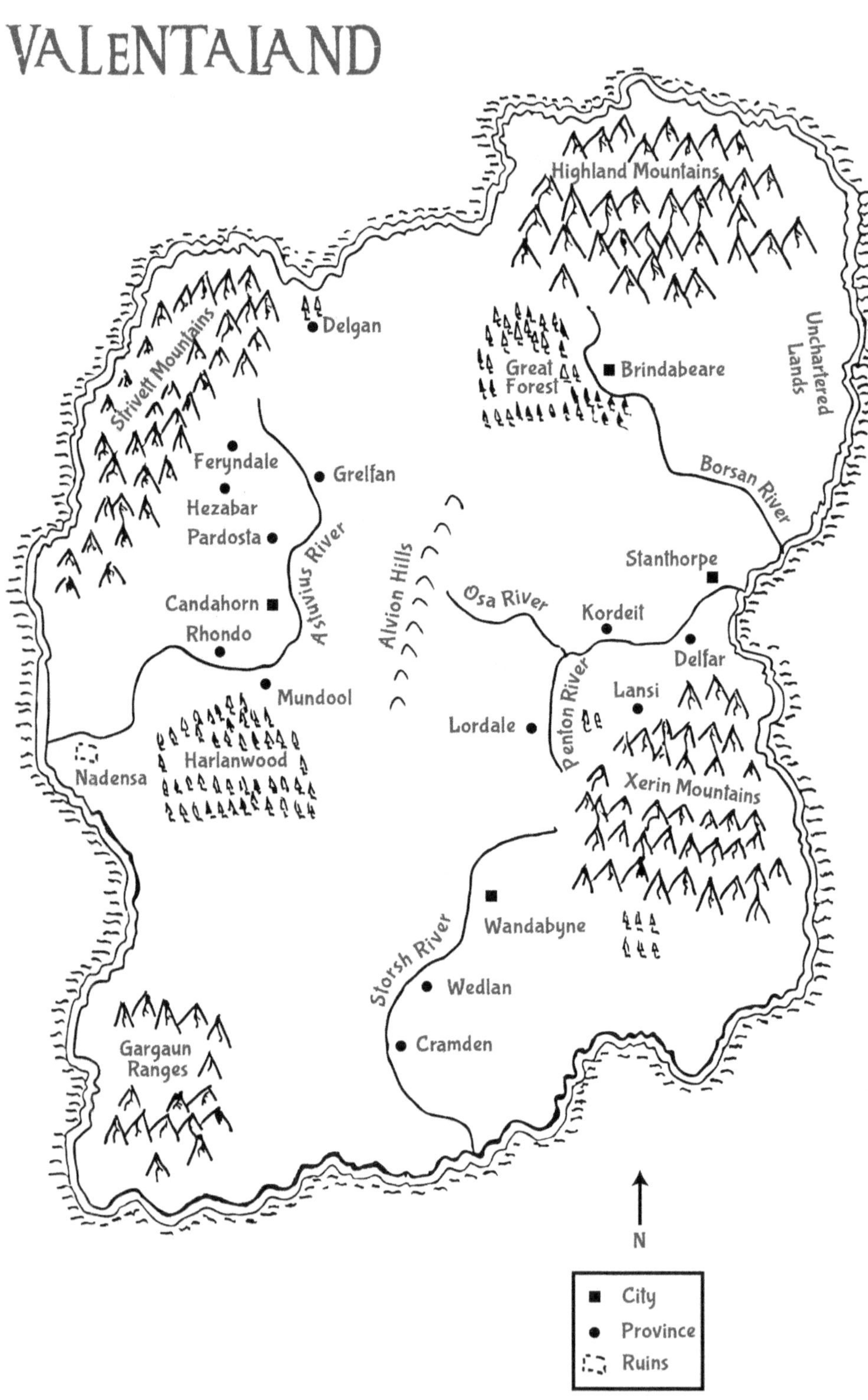

VALENTALAND
Highland Mountains
Uncharted Lands
Strivett Mountains
Delgan
Great Forest
Brindabeare
Feryndale
Grelfan
Hezabar
Pardosta
Borsan River
Candahorn
Alvion Hills
Osa River
Stanthorpe
Rhondo
Kordeit
Astuvius River
Delfar
Mundool
Lansi
Penton River
Lordale
Nadensa
Harlanwood
Xerin Mountains
Storsh River
Wandabyne
Gargaun
Ranges
Wedlan
Cramden
N
City
Province
Ruins

Chapter 1
TARGETED

With the afternoon sun for company, it had been a long, arduous ride. Relief washed over them when the clearing emerged ahead. Sweat gleaned on their faces; armour clung tight against their skin; limbs aching from their time in the saddle. Circling the perimeter, careful to leave no sign of their presence, they turned away, venturing west, before stopping among a cluster of trees.

Dismounting, they stepped away from the horses. Stretching their arms and turning slowly on the spot, the power entered their bodies. Sourced by their Lord from deep within the Fire Element, their muscles tingled as the warmth flowed into them, increasing their strength as it did so. At the same time, their appearance changed – all their armour turned to black; their faces now hidden under black war paint.

Adjusting to their new identities, all smiled inwardly at what they had become.

'And now,' said the leader, 'we wait.'

Swaying with the rhythm of the carriage, Princess Vanessa stifled a yawn.

'It's as though we're not getting anywhere,' she said.

Her companion nodded.

'I know. But there's nothing we can do about it.'

A tapping on the carriage window snapped the ladies out of their boredom.

'Everything comfortable in there?' asked one of the entourage, leaning as close to the carriage as he dared.

Vanessa smiled, moving close to the window, craning her neck to reach the small opening at the top.

'We're fine,' she replied. 'What's happening out there?'

Maintaining his position near the carriage, Royal Knight Dane Thorburn released the creature he'd been holding. With the exception of the scar under his chin, Dane looked like his father, the former Commander-in-Chief of the Brindabeare Army, in every way at eighteen years of age – standing over six feet tall, a lean yet strong build, short brown hair, and dark brown eyes that gave nothing away as they absorbed everything around them.

'We're making good time,' he said. 'I've sent Blaze to hunt. I'll be leaving to scout night camp shortly.'

Dane and his friend, Will Hevenshire, had been appointed Royal Knights some six months ago. Both had excelled during cadet training and played key roles in uncovering a plot by Firelord wizard Raegan and his Black Knights to invade Brindabeare and seize power.

With a choice of postings once they completed their extra training, both nominated to be part of Vanessa's personal entourage, which was why Dane found himself here at this very moment.

As the future ruler of Valentaland, Vanessa, now nineteen, was representing the King at official events throughout the land. They were making their way to the province of Feryndale, to swear in the new Governor.

Fifty strong, led by Commander Aidan Hindmarsh, the entourage had left Brindabeare, the ruling city of Valentaland, nearly two weeks ago, and were now a single day from Feryndale. The swearing-in ceremony would keep the party there a couple of days, before beginning the journey home. The entire trip would take just over a month to complete.

The carriage jolted over a bump in the road.

Vanessa continued looking out the window, straining to see into the distance. Slender, with long, light brown hair, she wore a long flowing azure dress, which matched her eyes.

'Is Will going with you?' she asked.

'No,' said Dane. 'He scouts in the morning.'

'You be careful,' the other voice called from the carriage.

'I'll be fine,' Dane answered.

The other voice belonged to Dane's mother, Mistress Marilena Thorburn, Vanessa's personal aide. Dressed in a light pink dress, with her dark hair, as always, pinned in a bun, she sat up straight, swaying with the carriage, maintaining her unruffled and officious appearance. On these journeys, Marilena liaised with Hindmarsh to ensure everything remained on schedule.

'When will Blaze be back?' asked Vanessa.

'Early morning would be my guess,' said Dane. 'She hasn't hunted for a few days, so she'll be hungry.'

A young eagle, Blaze had been assigned to Dane as a final part of his training. Travelling with the entourage, she searched for enemy riders and other potential threats, returning to either

Dane or Vanessa. In the short time Blaze had been in their service, her masters had quickly become attached to her.

'It will be good to reach camp,' said Vanessa, 'it's not much fun being in here for hours at a time.'

Dane laughed.

'I'll change places with you,' he replied. 'I'd welcome the chance to rest; to have everyone waiting on me, sipping cider and watching the land pass by.'

'We don't have anything to drink in here,' Vanessa responded, 'and it's less comfortable than you might think.'

'I'll still change places,' said Dane. 'Just to get out of the heat.'

'You're a Royal Knight, Dane Thorburn,' Vanessa replied, 'the last thing you should be concerned with is the heat.'

'You think I'm not worthy?'

'A Royal Knight has no concern for his own wellbeing. He cares only for who he is protecting.'

'And the Princess of Brindabeare, and the future Queen of Valentaland cares only for her people.'

'I'm well aware of my duties, thank you very much,' said Vanessa, a hint of anger in her reply.

'And I'm aware of mine,' said Dane, equally indignant.

'Enough! Both of you!' Marilena snapped. 'Really! Sometimes it's as though you're five years old again!'

Tapping the carriage a couple of times, Dane and Vanessa broke into laughter.

Looking at her smiling companion, and towards the voice outside, Marilena wore an uncertain, puzzled look on her face.

Gathering herself, Vanessa said, 'It was Dane's idea. He wanted to see how long we could argue before you'd lose your temper.'

Marilena's face went red for a moment, before relaxing. With a mischievous smile, she said, 'That's not very nice. And it's *exactly* what I'd expect from a pair of five-year-olds.'

'We needed something to pass the time,' said Dane.

A voice called from ahead of him.

'Dane, time for the scouts to go.'

Dane nodded.

'Time to go,' he said to Vanessa and Marilena. 'I'll see you at camp.'

Tapping the carriage one last time, Dane urged his colt, Thunder, to the head of the entourage.

Joining him were Commander Hindmarsh, and Royal Knight Harvey Rosenthal.

'Harvey knows the site,' said Hindmarsh. 'Make sure the area is secure, and ride back to the Advance Patrol when you're done.'

'Let's go,' said Harvey.

With a flick of the reins, Dane and Thunder took flight; Harvey and his mount right beside them. To their right, the sun was starting its evening descent.

Being the first time on the whole journey where he could set Thunder loose, Dane gave him free rein, letting the cool afternoon air shake the stiffness of the day's riding out of him. The entourage could only move as quickly as the carriage; little more than a slow canter.

Scouts checked resting areas and campsites, ahead of the Advance Patrol, who would establish and secure the proper perimeters before the carriage and the rest of the entourage arrived.

After a solid half-hour's ride, a clearing loomed ahead, and Harvey signalled to slow down. Easing Thunder to a walk, Dane and Harvey made their way into the clearing.

'We'll do a couple of circuits and push wider each time,' said Harvey. 'If you see anything unusual, point it out.'

They moved off in opposite directions.

Following his path, Dane walked a wide arc, counterclockwise, looking for a sign of anything out of place.

Meeting at the crossover point of their arc, it had been uneventful so far.

'Some saps and scrubs back there,' said Dane. 'I'm sure the Advance Patrol will make short work of clearing it.'

Harvey nodded.

'Finish the loop, but circle wider, so we cover more ground.'

'Agreed,' said Dane.

Approaching the halfway point of his circuit, a sound to Dane's right distracted him.

It sounded like – a horse?

But Harvey was at the opposite end of the circuit …

In the next moment he saw it, and it took his breath away.

Emerging from the trees in front of him, a Black Knight came into view. Glancing at Dane for a moment, both riders hesitated, each not sure what the other was seeing.

Realising he'd been discovered, the Black Knight took flight, spurring his mount hard.

Reacting on reflex, Dane sent Thunder charging after him.

Quickly at full speed, Dane rounded a bend in the path ahead. Eyes locked on the enemy, he urged Thunder on, dodging bushes and other obstacles, slowly gaining ground.

Drawing a knife from his gauntlet, he flung it towards the enemy rider, finding his mark with deadly accuracy.

Lodging in the neck of the Black Knight, the now lifeless body slumped forward a moment, before falling to the ground and disappearing. Stunned at what had just happened, Dane slowed Thunder to a walk. Drawing his sword, he scanned the area. Taking a couple of deep breaths, he realised he'd covered several furlongs chasing the Black Knight.

He heard movement to his right, an instant before three more came charging straight at him.

Reacting on instinct, he deflected the blow of one; another clipping his left arm as they passed each other; the combined force nearly unseating him.

Wheeling Thunder around to face his attackers, Dane drew a knife from his other gauntlet with his left hand, launching it side-arm in the same motion. Sailing through the air, it struck truly, reducing the Black Knights to two.

Thrusting Thunder into another assailant, Dane swung his sword with all his might. The Black Knight blocked the blow, raising his sword in front of his body with a moment to spare. Dane kept Thunder boring forward, swinging at his opponent, left and right, staying on the attack.

It was taking all the Black Knight's energy to stay in the saddle.

Not wanting to give an inch, Dane kept swinging, up, down, left and right, blow after blow, an endless barrage of strikes. One struck a gap in the Black Knight's armour, piercing the skin. With an anguished yell, he staggered in the saddle.

Dane struck again and again, and with a couple of final thrusts, the Black Knight fell from his mount, suffering the same fate as his partner. Before Dane could recover, an elbow from the leader, his remaining assailant, struck him so hard it sent him tumbling from the saddle. Hitting the ground with a thud, Dane gasped for breath, before rolling over and bouncing to his feet.

Looking around, he sized up his options.

Thunder was out of reach.

Harvey? Nowhere to be seen.

'You have made this more difficult than necessary,' said the leader. 'We had no wish to harm you. Lord Raegan wants you alive.'

Dane backed away.

'I have no care for whatever your Lord Raegan wants,' he said.

'Surely you realise you can't defeat me?' said the leader. 'You have nowhere to run, and your friend is dead.'

'I've taken three of you already,' Dane replied. 'I'll take my chances.'

Charging at Dane, the leader ran right over him, trampling him in the process. One, maybe two hoofs struck, sucking the air out of him as he slammed into the ground.

Barely conscious, Dane rolled over, gasping for breath.

Turning his mount, the leader, taller, stronger and more battle-hardened than Dane, started walking towards him.

'Now, perhaps, you will come quietly.'

Dane stood, barely able to keep his balance.

The leader laughed out loud.

'I will say this about you. You are determined beyond the measure of most men. I can see why Lord Raegan wants you alive. You will do well in his service.'

Noticing his sword in the grass to his right, Dane reached towards it and fell to the ground again.

'Tell Raegan,' he said, staggering to his feet, 'he'll have to kill me first.'

The leader laughed again.

Dane raised his sword.

'I'm serious,' he said, stumbling backwards.

Before he could steady himself, the ground crumbled beneath his feet and everything went black.

Chapter 2
AMBUSH

The entourage would arrive at the evening camp shortly. They were making their way back to Brindabeare, having completed formalities at Feryndale the day before. The ceremony had happened without incident. No one in Feryndale had been aware of anything unusual.

Vanessa had done her part; her composure formal and proper, despite the anxiety that kept seeping into her mind.

Looking out the carriage window, alone in her thoughts, her eyes remained locked on the way ahead.

Sitting opposite, Marilena was distraught, all pretense and protocol forgotten.

Where's Dane?

He'd been missing for nearly four days.

In front of Vanessa and Hindmarsh, Harvey had told them all he knew.

'I don't know what else to tell you,' Harvey had said. 'We were making our second circuit of the campsite, and he rode off into the trees and disappeared.'

'Why didn't you look for him?' Vanessa had asked, the sharpness in her eyes seeming to pierce the air as she looked at him.

'That's not my role, Princess. My role is to scout the camp.

I reported him missing when the Advance Patrol arrived, and after we established the camp, several of us conducted a brief search. When we knew the main entourage would be arriving, we had no choice but to come back and assist in making sure you were safe.'

Dane and Thunder had disappeared without trace.

Vanessa had insisted a search party be sent to find him.

Hindmarsh remained firm. Threats of demotion and other actions drew no sympathy.

'Princess,' he said at the height of Vanessa's arguing, 'with all due respect; would you have been as insistent about this if the missing scout was *not* Dane Thorburn?'

Compounding her plight, she couldn't convince Will to search on his own.

'But he's your best friend,' she'd said.

'I know. But if I don't follow orders, I could be dismissed.'

'You won't,' Vanessa replied, 'I'll take responsibility for it.'

Will could only shake his head, before apologising again.

'Don't worry,' he said, seeing the despair on her face. 'Dane's clever. He'll find his way back.'

Glancing out the carriage window; she saw Will to her right, taking his turn in the escort team. Slightly shorter and thinner than Dane, with black, wavy hair, he turned, surprised to see Vanessa looking hopefully at him. He shook his head. He'd neither seen nor heard anything since their last conversation.

Seeing Marilena slumped helplessly opposite, Vanessa moved to sit next to her, putting a reassuring arm around her.

'Don't worry,' she said. 'I know he's all right.'

'I hope so,' said Marilena. 'I hope so.'

Arriving at the campsite, the Advance Patrol went straight to work, busying themselves in securing the perimeter. Starting at one end, they rode in an arc to the right, a rider dropping off at regular intervals to conduct a detailed inspection of the surrounding area.

Brindabeare's rules were very clear. The perimeter is established fifty yards around the exterior of the camp, and the area outside the perimeter is to be cleared.

Unfortunately, the Black Knights waiting for them knew it too.

'I know he's all right,' said Marilena, despite her tears. 'I know he is.'

Vanessa nodded, squeezing Marilena's hand gently.

'I know,' she said, trying to mask the uncertainty in her voice.

Despite their growling stomachs, the food tray remained untouched. Looking out the window again, Vanessa saw the sun setting in the background.

A light flashed behind the carriage. Leaping into the corner of her vision, Vanessa strained to look behind her. Between the mass of Royal Knights escorting her, she saw it again – closer and larger than before.

What was it?

Before she could think further, a huge fireball erupted right next to the carriage. Slamming into the ground with earth-shattering force, Vanessa's world flipped upside down. Tearing a huge crater in the road, the fireball launched the carriage right off its path.

Vanessa was thrown from one side to the other, before coming to rest upside down.

Disorientated, she struggled to right herself. Through the broken carriage door, she saw more light flashes, each landing with the same force as the other; people yelling and screaming.

'Marilena, are you all right?' she asked.

No answer.

'Marilena!'

Vanessa heard a groan to her right.

Marilena rubbed her head and sat up.

'W-what happened?'

'I don't know,' Vanessa replied. 'But we have to get out of here.'

Before she could open the damaged door, a black-armoured arm reached in, tearing it from its hinges.

Vanessa screamed.

In the next instant she heard the sound of steel through flesh, followed by the thud of a body slumping against the carriage and sliding to the ground.

Will stuck his head inside.

'Come on!' he said.

Reaching in, he helped Vanessa and Marilena out of the carriage.

Outside, mayhem reigned.

The carriage lay cracked out of shape and useless. One of the blasts had separated the horsecar; none of the horses could be seen. Large holes littered the road where the fireballs had struck; dust clouds were choking the air, and bodies lay strewn everywhere. It was a full-scale attack by a team of Black Knights, and from what Vanessa could see, the Black Knights were winning.

'This way!' said Will.

Racing clear of the wreckage, they saw a couple of Royal Knights ahead, waiting with horses. Vanessa knew the routine. She'd practised it many times – now it was real. The three of them reached their mounts, and with a ring of guards around Vanessa and Marilena, the party took flight.

The aim was simple – get as far away, as quickly as possible.

They made it only a short way before three Black Knights came at them. Will and the other Royal Knights drew their swords.

Will swung at his opponent, boring his horse forward at the same time. Again, the objective was clear – occupy and defeat your opponent as quickly as possible, allowing Vanessa to get away.

Vanessa had to stay in control of herself; reacting instinctively to what she saw – and escape at the first opportunity – with or without an escort.

It took Will a couple of swipes to defeat his opponent. Around him, it looked an even fight. Turning away, Will, Vanessa and Marilena fled.

They were close to the campsite. If they reached it, the scouts and Advance Patrol would help them escape. The noise of the fireballs was enough to rouse anything for miles, so with any luck they'd already know something was awry and be on alert.

Charging into a clump of trees, they raced on.

They hadn't drawn any pursuit, so the plan appeared to be working.

Their joy was short-lived.

Emerging from the trees up ahead another group of Black Knights confronted them. Swords out, they were on them in a flash. Reacting on reflexes, Vanessa and Marilena veered to the left, racing further into the trees.

'Stay with me!' Vanessa yelled.

The trail twisted left and right. Leaning forward in her saddle, Marilena followed closely at Vanessa's heels. It was taking all her effort to keep up.

The noise behind them drifted away, but they kept their pace. Not until they'd ridden for another few minutes and found the perimeter of the campsite did they dare slow the horses.

Puffing and panting, they took shelter in a clump of trees.

'What happened back there?' Marilena asked. 'What are we going to do? We're helpless out here.'

Vanessa put a hand on Marilena's arm.

'Don't worry. We'll get through it. We might have to stay here awhile, but we'll be fine.'

'Stay here? Out in the open?'

'Not in the open exactly,' said Vanessa. 'But here; wherever we are, until we're found. We can't risk riding directly towards Brindabeare with so many Black Knights on the loose. We'll have to make our way slowly, and camp out until someone finds us.

'Maybe some of the entourage will make it back. When Blaze returns, I'll send her for help, and a party will be dispatched from Brindabeare. Lord Frederick is bound to be able to find us, once he knows something is wrong.'

She prodded her horse forward. Marilena followed. Not looking where she was going, Vanessa's horse tripped on a dead branch, stumbling forward.

Looking again, she saw it wasn't a dead branch.

Marilena screamed.

It was the body of a Royal Knight – one of the Advance Patrol. Vanessa realised their predicament immediately.

The Advance Patrol had also been attacked, meaning Black Knights were here as well.

The sound of horses caught their attention. With no weapons of their own, they were helpless. They stood rooted to the spot, cowering in fear as they awaited their fate.

Through the trees, Vanessa caught sight of a Royal Knight's uniform; breathing a sigh of relief when she saw Will riding towards them. Her face broke into a smile when he arrived.

Shuddering to a stop, Will spoke with all the self-control he could muster.

'It's a wonder the whole forest doesn't know you're here,' he said. 'That scream would have been heard for miles.'

Despite what he said, Vanessa could see the relief in his face on seeing they were all right.

'Look,' she said, pointing. 'The Advance Patrol. They were attacked as well.'

Will glanced at the prone body in front of him.

'I don't know what's happened back there,' he said, 'but I was hoping we might find reinforcements here. We might have been able to head towards Brindabeare and get as far away as possible. Now I think we have no choice but to stay low. At least until we know what we're up against.'

Vanessa nodded.

'Do you think Dane was attacked?'

'With all that's happened, it's possible.'

Will nudged his horse forward.

'We'd better move. I think we should get to the other side of the camp.'

Following the perimeter to the left, at regular intervals they discovered the bodies of the Advance Patrol and the scouts – ten in all.

By the time they'd reached the other side of the camp their mood was considerably more sombre

'Someone's been busy planning this,' Will cursed. 'And they knew exactly what they were doing.'

'We've survived this far,' said Vanessa. 'Where are we going to camp?'

'I'm not sure. Somewhere over ...'

Before he could finish, with a *whoosh!* several flaming arrows landed in front of them. Emerging from the cover of the trees around them, they were surrounded by a group of Black Knights.

Will counted eight.

Closing in, four pointed swords at them; the others had arrows nocked and ready.

'Your sword,' one growled at Will.

Helpless, Will threw his sword to the ground.

'You won't get away with this,' said Vanessa. 'Lord Frederick will find me as soon as he discovers what's happened.'

The leader of the group rode forward. He hesitated a moment, before slapping her hard across the face.

'You will speak when spoken to,' he said.

Vanessa cried out in pain, blood trickling down her cheek.

In the next instant Will drew a knife from his gauntlet. He was a moment from unleashing it when he felt a sword in his back.

'Throw it, and you die.'

Will hesitated for a moment, before replacing the knife.

'Now,' said the leader, 'if you do this properly, and in an orderly fashion, you will not be harmed.'

Looking at Will and Marilena, he said, 'the two of you are surplus to our needs. Once we're through here, we will set you free.'

'As for you,' he said to Vanessa, 'Lord Raegan requests your presence, and we are to be your escort.'

Rubbing her face, Vanessa said nothing, resigned to her fate. Will stewed, full of rage, unable to do anything to help. Marilena's mind raced – racked with worry as she looked desperately at Vanessa.

'Before we depart, we have something we wish to reveal,' the leader added. 'You can see this has been a well-planned and well-executed attack. I'm sure you'd like to know how we were able to do it.'

Will bristled. If he had anything to say about it, those responsible would suffer a most painful fate.

'Some in Brindabeare were most accommodating to our requests for assistance.'

Vanessa flinched.

'We had help from many sources, including one I am sure will surprise you.'

Moving his horse back a couple of paces, a space opened in the group.

Out of the trees, astride a large grey horse, a Royal Knight emerged, walking slowly towards them.

Vanessa, Will and Marilena gasped.

The Royal Knight was Dane Thorburn.

Chapter 3
ROCK MITES

Eyes open.

    Nothing but darkness.

    Trying to turn his head – a searing pain rips through his body; then, nothing.

✧ ✧ ✧

Eyes open.

It's hot – the sun beats down.

A dry mouth and throat. The air is choked with dust.

An empty horizon blurs in and out of his vision.

Where?

Lifting his head – a scorching pain tears through him.

Trying to fight it …

Blackness.

✧ ✧ ✧

Darkness. Pain.

Light. Pain.

Hot. Pain.

Cold. Pain.

The pain – dull; aching; burning through his body.

Sweat glistens on his face.

Another attempt to move.
Pushing up with one arm, fighting all the way ...
Darkness.

Eyes opening again, Dane squinted against the sun. For a few moments, he lay still. He felt the pain rippling through him – his aching head; his body sore all over.

Where was he? How long had he been here?

The sun sat at the peak of the day, but his last memory – a fading sun?

Forcing himself to a sitting position, for a moment he thought he'd pass out again. Slowly shaking dirt from his hair, his vision blurred, everything wobbling from side to side. Blinking for a few seconds, he sat still; the throbbing headache and the aches and pains resetting themselves.

Images flashed in and out of his mind.

Vanessa was smiling.

She had a sword in her hand.

They were sparring?

At a campsite?

Which campsite?

He and Will and Vanessa were laughing around a fire?

Harvey – he and Harvey scouted a campsite together.

Thunder – where's Thunder?

Black Knights – had ... attacked?

Near the campsite ... they chased him, and he ... fell?

Where?

Here?

A cliff rose above him.

Whatever had happened, he found himself on a ledge at least twenty feet down. Looking out over the edge, he saw roughly the same distance to the treetops of the land below.

Something wasn't right. Feeling the aches and pains in his body, it felt like he'd been rolling down an embankment, a rocky hill of some kind, before falling and slamming into the ground. His legs were tingling, as though they'd been pierced with thousands of tiny needles.

Looking around, there were no other outcrops. He couldn't go up or down.

What was he going to do?

Standing, he swayed for a moment as his body and mind adjusted to the movement. A little groggy, but otherwise stable, he let his breathing normalise, taking several deep breaths as he steadied himself.

Running his hand along the surface of the cliff, it confirmed what he could see – hard and smooth; no way to get a hand or foothold.

In the next moment, a shooting pain pierced his arm, from his fingers, to his hand, all the way to his shoulder. Trying to move his hand away, he found it stuck; pulled against the cliff face.

The pain increased; tiny pricks biting and squeezing, tighter and tighter. Fumbling for a knife with his free hand, he found none in his gauntlets. With an effort he grabbed one from his leggings, stabbing at the surface.

A high-pitched squeal came from within the cliff. The pain in Dane's arm eased and he jerked his hand away. Stepping away from the wall, he held his hand in front of him.

Apart from tiny pinpricks and the lingering pain, his hand was fine. It was the same pain he'd noticed in his legs.

But how?

Dusting himself off some more, he moved to the cliff face again. Careful not to get too close, he studied the wall. Nothing gave a clue to what happened.

He poked the wall with his knife.

It was met by the same squealing sound he'd heard before.

Again, he prodded – same noise. He moved along the wall; touching, poking and scraping his knife as he went. Higher and lower, left and right.

There were squeals everywhere.

Something in the cliff is alive!

'I give up,' said Dane, the words increasing his headache. 'I can do this forever. You need to show me whoever, or whatever you are.'

Silence.

Dane stood there, waiting.

With a small *'pop!'* a tiny rock fell from the wall, followed by another and another; hundreds falling in quick succession. A few moments more and a large pile of rocks lay at Dane's feet, some the size of a small pebble, others a couple of inches round.

They began to move, rocking gently, back and forth, before leaping into the air. Legs, feet, arms and hands sprouted, before they landed gently on the ground. Others continued to fall from the wall.

Looking again, Dane saw the rocks had very small eyes, with a tiny slit for a mouth. They were rock mites, tiny creatures found in large, hard, rock-like surfaces. Despite his predicament, he found himself struggling to keep a straight face.

One of the mites, about half the size of Dane's thumb, jumped up and down a few times. Unsure what to do, Dane bent down.

'You tickle us,' the rock mite said in a faint, high-pitched voice.

Dane couldn't believe what was happening.

'You were hurting me,' he said, showing the cuts in his fingers.

The rock mite raised its hand.

Dane could just make out what were tiny fingers, with sharp prongs.

'You hurt me,' he said again.

'Food,' said the rock mite. 'Eat what touches us. No food in long time. Plants grow once. No more. All gone. Take food from above now.'

Dane looked at the rock mites around him. There had to be hundreds, maybe thousands of them.

He looked at the cliff face. What had been a smooth, shiny wall had now become a surface littered with holes.

'You take food from up there?' he asked, pointing to the top of the cliff.

The rock mite nodded.

'Take all of us. You fall when we pull food. We think you food. We reach and stop you. Try to stop you falling.'

Dane's eyes went wide in surprise. It made sense – why he felt he'd rolled down a rocky hill, and the lingering pain in his legs.

'You saved me,' he said.

As one, the rock mites talked and jabbered excitedly, jumping up and down.

'Thank you,' said Dane to the one who'd spoken to him. 'What's your name?'

'Titch,' answered the little rock.

'Thank you, Titch,' said Dane. 'Thank you all.'

Again, the rock mites talked in a babble of excited yelps and cries.

Looking at the cliff again, Dane saw the indents in the wall, reaching towards the top.

He bent down to Titch.

'I have to get to the top. Can you help me?'

Titch turned and spoke to the others. It was too fast for Dane to understand, but they all started yelping and chattering.

'Hand,' said Titch.

Dane held out his arm. Titch jumped into the palm of Dane's hand. Dane stood to his full height. Titch ran the length of Dane's arm, stepping onto his shoulder.

The other rock mites were scrambling up the surface of the cliff.

Walking to the wall, Dane saw there were now small niches and tiny ledges he could use for hand and footholds. Placing his right foot in one, he reached above his head with his left hand.

Dizzy for a moment, he steadied himself.

Next, he secured his right hand and left foot. He heard what he thought was a whistle from Titch and looked for the next foot and handholds.

In the next moment, new outcrops appeared as the rock mites moved around the wall; giving Dane the holdings he needed to climb higher.

The rock mites could appear from anywhere within the cliff face. Out of the corner of his eye, Dane saw Titch jumping up and down. The whistling noise was still there.

Resting a couple of times to counteract the dizziness and the aches in his body, he reached the top in a few minutes; scrambling over the ledge, back on hard land. Glancing over the cliff, he saw the rock mites sticking out from their places in the wall.

He could hear a high-pitched noise; they were all yelling excitedly again. If he didn't know better, he could have sworn they were waving at him.

He felt Titch jump off his shoulder, landing on the ground in front of him.

'Thank you,' he said. 'Thank you all.'

Titch fell on his face before springing back up. Dane guessed Titch had just tried to bow.

'Wait a moment,' said Dane.

In the long grass in front of him, he found a couple of large plants, uprooted them and walked back to the ledge. Bending down, he placed them in front of Titch.

Titch jumped up and down, delirious. Dane pushed the plants gently over the edge, leaning them into the wall. In an instant he could feel them being pulled from his hands and released his grip. Sure enough, they were now fastened against the cliff face, a feast for the rock mites.

He moved away from the cliff.

'Goodbye Titch,' he said.

Titch pitched forward again, righted himself, and with a wave disappeared over the edge.

Turning around, Dane scanned his surroundings, trying to work out where he was. Wobbling for a moment, he stood still; trying to settle the aches in his body and clear his head.

Images of Black Knights flashed in and out of his mind. Everything was a blur, impossible to understand.

Retracing his thoughts, he tried to remember.

He and Harvey were scouting.

What happened to Harvey?

They'd told him – they'd said he was ... dead?

Checking his armour, he took stock of the weaponry he had left. Apart from his sword and gauntlet knives, the other pieces were there; the small sword in his back, and the knives in his leggings.

Drawing his small sword, he walked towards the trees ahead.

He thought of Thunder … where could he be?

In the trees now, heading to his left, there was no trail here.

Without really knowing why, he turned to his right, crossing a small clearing, before heading into a thicket of trees. It was darker here, the canopy thick enough to block the sun.

Turning to his right, and then to the right again, he heard a muffled noise in front of him. Something was moving; struggling against whatever was holding it.

Following the noise, the undergrowth grew thicker with every stride. Now turning left, a wall of vines and leaves confronted him, strung from a branch at least ten feet tall, all the way to the ground.

The whickering sound came from behind the vines.

In an instant he knew.

Cutting his way through, he saw Thunder, tangled in the vines of a strangler plant. Climbing trees, stranglers extended their mass of vines and leaves like tentacles, trapping anything that walked into it. They weren't strong enough to kill a horse – Thunder was restrained rather than trapped.

Hacking his way ahead, Dane forced his way through, and cut the vines caught around Thunder's legs.

Dane walked him away from the strangler and checked him over.

'Am I glad to see you!' he said.

Thunder nuzzled against him.

Restoring his sword, Dane climbed into his saddle.

Glancing at his surroundings, a question made its way into his mind – *where am I?*

Chapter 4
CAPTURED

Finding the way back wasn't going to be easy.

He'd never been in this area of the land. Unlike others who had been on these journeys before; he was seeing everything for the first time. And after adding all that happened after chasing the Black Knight, along with a throbbing headache; he had even less of an idea as to where he was, and how to get back to the trail that would lead him to the campsite.

Thinking through his options, he realised his best chance was to start where he'd emerged from the cliff face and work out his bearings from there. In a couple of minutes, he found the patch of ground where he'd pulled the plants for the rock mites. Turning away from the cliff, he looked at the land in front of him. Nothing stood out. Not the slightest clue.

'What do I do now?' he said out loud.

Straining his eyes, he looked again; trying to remember how he ended up here. The last thing that happened before going over the edge of the cliff – the Black Knights ... no, not Knights; *Knight* – there had been only one of them.

In an instant it came flooding back.

I killed the others ...

There should be armour – somewhere around here.

Leaning down, he walked Thunder forward, scanning the ground within his field of vision.

About fifty yards into his walk, he saw it.

Empty pieces of black armour – near a group of trees ahead.

Instinctively, he knew he would have emerged on the open stretch of land he'd just covered from somewhere among those trees. With more confidence, he started turning in an arc to his left.

A few moments later, he saw the trail.

He'd found it – his way back to the campsite.

Resisting the urge to charge ahead, he kept Thunder to a slow pace, eyes and ears alert for any sight or sound that might give a hint as to what lay ahead. Without knowing how long he'd been on the ledge before he woke up, he had no way of knowing what may or may not be at the campsite once he arrived.

It took a few minutes for the campsite to emerge ahead of him.

There were no sounds, nor signs of movement.

Looking around, his first thought was to walk the perimeter; the same way he would if he were in the Advance Patrol.

Starting his circuit, a thought struck him.

If the Advance Patrol has been here, why is it such a mess?

After only a few steps, Thunder hesitated, shaking his head. Dane looked down.

A body!

Recoiling in shock, he thought of Harvey. The Black Knight had said he was dead.

Jumping from the saddle, he turned the body over.

A Royal Knight – but not Harvey.

It was Hendricks; one of the more experienced in the entourage.

Hendricks must have been in the Advance Patrol, which meant *the Advance Patrol were attacked!*

Which way now?

To Brindabeare, or Feryndale?

Vanessa!

Is she safe?

A jumble of thoughts poured through his mind as he continued staring at Hendricks's lifeless body.

'Observe the area,' he said out loud, almost by reflex, hearing the voice of Officer Parnsworth, his cadet training commander.

The words calmed him for a moment, pulling him away from his thoughts:

'In the aftermath of battle, observe the area. Cover as much ground as you can. Assess the casualties, note everything you see, anything that may be useful, no matter how small it may seem. Observe it and remember it – so you can give a precise description of what you saw.'

The task was set.

Moving the body to the base of a tree and covering it with foliage, he marked the tree with his sword. That would do for now.

Continuing around the perimeter, Thunder stopped again.

Another body.

The same as Hendricks – attacked from behind; killed before he had a chance to defend himself.

It had to be the Advance Patrol...

Are they all dead?

Is the enemy still here?

Edging Thunder forward, he continued his circuit.

He didn't need to complete the entire lap before he knew the outcome, but he did it anyway. Taking in the enormity of what he found, his mind raced.

The Advance Patrol and scouts were dead – every one of them. Killed by a single wound to the back of the head. They'd been clearing debris when they were struck.

Noting where and how he'd found them; Dane knew they'd been attacked where they wouldn't be seen by another in the patrol. It had been a deliberate, well-planned assault. They were probably attacked within moments of each other; with no chance to know what was happening; no chance for escape.

That meant they'd been attacked by at least *ten* Black Knights!

If the Advance Patrol and scouts were dead, what happened to the entourage?

This attack had happened *before* the entourage had arrived.

Putting it all together, his mind filled with dread – he'd been attacked on the way to Feryndale; the Advance Patrol were attacked – *the entourage was attacked!*

But where?

If none of the Advance Patrol reported to the entourage within a mile of its arrival at the campsite, the entourage would retreat for two miles, and a search team would investigate.

Did the entourage make it this far?

Did they retreat?

Were they attacked before or after Feryndale?

If it happened after Feryndale, that means I was stuck on that ledge for … at least four days.

Four Days!

So much could have happened in that time.

Had they survived?

At full strength, the entourage was fifty strong. Even with the Advance Patrol and scouts eliminated, that left them with forty – forty Royal Knights. All of whom were sworn to protect Vanessa with their lives.

Vanessa!

Is she all right?

He needed to get to the road – it would give him another set of sights to check.

It didn't take long to find it.

He slowed on approach, not wanting to appear in the open until he felt safe. Listening for a few moments, he heard nothing to cause concern.

Feryndale was the closer settlement; so it made sense to search in that direction first.

He found a small branch; staking it so he'd know when he found this point again.

Heading off at a gentle pace, he wasn't sure how far he'd follow the road before turning back. Two, maybe three miles.

The sun was setting now, which didn't leave much time.

Eyes peeled; he kept a steady pace.

Nothing after the first mile; no carriage tracks in the road.

Wait – *that's a sign.*

He came to a stop, collecting his thoughts.

If the Advance Patrol were attacked setting up the camp, and there were no fresh tracks in the road, it meant one of two possibilities – either the entourage had retreated to Feryndale – where they might be safe; or they were attacked *before* they reached the campsite!

One way or the other, he had to find his way to Feryndale.

At a slow gallop, he headed in that direction.

After about a mile, something in the distance caught his attention. A light was reflecting off it.

On a road in the middle of nowhere?

Spurring Thunder to full speed, he covered the ground quickly.

On approach he saw it clearly, a mass of twisted metal.

Vanessa's carriage!

It lay upside down, by the side of the road.

Heart racing, he covered the remaining ground, shocked at the destruction around him. Dismounting, he leaped onto the overturned wreck. A door had been torn completely away. The carriage lay empty.

Jumping down, he studied the surroundings.

Huge holes littered the ground. Fallen horses, Royal Knights and empty black armour were everywhere.

So, there *had* been a battle – a fierce one.

From the number of bodies, it looked as though the Black Knights had won, or at least inflicted serious damage … and Vanessa was gone.

Vanessa's gone!

Did she escape?

Is she safe?

In a battle like this, she would have been lucky to escape – very lucky.

Pangs of guilt flowed through him.

'No!' he screamed. 'No, no, *no*, no, No!'

Tears streamed down his face; his head ached worse than ever; a smith's hammer battering against a wall in the back of his mind.

'I should have been here,' he said, burying his head in his hands. '*I should have been here!*'

His thoughts were distracted by the sound of horses approaching.

Looking up, he could see five, maybe six riders. Another glance and their uniforms were visible – Royal Knights.

Standing by the carriage, he waited for them to arrive. As they approached, he saw them draw their swords.

Why were they in an attacking formation?

They could see who he was, so why were they …

The horses shuddered to a halt, surrounding him. Six Royal Knights, swords drawn, pointed at him.

He recognised them immediately – other members of Vanessa's entourage. A mixture of relief, surprise and bewilderment washed over him.

'Richard?' he said. 'Byron? What are you …?

'Silence!' said the leader of the group. 'In the name of King Winston Meriwether, Ruler of Brindabeare, Supreme Ruler of Valentaland, I arrest you on the charge of treason and conspiracy to aid and abet the kidnap of Princess Vanessa, heir to the throne.'

Chapter 5
TWISTS AND TURNS

Alone in her cell, Vanessa had no idea where she was.

Bound at the wrists and blindfolded since her abduction, other than sensing night turn to day and back again, she'd had nothing to guide her about where she was going or how long she'd been riding during the journey to the dark cell she'd been dumped in.

Alone ever since, she'd had little to do other than think through the events that resulted in her current predicament.

It had been a well-planned and carefully coordinated attack.

To defeat the entourage – a team of Royal Knights no less, so easily and completely, it seemed as though the enemy knew exactly where she would be at the exact moment of the attack – not only surrounding them, but cutting off all avenues of escape.

How did they know?

How did they do it so comprehensively?

Traitors?

Possibly – but who?

Raegan had his Black Knights and others willing to do his bidding, and there were others she'd heard about who had been forced to help him against their will.

They want *me to think it was Dane.*

Never!

But who?

And what now?

Thwarted some twenty years ago in his efforts to become High-Governor of Brindabeare; seeking to use the position as a means to seize power of the entire land, Raegan had been plotting his revenge ever since.

One of two wizards remaining in all Valentaland, and the brother of Lord Frederick, the one chosen as High-Governor over him, Raegan was a Firelord – the source of his power and sense of being coming from the fire element; one of the four Ruling Elements of Nature (earth, air, fire, and water) governing the state of the entire land and all living things.

Lord Frederick had taught Vanessa about the complexities of the elements, how they worked in isolation and how they mixed with each other. Whether dominant in one element or another, wizards possessed characteristics of all: each element possessing unique traits that, among other things, counter-balanced those of the others.

Over time, a wizard became dominant in one, maybe two. In rare cases, one became a Masterlord, equally dominant in all elements. No two wizards were ever the same; their interaction with the ruling elements and their ability to draw from them were unique to each individual.

In some, the desire for the features of their dominant element to be all empowering led to the suppression of the counterinflu-ences of the others, allowing the light and dark side of the domi-nant element to flourish.

Characteristics within the fire element include courage, forti-tude, zeal and tenacity.

Wizards dominant in fire face danger without fear; they're resolute in the confidence of their actions and determined to succeed.

However, when unchecked, determination to succeed gives way to succeeding *at any cost*. This in turn rouses emotions such as deceit, spite, anger and revenge towards those who stand in their way.

It was just so for Raegan – nothing mattered but his ambition to rule the land – and it was why she now sat in a cold, dark cell, waiting for whatever he had planned for her.

Noises outside snapped her away from her thoughts.

Footsteps, jangling keys, and the groan of the door of her cell being opened. Rough hands grabbed her, hauling her to her feet without a word.

Led down a couple of passageways and up several flights of stairs, she walked down a couple hallways before being led into a room and thrust into a chair.

'Remove the bindings,' a voice commanded.

Vanessa felt rough hands grab her wrists as a knife cut the rope restraining her hands. Another pair of hands grabbed her from behind, tearing the blindfold away with a swift, sharp tug.

Rubbing her hands and blinking her eyes to adjust to the light in the room, she looked at her adversary, seated opposite.

Dressed in black and wearing his red Firelord cape; Raegan's dark eyes sat silent and alert as he stroked his beard, looking at his prisoner like a wolf sizing up its prey.

'You must be hungry,' he said, nodding to the meat, poultry, fish, fruit, and cheeses spread in front of them. 'Please, eat.'

Vanessa stared at her empty plate.

Raegan shrugged his shoulders.

'Suit yourself. But know this will be your last chance to enjoy such a meal.'

Vanessa looked at Raegan, pure hatred on her face.

'What are you planning to do?' she asked. 'Kill me?'

Raegan lowered his goblet.

'There is no need for anger. If I had wanted to kill you, you would not be sitting before me.'

Vanessa stared down her captor.

'Lord Frederick will find me, and you will be captured and killed, once and for all. So, I don't want your food or drink,' she said, swiping her hand across the table, dumping the contents on the floor.

Calmly lowering his goblet, Raegan stood, pointing a finger at Vanessa and walking around the table towards her.

Vanessa felt her neck tighten. The air around her dried up. The force pressing against her neck increased. In the next instant she found herself choking, gasping for breath. By the time Raegan reached her, she was close to collapse.

'If I press a little more, you will pass out,' he said. 'Although you can't feel it, there is enough air in your body to keep you alive; and I want you to listen very carefully to what I have to say.'

Gasping for air, struggling more and more to breathe, Vanessa started seeing blurred images around her.

'Look at me when I am talking to you,' said Raegan, grabbing her by the hair, forcing her to meet his gaze.

Vanessa's eyes were bulging with fear.

'I assure you, you will not be found, unless I allow it.'

Reaching into his pocket, he took out a necklace.

'Recognise this?'

Vanessa forced herself to nod. Until that moment, she hadn't realised it had been taken from her.

'This ensures Frederick will never find you. While it remains in my possession, I can project images of you anywhere I please. So, you can forget any notion of a gallant rescue.'

Lowering his hand and releasing the choker hold, Vanessa slumped to the table, gasping fresh breaths of air. She looked at Raegan, tears streaming down her face.

'What are you going to do with me?'

Raegan walked to his seat and sat down. A flick of his hand restored the scattered food to its place.

'At the moment I'm offering you a meal,' he replied. 'I suggest you eat something.'

Glancing at the food in front of her, Vanessa's stomach growled with hunger. Despite her misgivings, she helped herself to some meat and bread, and poured herself a drink.

'I knew you'd see things my way,' said Raegan. 'And I won't tell anyone if you try the wine.'

'What are you going to do with me?' Vanessa asked again.

'Leverage,' said Raegan. 'I have something your father desires. We will see just how much you are worth to him.'

'You won't get away with this. No matter what you do, Father and Lord Frederick will find me.'

'I doubt it,' said Raegan. 'I doubt it very much. In time, you will see that I am right.'

'They've stopped you before,' said Vanessa. 'When you killed Dane's father; and the last time, when Dane found your men storming the castle. Both times we stopped you.'

Raegan looked at Vanessa, deep loathing on his face.

Rocking back, Vanessa raised a hand to her throat, hoping she wasn't going to be choked again.

'This is different,' Raegan said through gritted teeth. 'Very different.' He stood, leaning over the table towards her. 'This time, I have something they want. They will have to come to me, and do as I say if they wish to get it back.'

Pacing the room, he went on, talking to himself as much as anyone else.

'I admit it was somewhat rash and foolish the first time; although, in killing that meddlesome Gil Thorburn, I didn't fail entirely. And the last time ...'

He trailed off, doing his best to contain his anger.

'The last time ... well, the aim of that plan was to see how well the castle was defended. So, despite young Thorburn's efforts, it was not a total failure.'

Stunned at the audacity of Raegan's comments, Vanessa took a large sip from her goblet; using it to mask her emotions, allowing her a moment to choose her words carefully.

'You failed,' she said. 'You thought you'd walk in and seize the castle. We defeated you; the city is better defended than ever before, and we know who your allies are. We had our suspicions, and now we know. In time we will defeat them – and you. Once and for all.'

Taking another sip, Vanessa stole a glance around the room.

Swatting the goblet from her grasp, the contents spilling everywhere, Raegan leaned in close.

'You take me for a fool?' he said, following her gaze. 'There is nothing here that will give an indication as to where you are.'

'One of the provinces aligned with Candahorn,' Vanessa guessed. 'They will search all of them.'

'They may well,' said Raegan. 'But who is to say you are in any of those locations? Who is to say you will remain here? They will search, and search, and search. Images of you will appear in the most unlikely places, and they will send parties to all of them. All the while, you will be wherever it is I wish you to be, and quite unreachable.'

A Black Knight appeared at the doorway.

'Yes?'

The Black Knight hesitated.

'My Lord,' he said, 'I have news.'

'There is no need for concern,' said Raegan, glancing at Vanessa.

The Black Knight nodded, still hesitant.

'Very well,' he said. 'Our search has found no trace of the Thorburn boy.'

Vanessa's heart leaped – *Dane!*

Raegan felt his anger boiling inside him.

'I will never understand how he avoided capture,' he snarled. 'There were four of them. *Four of them!*'

'Yes, my Lord,' the Black Knight replied. 'Once he went over the cliff and they saw him motionless on the ledge below, it was assumed the fall had killed him.'

'And that was the mistake!' said Raegan. 'I have no desire to hear a repeat of how he *disappeared.*'

'W-would you like me to expand the search party?' asked the Black Knight.

'No, I would not,' said Raegan 'Leave us. Now!'

With a relieved nod, the Black Knight left the room.

Raegan slammed his fist on the table.

'That Thorburn boy has more lives than a three-headed serpent,' he cursed.

Vanessa's face broke into a wide smile, a wave of jubilation coursing through her; allowing her to draw strength in her own predicament.

Dane's alive!

'I wouldn't be too pleased if I were you,' said Raegan.

'Dane escaped,' said Vanessa. 'Before your men kidnapped me. I knew it wasn't him. You tried to make everyone think it was, but it wasn't.'

'I'm afraid it will hurt, more than help him. Like his father, he has proven to possess rare abilities, even at his age. He has become an obstacle in need of removal; in one way or another. Upon his capture, in time, I was hoping he would see reason, that I would be able to channel his abilities to serve me.'

'Never,' said Vanessa. 'Dane would never turn against Brindabeare.'

Raegan nodded.

'You may be right about that,' he conceded. 'But surely you weren't foolish enough to think I would not have an alternative plan? Why else would I project his image to the scene of your capture?'

Vanessa hesitated.

'But it was an image ... it wasn't him. We know that.'

'*We* do,' said Raegan. 'You and I. But who else? You are here with me, with no means of being able to tell anyone.'

'You didn't catch him,' she said. 'That means he's all right.'

'Does it? Where will he go?'

'To Brindabeare,' she said without hesitation.

This time it was Raegan's turn to smile.

'I'm disappointed in you,' he said. 'You have not thought this through.

Part of my leverage in convincing young Thorburn to serve me, was to make sure he would not be able to serve you or anyone else. What better way to do that than to have the entire city turn against him?'

'That would never happen!' said Vanessa.

'I'm afraid it will,' Raegan replied. 'All of Brindabeare think he's a traitor. Everyone who survived the battle will swear he led the force that captured you.'

Vanessa's jaw dropped.

'What's in store for him, should he return to Brindabeare, will serve my needs as well as if I had sent him myself. I expect he will hang within hours of his return.'

Chapter 6

PRISONER

The party arrived at the first gatehouse. News of their return had been relayed in advance, but official protocols had to be followed.

'Royal Knight Ernest Honeywood and party, returning from the scene of the kidnap of Princess Vanessa, with a prisoner.'

The guards at the gate craned their necks.

'I'm not a prisoner!' Dane yelled. 'I've done nothing wrong!'

Not for the first time since his arrest, his comments were met with a slap across the face from one of his guards.

'We did not give you permission to speak,' his assailant replied.

With his hands tied since capture, Dane could offer nothing in defense. He absorbed the blow, staring defiantly at the knight who'd struck him.

The Chief Guard nodded.

'You may proceed.'

The party moved through the gatehouse, into the city proper.

Dane was surrounded. The six who'd arrested him were in a tight bunch around him, accompanied by more knights from the castle.

As he was led forward, he could hear a dull roar coming from the road ahead.

47

People lined both sides of Main Street, the largest road in the city, yelling, jeering and screaming obscenities at him.

'Traitor!'

'Murderer!'

'Hang him!'

'Kill him!'

Dane hung his head.

He couldn't believe his ears. In the minds of the people he was guilty. He caught glimpses of some he knew, who should know better. None offered anything in the way of support, not even a sympathetic nod.

His captors sat proudly in their saddles, revelling in the glory at having caught one of the masterminds of Vanessa's kidnapping. Once or twice, one of them reached over, grabbing him by the hair, roughing him up and throwing him forward in the saddle. Time took an age to pass while they wound their way to the castle.

At one point, he caught a glimpse of three youths his own age: Martin Fenwick, and his cohorts, Vincent Winslow and Austin Harrop. Fenwick had held a grudge against Dane since childhood, and during training, had tried several times to set Dane up for fail-ure. Not only had Dane overcome those setbacks, he'd turned the tables during last year's Tournament of Knights, when Fenwick had been caught cheating in the final event.

Now the tide appeared to have turned again, with Fenwick sporting a huge smile as Dane passed by.

'What you've always deserved Thorburn!' he yelled. 'I'll be sure to have front seats at your hanging!'

Once past the castle gatehouse, they travelled the length of the main courtyard, before turning to the left and stopping at a side entrance towards the rear of the castle.

Dane didn't need to think twice to know where they were – the entrance to the castle's dungeon.

Stablehands helped his captors dismount, leading their horses away. They stood to attention, closing ranks around him.

In front of everyone stood General Laramer Silvers, Commander-in-Chief of the Brindabeare Army. Dane knew the General well; as a young boy growing up in the castle, and more recently, having served under his direct command as a member of the Royal Knights.

In full regalia, the General was an imposing sight. Well over six feet tall, his physical presence alone was intimidating, and he carried himself with an air that commanded respect from those who served him. Not for the first time, Dane felt as though Silvers was looking right through him, boring into his heart and soul.

Dane saw the hate in the General's eyes; the contempt, the anger.

'Get the prisoner off his horse,' Silvers growled. 'And remove those gauntlets and leggings. I will not have a traitor disgrace the markings of a Royal Knight.'

Before Dane could react, a hand reached up, wrenching him from the saddle. Another pair of hands tore off pieces of his armour. For good measure, the two handling him threw him to the ground, a couple of kicks to his ribs finding their mark.

Coughing and spluttering, Dane staggered to his feet.

'General,' he gasped. 'I'm innocent. It's a mistake, I didn't ...

Before he could finish, a stinging smack across the face sent him reeling to the ground once more. Curling himself into a ball as best he could, he absorbed more kicks to the body.

'You will not speak to the General that way!' roared the Royal Knight who'd struck him.

'Enough!' a voice commanded.

The beating stopped immediately.

The voice belonged to Lord Frederick, Masterlord wizard and High-Governor of Brindabeare, the most important person in the land after the King. Dressed in dark grey, his multi-coloured Masterlord cape billowing behind him, and Scarafuse, his all-powerful sword strapped to his side, he had an aura and strength about him that exceeded all; including Silvers, who stood to his left.

Next to his brother, Lord Frederick would be slightly shorter, his hair and beard a little longer; his face showing a relaxed, composed intensity, as opposed to Raegan's smouldering anger.

Lord Frederick had been a friend and mentor to Dane his whole life; saving him from Raegan's wrath the night Raegan killed his father, and more recently, when Raegan had tried to kill him in the Great Forest.

For the first time since his arrest, Dane felt safe.

Relief swept over him.

With Lord Frederick here, he'd get a chance to explain what happened. He'd be a villain no longer.

'Lord Frederick! Thank goodness. I was attacked by Black Knights. I found Vanessa's carriage. I had nothing to do with it!'

Lord Frederick raised his hand.

'Enough. You will have an opportunity to explain yourself at the trial.'

Dane couldn't believe it.

They were going to go through with it!

He would face trial in front of the Brindabeare Council. Only one outcome awaited those found guilty of treason – hanging.

Looking despairingly at Lord Frederick, he met a cold, hard stare. He saw no look of recognition from the great wizard, no hint of any relationship between them.

'Escort the prisoner to his cell,' Lord Frederick commanded.

The Royal Knights on either side of Dane grabbed him by the arms, walking him towards the entrance to the dungeons.

'Lord Frederick,' Dane pleaded, 'Lord Frederick, please!'

Nothing.

Pushed inside, he was led down a long corridor, harried down a series of stairwells and passageways, before coming to a large empty cell in the bowels of the castle.

Untying him, his captors flung him inside, locked the door and walked away.

Grabbing the bars of the door, Dane screamed, 'I'm innocent! I had nothing to do with it! I'm innocent!'

Bouncing off the walls, his cries were met with silence.

The cells around him were empty. Large, heavy doors were at each end of the passageway, bolted from the outside.

Defeated, he slumped to the floor.

It was hopeless.

At the moment he didn't have a friend in the world. With Lord Frederick against him, there didn't appear to be a way out of this. No matter what he said at the trial, they'd find him guilty – of treason, kidnapping and whatever else they wanted to charge him with.

How could they think such a thing?

The city and people he loved were abandoning him.

It was impossible, but true.

Why?

Why?

The rumble of an opening door snapped Dane out of his misery. He jumped to his feet, craning his neck to see down the passageway.

Footsteps approached.

'Who's there? Who is it?'

Dane shook the cell door.

'Who is it?' he asked again.

A guard bearing food and water stopped in front of him.

'If you want to eat, move to the back of your cell.'

Dane hesitated.

'You get one chance,' the guard said. 'Move to the back of your cell and face the wall.'

Dane stepped away from the door.

The guard pushed a tray through a gap cut in the bottom and walked away.

'Wait!' said Dane. 'I'm innocent!'

The guard's footsteps disappeared down the hallway, and the door at the end slammed shut, leaving Dane alone again.

Slumping to the floor, he looked at the food tray. Despite his predicament, his stomach growled. He couldn't remember the last time he'd taken a meal. Stale bread, cheese, and a cup of water – it would have to do.

Alone with nothing but his thoughts, time dragged on. A lone torch flickered on the far wall, his breathing the only sound.

Thoughts clogged his mind.

Where's Vanessa? Is she safe?

Why does everyone think I'm a traitor – even Lord Frederick?

Over and over it went, again and again.

No answers came, and several lonely hours passed before he finally fell asleep.

Surrounded, the darkness of the night concealing the size of the enemy force around them, they had no chance of escape.

'We offer this once,' said the lead captor. 'Throw down your weapons, now; or die.'

The group hesitated, looking at each other nervously, unsure what to do. Their Commander was dead, cut down at the onset of the attack.

'We will never surrender,' said one, reaching for his sword.

Before he could unsheathe, he felt a searing pain in his back, before everything went dark, and he fell forward in his saddle, dead. Others near him suffered the same fate – cut down, even though they had made no move to attack.

'Very well!' said the Junior Knight. 'I surrender.'

Slowly drawing his sword, he threw it to the ground.

'Dismount,' said one of his captors.

The Junior Knight did as he was told.

Two captors approached, towering over him, grabbing him and reaching into gauntlets, leggings and behind his back. Completely disarmed, one captor held him while another punched him hard in the stomach, following with a kick to the ribs as he fell.

Coughing and wincing in pain, the Junior Knight lay motionless, apart from his laboured breathing.

'You belong to Lord Raegan now,' the lead captor said to the rest of the group. 'Surrender and disarm; or die. I will not ask again.'

With nervous looks, the rest of the party complied.

A short time later, beaten and humiliated, they stood in a line, hands tied to the one in front.

'You're a coward,' one spat under his breath to the Junior Knight as they were led away. 'We would have found a way to defeat them.'

Staring straight ahead, the Junior Knight said nothing.

'I have her,' said Raegan ...
'I have her, and there's nothing you can do about it.
He ran towards them, pounding against an invisible wall ...
'Dane!' she screamed...
"Vanessa! ... Vanessa!'

A rough hand seized Dane by the hair, jolting him awake and hauling him to his feet. Another guard grabbed his hands, slapping them in shackles.

Dazed and confused, he looked around. Vanessa, Raegan, and the invisible wall were gone. He saw a guard on either side of him, grabbing him by the arms and leading him from his cell.

'Where are you taking me?'

The question went unanswered. Led down the passageway, a door at the end lay open, and they continued along a corridor to the left. They saw no one else on their journey; turning left and right, down several corridors, before coming to a large, open room.

Flung inside, Dane went crashing against a table. The door slammed shut behind him.

Dane had no idea where he was. The room was larger than his holding cell, and with the door closed, the small sliver of light in the room made it hard to see more than the outlines of the four walls.

For a time, nothing happened. Dane sat at the table, his head in his hands, mulling things over and over in his mind.

What was going on?

The door burst open and two men entered. Dane recognised the first immediately – Maurice Fairbrother, a member of the Brindabeare Council, the city's ruling body. He was accompanied by a guard, an imposing figure next to the much older, shorter, more rotund councillor.

Fairbrother took a seat at the table, running a hand through his the greying hair on his balding scalp.

'It will work better for you if you tell me exactly what happened,' he said. 'How the kidnapping was organised, who helped you, and most importantly, where the Princess is being held.'

'I had nothing to do with it!' said Dane. 'Surely you know that! I was attacked by Black Knights when I scouted the campsite. I fell down a cliff and was knocked out for at least four days. I was on my way to Feryndale when I found the carriage. No one has given me a chance to explain.'

Fairbrother leaned closer.

'It's no use,' he said. 'We know you were involved. You were seen at the kidnapping, aiding the Black Knights, and you were caught returning to the scene. Your trial and guilt are a formality. If not for the decrees of the Valentaland Charter, you would have swung from the noose well before now.

'Let's try this again. I want a full account of how the kidnap was organised, who was involved and where the Princess is being held.'

'I wasn't involved!' Dane yelled. 'I had nothing to do with it! Nothing! I have no idea where she is!'

The guard grabbed Dane by the hair, twisting his head awkwardly.

'Answer the questions,' he said.

'I had nothing to do with it,' said Dane, trying to grab at the arm pulling his hair.

Dragging Dane out of his chair, the guard wrapped his free arm around Dane's neck.

'Wrong answer,' said the guard.

'I ... don't ... know ... anything,' said Dane.

Fairbrother nodded. The guard released his grip and Dane slumped in his chair. Gasping fresh gulps of air, he looked pleadingly at Fairbrother.

'I see you are not interested in telling the truth,' said Fairbrother. 'I will leave you with Bowers for a while and see if that changes your mind.'

He stood and left the room.

Alone with the guard, a tall, heavy-set, man-mountain with arms that looked more like tree trunks, Dane knew how this would play out. It would be a battle of wills. Bowers would try and break him; wear him down and get the information they thought he had. Given his innocence, he could do nothing other than absorb whatever Bowers tried on him – no matter how painful it might be.

Slumped in his cell, Dane rubbed his neck. Aching all over; his face, arms, chest, sides, and legs were bruised and sore. His latest session with Bowers had been no different to the last.

He'd been slapped, twisted and contorted every which way but he'd doggedly proclaimed his innocence.

'Where is the Princess?' Bowers yelled, over and over, pummeling Dane around the room, striking him at will. 'Who helped you organise the kidnapping?'

Slaps, punches, kicks. To his face, chest and stomach. Thrown against a wall, over the table, on to the floor, dragged to his feet.

Over and over; and on and on.

Despite the beatings and the yelling, Dane held on. He made no attempt to resist, and with his wrists shackled, he could do nothing more than raise his arms, trying in vain to protect his face against the much stronger man.

Sometimes he felt on the brink of collapse, but he'd held his nerve. As the days passed, he found the beatings were somehow sustaining him. He'd be thrown back in his cell, a beaten lump of flesh and bones; and yet, despite the physical pain, he felt his mental strength growing.

Each day, the routine repeated. The only people he saw were the guards who brought his food, those who escorted him to the 'battleground' and Bowers.

Marking the ground in his cell after each session, he claimed a 'victory' in his mind, having survived another day. There were now six markings on the floor.

Hungry and thirsty at the end of each day, he'd managed to stomach the stale food they gave him.

Hearing the door open at the end of the corridor, he stood, moving to the back of his cell as he'd done every other day.

This time, he heard voices – familiar voices.

'Well, well,' said the first voice. 'Locked up, waiting to be hanged. Just where he should be.'

Dane couldn't believe his ears.

'Fenwick?' he said. 'What are you doing? How did you get in here?'

'With me,' the other voice replied.

'Who?' said Dane. 'Harrop?'

'Yes,' said Fenwick. 'Our friend Harrop works with Bowers. And while he hasn't been part of your interrogations, he's heard them all; and told me what a weak, sniveling coward you are. Begging for mercy at every turn.'

Dane felt his anger rise momentarily, before, overcome with exhaustion, he said meekly, 'whatever you say, Fenwick. Just put my food down and leave me alone.'

'I think not,' said Fenwick.

Keys tingled as Harrop unlocked Dane's cell, and with his friend standing guard, Fenwick strode in. Reaching down, he grabbed Dane roughly by the shoulder, hauling him to his feet.

'You've got what's been coming to you,' said Fenwick, kneeing Dane in the stomach.

Dane fell to the ground, crouching into a ball, doing his best to protect himself.

'That's for the tournament!' said Fenwick with a kick.

'That's for mucking out your stable!' he said, stamping on Dane's ribs.

'That's for keeping me out of the Royal Knights!' he added with another kick.

'You should stand up and fight like a man!' he yelled, kicking Dane again. 'But, as usual, you're nothing but a coward.'

Fenwick stepped back, looking at Dane, who lay gasping and wheezing on the floor.

Dane glanced at the thin, weasel-like face of his attacker; too battered from all the beatings he'd taken to do anything.

Harrop stood behind Fenwick, his large, bulky frame blocking the door, a wide grin on his face.

'Pathetic,' Fenwick spat. 'But far be it for me to deny a prisoner his rations.'

Taking the food tray from Harrop, he dumped the contents over Dane.

'Enjoy your last night among the living,' said Fenwick, stepping out of the cell.

Crumpled on the ground, facing the back of his cell, Dane heard the door shut behind him, the key turn in the lock, and the fading footsteps and laughter of his attacker.

Breathing heavily, rolling himself slowly into a sitting position, he slumped against the back wall of the cell.

Just another beating, he thought, letting his mind wander.

Where's Vanessa?

Do they know anything about where she is?

They've got nothing from me, but has anyone found anything?

He found himself drifting off to sleep when a new light in the hallway distracted him.

He'd seen it before. Not here, but somewhere else. He knew this light - small, yet strong enough for the person using it to see a short distance.

Despite his aches, Dane leaped to his feet.

'Lord Frederick!' he said softly.

A moment later the wizard stood in front of his cell.

'Thank goodness! Are you going to let me out? I'm innocent! You couldn't say it in front of the guards, but you know I'm innocent! Please, get me out of here!'

Lord Frederick raised his hand.

'I'm sorry,' he said. 'I cannot release you. You are a prisoner accused of treason.'

Dane felt his throat go dry. His eyes gaped and his mouth fell open.

'Yes,' said Lord Frederick. 'I'm afraid the trial will have to proceed.'

'Vanessa? Have you found her?'

'We know nothing of her whereabouts,' Lord Frederick replied. 'Other than she was captured. Presumably, she is now Raegan's prisoner.'

'Mother?' said Dane in a rush.

'Will escorted her to safety.'

Dane nodded.

'Good,' he said. 'You know I'm innocent. I was attacked myself. I fell down a cliff. I don't know how long I was there. The rock mites helped me. I found the camp. The Advance Patrol were dead – ambushed. I'd just found Vanessa's carriage when they arrested me.'

Lord Frederick nodded.

'I believe you,' he said. 'Unfortunately, apart from your mother and Will, the surviving knights in the entourage say you are a traitor.'

'Why would they do that?'

'All of them swear they saw you in the company of the Black Knights who captured the Princess.'

Dane's eyes widened in disbelief.

'That's not possible,' he replied.

'I'm afraid it is,' said Lord Frederick.

Reaching through the cell bars, he touched Dane on the arm. In the next instant a thin wisp of green smoke rose from the floor, and two exact images of Dane appeared, one on each side of Lord Frederick.

Dane's heart sank.

Now he understood.

Raegan had projected a duplication of his image to the scene of the kidnapping. Unfortunately, he also knew there was nothing he could say or do to prove it.

Chapter 7
ON TRIAL

A rough hand shook Dane awake.

Rubbing his eyes open, he noticed a tray at his feet. There were more helpings than usual. A couple of guards were in attendance, one with his hands full.

'Eat and put these on,' he said, placing a set of clean clothes at Dane's feet. 'You will not go to trial looking like a rat; even if that is what you are.'

The guards left.

Today was the trial.

The wait was over.

Today he would be found guilty and hanged.

The hopelessness of his fate washed over him.

It would only be a matter of hours now.

Everyone in the court would be against him.

He knew the councillors personally, but it gave him no comfort.

Convinced of his guilt, Fairbrother had sanctioned the beatings he'd suffered at the hands of Bowers and his cronies.

Lindstrom, his one-time tutor, would offer nothing – formal and proper in everything he did.

Medhurst had never liked him, and Dane knew he'd be in his element; lauding himself over all present, his loud, condescending voice echoing though the chamber, full of hunger and relish at the prospect of passing the sentence to hang.

Hindmarsh wouldn't help. A few years older than himself, Hindmarsh had quickly progressed to his current position, and in addition to his physical prowess, Dane had experienced his meticulous eye for detail firsthand – his eyes searching and probing, seeing what others did not. Hindmarsh would give a full and comprehensive account of everything he'd seen, all the way down to the texture of the leaves on the trees, if asked.

No matter where he looked, it seemed hopeless. With no way to prove his story, the overwhelming evidence others would present would drown his version of events.

He wasn't afraid of dying – every knight strived to serve his King with honour and valor, with no hesitation at the prospect of laying down his life in battle.

But for a knight, *any* knight, to be hanged as a traitor – there was nothing more dishonourable than that.

Dane's position was even worse – the son of the great Gil Thorburn; perhaps the finest to ever serve in a Brindabeare uniform, was to die a traitor.

What would become of Marilena?

How would she cope with the shame?

Would she be forced out of the city – an outcast – because of him?

Unable to touch his food, he changed his clothes and waited.

Five guards arrived, one bearing shackles.

Dane held out his hands.

The group headed towards the main council chamber, which would serve as Brindabeare's courtroom. Royal Knights manned every point of the walk; eyes locking on Dane as he passed.

The party reached the entrance to the council chambers. Muffled sounds came from inside, before, with a rush, the doors were thrust open.

Dane had been in this room before, but today it was different. Instead of a large table in the centre, the councillors were seated on a dais at the far end.

Apart from a centre aisle, the rest of the room was full of seats. A deathly silence filled the chamber as the guards led Dane towards the dais.

Every eye was trained on him. Their expressions were the same he'd seen while being led through the city.

Hate.

Loathing.

Disgust.

Lindstrom moved to the centre of the dais. His face layered with the wrinkles gained from a lifetime of study, he spoke in his usual dutiful, direct voice.

'We are gathered today to witness the trial of Dane Thorburn, who is herewith accused of treason, for his role in the recent kidnap of Princess Vanessa Meriwether, heir to the throne.'

Dane glanced at the King, who stared him down with his daughter's eyes and a look on his face as hard as stone. While the King possessed neither the physical presence of the General, or the inborn power of Lord Frederick; his demeanor, radiance and presence oozed leadership and strength, leaving no one in doubt as to who ruled the land.

Stealing a glance at Lord Frederick, Dane saw him wearing the same look as the King; but as their eyes met, Dane felt the slightest hint of a smile.

'Councillor Medhurst will outline the King's case against the accused.'

Striding to the centre of the dais, trying in vain to stand taller with each step, Medhurst puffed his chest out, and addressed the chamber.

'Dane Thorburn is accused of conspiring to kidnap Princess Vanessa Meriwether during her recent journey to Feryndale. That he assisted the wizard Raegan and his Black Knights in an ambush of the Princess's escort in the early evening of the day in question.'

Dane turned his mind away from Medhurst, trying one last time to think of a way out of this mess. There had to be something he could say, something he could find that would prove the truth of his story.

He went over it one more time, the events rolling through his mind.

Scouting the site; the Black Knights; the cliff; the rock mites, finding Thunder.

Something flared inside him for the first time.

Thunder ...

Dane felt a jab in the ribs.

Everyone was watching him.

Medhurst looked on impatiently.

'Well?' he said. 'How do you plead?'

Dane stood, locking his eyes on Medhurst and the King.

'Not guilty,' he replied.

Shouts broke out in the room.

'Liar!'

'Guilty!'

'Hang him!'

'Very well,' said Medhurst when the noise died down. 'I call my first witness, Commander Aidan Hindmarsh.'

Faces turned to the entrance.

Hindmarsh strode into the room, stopping at the foot of the dais.

'You are Commander Aidan Hindmarsh?' asked Medhurst.

'I am,' Hindmarsh replied.

'You were the Commander in charge of Princess Vanessa's escort?'

'I was.'

'Please describe the events leading up to the kidnap of Princess Vanessa.'

Hindmarsh recounted his story.

'I see,' said Medhurst once he'd finished. 'Commander, it appears to have been a detailed and well-planned attack. Would you agree?'

'Regrettably, I do,' said Hindmarsh. 'The balls of fire landed in the exact places where they would do the most damage. We'd never seen anything like it. It caught us completely by surprise. We had no time to react and were overwhelmed by the nature and scale of it.'

'Would you say,' said Medhurst, 'that to have been able to know exactly when you would arrive at the attack point, and thus be able to inflict so much damage so quickly, the enemy would have needed to have someone inform them?'

Hindmarsh nodded.

'It was so well executed, not just in light of the fireballs, but also in the way the enemy surrounded us and cut off all our avenues of escape. From the very moment we were attacked, they completely outflanked us, taking away any chance we had of escape.

'For a brief moment I thought we'd been able to escort the Princess away, but the areas beyond the attack point were so well manned, they captured her quite easily. I don't believe it would have been possible to execute such a well-orchestrated and well-timed attack, unless they had someone informing them of our movements.'

'Indeed,' said Medhurst, warming to the task. 'Tell us, Commander, during your party's efforts to save the Princess; in addition to the Black Knights, did you see anyone else in the enemy force?'

'I did.'

'And who was that?'

Hindmarsh pointed at Dane.

'Dane Thorburn,' he said.

'And yet, he had not been seen since you sent him to scout the campsite?'

'That's correct.'

Medhurst smiled.

'Commander, while it is not appropriate for you to reveal all about how you organise and manage the Princess's escort, would you please tell the court how you arrange your scouting patrols?'

'In most cases,' Hindmarsh replied, 'the scouts know the area and have travelled the land we are covering on several occasions.'

'And yet,' said Medhurst with emphasis, 'the accused was on his first assignment outside the city, and volunteered to be in the scouting party on the night he disappeared?'

'That's correct,' said Hindmarsh.

Dane seethed as he saw the way Medhurst was manipulating Hindmarsh – asking questions in a manner designed to paint him in the worst possible light.

He saw Medhurst smile knowingly once more.

'And tell me, Commander, isn't scouting one of the more menial tasks? One for which your knights would not willingly volunteer?'

'Royal Knights don't hesitate to complete whatever task is assigned to them,' said Hindmarsh.

'But in your opinion,' said Medhurst quickly, ignoring Hindmarsh's response, 'why would the accused have been so eager to scout the Princess's campsite on the afternoon in question, if not for the opportunity it presented him to escape and meet with the Black Knights involved in the attack?'

'I can't say for certain,' said Hindmarsh. 'But it certainly provided the best opportunity to abandon the entourage.'

'Indeed it did,' said Medhurst. 'Commander, how many of your party survived the attack?'

'Including myself and excluding the accused; eight,' said Hindmarsh.

'Eight?' said Medhurst. 'From a party fifty strong?'

Hindmarsh nodded.

'Let all know,' said Medhurst with relish, 'that over forty Royal Knights died during the attack that resulted in the kidnapping of our Princess – an attack aided and abetted by the accused!'

Roars of outrage filled the chamber.

'Traitor!'

'Shame!'

'Hang him!'

'Commander,' said Medhurst, 'did you see the accused attack any of your party? The very men who trusted him as one of their own?'

Hindmarsh nodded.

'I did,' he said.

More howls of fury filled the chamber.

'And how do you feel about that?' asked Medhurst.

Hindmarsh glanced at Dane for a moment before answering.

'It sickens me to my very soul,' he said. 'Such action is contrary to everything a knight stands for.'

'Thank you, Commander Hindmarsh,' said Medhurst, barely able to contain the excitement in his voice. 'You may leave.'

Dane's mind filled with dread. It could not have gotten off to a worse start. Hearing Hindmarsh's testimony, he hadn't the slightest doubt all in the chamber hated him more than they did already, their eyes dripping with anger and outrage, ready to see him hang.

How could he possibly survive this? Every other witness would say the same things as Hindmarsh.

He caught Lord Frederick's eye again. Like before, he saw that strange hint of a smile; like a knowing wink, as though Lord Frederick wanted this to happen exactly as it had.

'I call Royal Knight Harvey Rosenthal,' said Medhurst.

Dane turned to see Harvey walking towards the front of the chamber. The Black Knight had said Harvey was dead. Any relief he may have felt that Harvey was alive vanished with the look of loathing Harvey gave him as he passed.

Medhurst took his time exploring the sequence of events around scouting the campsite, in order to corroborate what Hindmarsh had said.

'And you searched the campsite, the perimeter and surrounds and found no trace of him?'

'None at all,' Harvey replied. 'The Princess was very insistent, yet we found nothing. He deserted me, and when I saw him again, he was escaping with the Black Knights.'

Dane cringed.

Another wound – to be accused of deserting another knight. It was the least of the charges against him, but it hurt all the same.

'Thank you,' said Medhurst with a satisfied smile. 'You may go.'

Medhurst looked at Dane, a triumphant grin on his face. He was in his element, knowing he had his case won, determined to milk it for all its worth, basking in the glory of the moment.

'I call Royal Knight Richard Lovell,' he said.

Lovell offered Dane no hint of recognition as he walked past.

The sequence of events repeated.

'And you saw the accused kill one of your colleagues?' asked Medhurst when Lovell finished.

Lovell nodded.

'I did,' he said. 'Royal Knight Gordon Oppen was my closest friend. We'd trained as cadets together, serving in the same regiment, before being promoted to the Royal Knights. A knight of impeccable character. He has a wife and child.'

'A wife and child now abandoned, due to the actions of the accused,' said Medhurst without a hint of sympathy. 'Thank you for your testimony.'

'I hope you *hang!*' Lovell spat at Dane as he made his way from the chamber.

Wincing, Dane closed his eyes, but said nothing.

'I call Royal Knight Byron Southwell,' said Medhurst.

As more witnesses came forward, Dane turned his mind back, searching desperately, one last time, for something that might help him.

Thunder ... something about Thunder bothered him.

What *was* it?

'I call Mistress Marilena Thorburn,' Medhurst announced.

Dane snapped himself away from his thoughts – *Mother!*

He hadn't seen her since leaving to scout the campsite.

His face turned to despair at the sight of Marilena making her way slowly towards the front of the room. Gaunt and withdrawn, it looked as though she hadn't eaten in days. Her face was pale, and he could see she'd been crying.

Dane felt sick to the pit of his stomach.

'No!' he yelled. 'She doesn't have to see this!'

Marilena looked at him and broke down. Sobbing uncontrollably, she collapsed.

Dane sprang to his feet.

'Mother!'

A swift punch to the stomach sent Dane reeling into his seat. Two sets of hands clamped down on him.

A couple of guards helped Marilena to her feet. Looking as though she'd collapse again, the guards held her upright.

'State your name,' instructed Medhurst.

'M-Mistress Marilena Th-Thorburn,' Marilena sobbed, her voice just above a whisper.

'Mistress,' said Medhurst, 'I see this stresses you, so I will get straight to the point. On the night of the Princess's kidnap, apart from the Black Knights, who else was with them?'

A hush fell over the courtroom.

Marilena hesitated.

The courtroom waited with bated breath.

'Mistress, please answer the question.'

Marilena opened her mouth, but no words came out.

'If you can't speak, just point,' said Medhurst.

Marilena hesitated again.

'No,' she said finally.

Medhurst smiled.

'Mistress. I understand how you must feel,' he said.

Dane boiled inside. At that moment he wanted nothing more than to punch Medhurst in the face and wipe the smug look off his face.

'But I remind you,' added Medhurst, 'if you do not answer the question, I will have you arrested and thrown in prison, and tried for treason in the same manner as the accused. I ask one more time. If there was anyone you saw apart from the Black Knights who was in any way involved with the kidnapping, either tell us who it was, or point him out.'

Marilena wobbled, ready to topple over again. With an almighty effort she started to turn towards Dane.

Dane couldn't believe what was unfolding. In what seemed like slow motion, he and everyone in the chamber saw Marilena turn and point at him.

Everyone in the room gasped.

A moment later pandemonium broke out.

'His own mother!'

'His mother says he's guilty!'

Marilena screamed, collapsing to the floor.

Eventually the noise died down.

Medhurst wore a grin as wide as a chasm, knowing he'd sealed Dane's fate.

The guards carried Marilena out of the room.

Watching her leave, Dane's heart ached. If he ever got out of this, he'd make sure Medhurst would pay for what he'd just done.

Once again, Dane saw the hint of a smile on Lord Frederick's face, in such a way it appeared to be directed to him alone. Torn by what he'd just seen, Lord Frederick's reaction made no sense.

'I call Royal Knight Will Hevenshire,' said Medhurst.

Dane strained to see as the doors swung open and Will walked into the room. Will looked uneasy at what he was going to have to do. He strode to the front of the room and stopped in front of Medhurst.

'State your name.'

'Royal Knight Will Hevenshire.'

Medhurst went straight for the kill.

'And you were with the Princess and Mistress Thorburn when the Princess was captured?'

'I was,' Will answered.

'And apart from the Black Knights, who else was with them? Who else played a part in the kidnap of the Princess?'

Will hesitated.

'You will answer the question,' Medhurst ordered, 'or I will have you thrown in prison and tried for treason.'

Will took a deep breath.

'It appeared as though I saw Royal Knight Dane Thorburn.'

Medhurst's face was aghast.

'You *appeared* to see Royal Knight Dane Thorburn? What do you mean '*appeared*'? Either you saw him, or you didn't. Which is it?'

'Well,' said Will, 'it *looked* like Dane, but it didn't seem to *be* him.'

Dane listened intently. For the first time since his capture, someone was standing up for him. He knew Lord Frederick believed him; now Will was the first to argue for him in public. It wasn't much – but it was something.

Medhurst wasn't going to let Will off though.

'I say again. You either saw him or you didn't. Which is it?'

Will hesitated.

'I think I saw him,' he said. 'But somehow, it wasn't him at all.'

'Enough!' Medhurst yelled. 'Clearly you are trying to save your friend. Well let me tell you something, *Royal Knight* Will Hevenshire. This courtroom has heard the testimony of eight witnesses, including the mother of the accused, who all say they saw him at the scene of the crime.

'In failing to answer the question, I arrest you on the charge of treason. Guards!'

'One moment,' said Lord Frederick. 'I would like to ask Royal Knight Hevenshire a couple of questions.'

'Lord Frederick,' Medhurst stammered. 'This is highly unusual.'

'Nonetheless, if the King has no objection?'

The King nodded.

Lord Frederick turned to Will.

'Royal Knight Hevenshire, did the person who appeared to be Dane Thorburn speak at all.'

'No,' said Will. 'He didn't say anything. To me, or anyone.'

Lord Frederick nodded.

'And what colour was the horse of the person who appeared to be Dane Thorburn?'

Will's face went blank.

Dane stared, dumbfounded.

Everyone in the courtroom wore the same stunned look.

Dane was on the verge of being found guilty, and Lord Frederick wanted to know the colour of the horse he was riding?

'Lord Frederick,' said Medhurst, stunned at what he'd heard at his moment of triumph. 'Surely the question is not relevant.'

'Royal Knight Hevenshire will answer the question,' Lord Frederick replied.

Everyone waited, wondering what Will was going to say, and what it could possibly mean.

'The horse was grey,' he said.

Snap!

Like a bolt of lightning across a dark sky, a chain of thoughts exploded in Dane's mind.

In an instant he found what he'd been searching for.

He could prove the projected duplication was real!

Murmurs rippled through the room. No one except Dane, Lord Frederick and maybe Will understood what had just been revealed.

Lord Frederick smiled.

'Is this your final witness Medhurst?' asked Lord Frederick.

'Y-yes,' Medhurst replied. 'Royal Knight Hevenshire, you may go. But don't go too far. Once we finish here, we will be looking for you.'

'That is quite out of line, Councillor Medhurst,' said Lord Frederick. 'It is no one's place to threaten a man unjustly.'

Medhurst took a couple of deep breaths, controlling his boiling anger as best he could.

'Royal Knight Hevenshire,' he said. 'Leave.'

'If it pleases the court,' Will replied, 'I would like to stay.'

The King nodded.

Will took a vacant seat on a stool a few rows behind Dane.

'Very well,' said Lindstrom. 'I believe we are ready to hear from the accused. Would the accused please stand.'

The hands restraining Dane released their grip.

'State your name,' said Lord Frederick.

'Royal Knight Dane Thorburn.'

Jeers and howls of protest echoed through the courtroom.

'Traitor!'

'You're no Royal Knight!'

'You're a disgrace!'

'You'll hang for this!'

Lord Frederick raised his hand and the noise died down.

'Royal Knight Thorburn, please recount, in as much detail as possible, what happened from the time you were sent to scout the campsite, until the time you were apprehended.'

Taking his time, Dane recounted his story, stopping a couple of times when shouts of protest drowned him out. Remaining calm throughout, he covered every detail; no matter how many taunts and jeers, no matter how absurd his story sounded.

'Thank you,' said Lord Frederick when Dane finished. 'And how do you explain accounts of the witnesses brought forward by Councillor Medhurst; all of whom say you assisted the Black Knights during the kidnapping?'

'He's lying!' a voice yelled.

Lord Frederick waited for Dane to answer, the same knowing hint of a smile in his eye.

'It was a projected duplication,' Dane replied.

Faces in the court went blank.

'Please, explain what you mean,' said Lord Frederick.

'Raegan took something that belonged to me and used it to project my image on another person – a Black Knight at the kidnapping. That would make everyone who was there think it was me.'

Screams filled the courtroom.

'Liar!'

'You can't prove it!'

'A likely story!'

Lord Frederick raised his hand, and the noise faded away.

'Let me ask another question,' he said. 'What is your horse's name?'

Faces in the room went blank again – what was it about the horse?

'Thunder,' Dane replied.

'Describe him for me.'

'He's a little over three years old. I've had him since he was a weanling. We've been through a lot together.'

Lord Frederick nodded.

'Yes. We all know Thunder. We've seen you escorting the Princess on her rides, patrolling the city as a part of her escort, and many other times. We even saw you on Thunder when you were led through the city several days ago. Is there anyone here who can testify they have, at one time or another, seen the accused on his horse?'

Heads nodded.

None had any idea what it meant, but all agreed – they knew Dane and Thunder.

'One more question,' said Lord Frederick. 'What colour is he?'

Everyone in the courtroom answered in their mind.

His heart leaping, Dane said the answer in a loud, clear voice.

'Black.'

'Black,' Lord Frederick repeated. 'Does everyone here attest to the fact that Thunder is a black horse?'

As one, all in the chamber nodded.

Dane had a huge grin on his face. Although they didn't realise it, everyone in the room had just proved his innocence.

'Thank you,' said Lord Frederick. 'Now, allow me to recount what you have heard. All witnesses called by Councillor Medhurst testified they saw Royal Knight Thorburn in the company of Black Knights at the scene of the Princess's kidnapping.

'Royal Knight Thorburn has testified as to what happened since he was sent to scout the campsite, up to the point of his apprehension by our Royal Knights.

'The respective versions provide an interesting contrast as to Royal Knight Thorburn's involvement in the kidnapping of the Princess; and to this I would ask a question that has not been considered until this point – namely – if Royal Knight Thorburn had been involved in the kidnapping, why would he then return to the scene some days later, when, had he been in league with Raegan and the Black Knights, there would be no reason for him to do so?'

Nervous chatter broke out.

For the first time since his capture, Dane saw confusion on the faces of everyone present. Smiling to himself, he waited for Lord Frederick to continue.

'Royal Knight Hevenshire testified the person he saw *appeared* to be Royal Knight Thorburn, although it didn't seem to *be* him. Royal Knight Hevenshire also recounted the person who appeared to be Royal Knight Thorburn did not speak at any time.

'And finally, during his testimony, Royal Knight Hevenshire informed the court the person thought to be Royal Knight Thorburn rode a *grey* horse, when in fact we *all* know, as you yourselves have verified just now that Royal Knight Thorburn's horse, Thunder, is *black!*'

The court let out a collective gasp.

Oh my goodness!

As one, they realised they'd been wrong.

Blinded by the outrage of Vanessa's kidnapping; the accounts of Dane with the Black Knights, and his capture and imprisonment, they hadn't considered for a moment he might be innocent.

Now, as clear as the day outside, everyone knew Dane's story was true – he'd been attacked by Black Knights and his image projected to the scene of the kidnapping, so everyone would think it was him. What Raegan had failed to do was project Thunder's image.

Lord Frederick turned to the King.

The King strode to the centre of the dais.

'I find the accused cleared of all charges,' he said. 'Royal Knight Thorburn's name is to be cleared of this incident. Royal Knight Thorburn's status is to be reinstated without further delay.'

The King, Lord Frederick and councillors departed through a door adjacent to the dais. The rest of the chamber burst into conversation, eagerly recounting what had just happened.

Will walked over and waited for the guards to remove Dane's shackles, before shaking hands and wrapping him in a bear hug.

Dane grinned at his friend.

'Thanks.'

'Don't mention it,' said Will. 'You can repay me later.'

Chapter 8
A DARING DASH

The group finally came to a stop. They'd been travelling since daybreak, maintaining a steady pace. With the cloud around her, Vanessa had no clue where she was. Surrounded by a thin, dark mist, she could see only a couple of feet in any direction.

Guarded by a group of Black Knights, not a word had been said during the entire journey.

It had become a routine.

Awake before daybreak; travel until the high point of the sun; rest; travel into the afternoon; rest; travel until sunset; stop somewhere under the cover of darkness to spend the night. On some days they slept in the open; others, when they arrived at a province, or whatever the settlement happened to be, the night would be spent in a cold, hard cell.

She had not seen Raegan since dining that one night at his table, wherever that may have been.

A hand reached up, dragging her out of the saddle.

Stifling a scream as her body twisted awkwardly, she shrugged herself free of the Black Knight's grip.

'When all this is over, you and your friends will die. I will see to it personally.'

Grabbing her arms, the Black Knight pulled her within inches of his face.

'You will not speak unless you are spoken to,' he said, squeezing his hands tighter.

Vanessa winced under the Black Knight's grip.

'Do you understand?' he asked, increasing the pressure on her arms.

'*Yes!*' Vanessa screamed.

The Black Knight threw her to the ground.

'Very well. It's important you realise who is in charge now. You bear no title, no rank, no relevance. We answer to Lord Raegan only, and it is purely by his will that you live.'

Vanessa said nothing.

'There,' said the Black Knight, pointing to a boulder about twenty feet from where they were standing. 'We will collect you when we are ready to continue.'

Defeated for the moment, Vanessa walked slowly to her resting place. Stale bread and cheese, and a small waterskin were waiting. It would do nothing to calm her appetite, but it was better than nothing at all.

Leaning against the boulder, she undid her hair and shook it out, before slowly resetting it.

She noticed the torches, staked in a circle, about thirty feet in diameter. Outside the perimeter, she could see nothing apart from the misty cloud masking everything beyond it.

Each torch reached about a foot from the ground, emitting thin wisps of grey smoke.

It had to be something Raegan created.

The reasons for not allowing her to be aware of her surroundings were clear enough.

Did the cloud hide the entire party? A group of ten or more Black Knights travelling together would be sure to draw attention.

She stretched her arms, rubbing out the aches where the Black Knight had grabbed her. She'd remember that one; he appeared to be the leader, and although she couldn't say for certain based on his appearance; judging by his voice and the way he carried himself, she had a feeling he'd been one of her assailants the night she'd been captured.

In what seemed no time at all, one of the group made his way over, leading her back to the horses.

She offered no protest – now wasn't the time.

'Aaaaargh!'

'I will ask again. Where are the other patrols heading?'

Gasping for breath, the Junior Knight looked helplessly at his assailant.

'I ... don't ... know,' he said.

'That is not the answer I'm looking for.'

With a nod to his companion, the Junior Knight's captor grabbed him by the hair, pulling and bending his body back as far as he could.

Kneeling, with his hands tied behind his back, the Junior Knight could offer no resistance to the way his captors were contorting him, or against the punches to his exposed ribs he received at the same time.

'Aaaaargh!' he screamed again.

It had been like this for half an hour. Cuts and bruises were blotching his face, blood seeping into and matting his hair. Stripped of all protective armour, his chest, sides and back were taking a heavy beating.

'You are either very stubborn, or you really don't know,' said the first captor.

'Please,' begged the Junior Knight.

Another punch to the ribs.

'Please! Stop!'

'We will stop when you answer the question. How many other patrols have been dispatched? How many are in each patrol? And where are they headed?'

'I ... said ... I ... don't ... know. Why ... won't ... you ... believe me?'

Another punch to the ribs.

'Because we don't trust Brindabeare filth to tell the truth.'

Releasing his grip, the first captor pushed the Junior Knight forward.

With no strength left, the Junior Knight collapsed to the ground.

'He's out,' said the second captor.

Both men grabbed the Junior Knight by the shoulders, hauling the limp body to its feet, dragging him down the narrow corridor.

Stopping at a cell door, they waited for it to be opened, before throwing him inside.

Murmurings broke out among the other prisoners.

'Is he dead?' asked one.

'If he is, they would not have brought him back,' said another.

The day had unfolded the same as the others.

They'd arrived at their afternoon break; shorter than the middle of the day, but a chance to rest, nonetheless.

The window of opportunity would be small. If the moment passed, she would have to wait another day.

The Black Knights tethered their horses. Vanessa waited patiently while two approached; one taking control of the horse, the other reaching up and wrenching her out of the saddle.

Twisting and turning awkwardly as usual, this time she collapsed in a heap on the ground, lay motionless, and began counting to herself.

One ... two ... three ... four ... five ...

'Get up!' the Black Knight ordered.

Six ... seven ... eight ...

'I said, get up!'

The Black Knight reached down, grabbing her by the arm.

In the same instant she struck.

Turning her body as his hand gripped her arm, Vanessa sprang to her feet, swinging her other hand in the same motion, smashing the rock she'd been holding into the face of her captor.

With a scream, he collapsed to the ground.

Seizing her chance, Vanessa leaped aboard her horse, turning and kicking the other Black Knight, tearing the reins from his hand, and taking flight.

It took a couple of moments for the others to realise what had happened. By the time they reacted, she'd reached full stride.

As one, they jumped to their feet, racing to the horses.

Vanessa pulled another rock from a pocket, throwing it at a torch. Falling to the ground, a hole opened in the misty cloud, a corridor appearing with clear surroundings ahead.

With a surge of adrenaline, she urged her mount through the gap, riding for her life.

Her assailants yelled behind her.

Squinting into the fading sun, it took her a moment to get her bearings. Seeing real light for the first time since her capture was almost dizzying.

The first objective was escape – then figure out everything else; where she might be, where she needed to go. Seeing some cover to her right, she veered in that direction.

The Black Knights split into groups, riding to the left and right, seeking to outflank her and drive her towards one group or the other.

'Alive!' the leader shouted. 'She is to be taken alive!'

Vanessa went further into the trees, weaving her way in and out, swerving so hard at one point she nearly unseated herself. She could hear shouts to her right, so she cut back the other way, riding away from the noise.

She wasn't sure what lay ahead, but her main concern was keeping the distance between herself and the Black Knights. She'd been on this horse for days, and although it wasn't her own mount, she felt it responding to every flick and turn of her wrists, seemingly grateful to be given the chance to run at speed.

The Black Knights to her right were closer; in a short time, they'd be within striking distance. Riding harder, a fallen tree loomed in her path. With no time to think, she didn't hesitate, riding to it at full speed and hurling herself over. Her horse jumped truly, its hind legs grazing the fallen log as it went over.

She heard a groan behind her. The log appeared to have claimed at least one Black Knight, and for a moment she thought she'd lost them all, until she caught their voices – still in pursuit, but not as close as before.

The foliage was thicker now, slowing her progress. Without a clear path, she had to force her way ahead, cutting her own trail.

She caught sight of the Black Knights on her left, several yards away, striving to get ahead of her, so they could close in and force her towards the other group. Turning away from them slightly, she saw the way ahead drop a couple of feet, heading downhill about fifty yards, before levelling out again.

Using this to advantage, she made her next move, veering slightly to her right as she travelled down the slope, urging her mount to go faster.

It brought the result she'd hoped for. Her change of direction and the downward slope of the terrain gave an additional burst of speed, allowing her to increase the distance between herself and those chasing to her left; taking away the distance they'd claimed in trying to outflank her.

Straightening after another fifty yards, the distance between herself and her pursuers on both sides was now the same. The Black Knights had lost the advantage of hunting in two packs.

The undergrowth had thinned again. Straining her ears, she heard no noise behind her – no shouts from the Black Knights, no sound of hooves.

For the first time, she dared to look back.

She saw nothing to her right or left.

Another burst of energy surged through her. Spurring her mount again, she rode on, emerging into a small clearing. With no visual clues to know where she might be, she could do nothing more than continue straight ahead.

After another couple of minutes, she looked back a second time. She saw nothing, heard nothing.

Daring to slow down; first to a slow gallop, then to a walk, she listened again.

No shouts.

No horses giving chase.

Taking a couple of deep breaths, she dared to wonder.

Have I done it?

Have I escaped?

The plan was sound. Using the routine of the day to her advantage, and offering no resistance, she'd lulled the Black Knights into a sense of boredom and familiarity.

If she came across as no threat, she knew they'd let their guard down sooner or later.

Seen to be no threat, they wouldn't be as vigilant in watching her – not the way they would if they thought she'd try to escape at any moment.

They, like others, probably thought such ideas and thoughts beyond her – that she'd have no aptitude in military affairs, no physical capabilities.

Dane had told her it was a good thing, something that may come in useful one day.

'Let them think you're weak, and when the time comes, use it to your advantage.'

She'd now done that very thing.

Straining her ears, she listened for the slightest sound.

Dead silence.

It was almost too quiet...

'There she is!'

She heard the voice – faint; but audible just the same. At the same time, she saw a group of four in the corner of her eye.

Taking flight once more, she raced away.

The terrain started dropping again; lower and lower, until she caught sight of a water crossing ahead.

About twenty yards wide, the approach was slippery and muddy. Instead of crossing straight over, she veered to the left. With the water barely over the hooves of her horse, the move cost her no time. Spotting a solid, grassy exit point, she was about ten yards to the left of her entry when she left the water, leaving no clue behind. With any luck, this would confuse the Black Knights, if only momentarily, giving her precious seconds to put more distance between them.

Heading further in the direction of her exit, through some brush and undergrowth, she disappeared into another cluster of trees. The voices had gone again, giving her renewed hope.

With the sun fading quickly, it would soon be dark.

Guessing the Black Knights had left their torches and arrows at the rest point, she knew her chances of escape would be better if she could avoid them until nightfall.

Working a new plan in her mind, she rode on, maintaining the distance from her adversaries. Sweat poured off her, yet she felt nothing, running high on adrenaline.

The land was a mixture of clearings and trees, and even now, there were no clues as to where she might be. She kept going, still focused on her escape, and at the same time starting to think about what she would do once she'd lost her pursuers.

Several minutes passed, the sun slipping below the horizon; a few more, and the night sky would be out.

To her right she noticed a denser cluster of trees. Heading towards it, something familiar caught her attention, and she slowed down.

Sure enough, clearly visible to her, it was there – a scuttler's portal.

Forest foragers who live in the ever-expanding caves they dug to hoard their collection of rocks, sticks and other treasures, scuttler's caves were invisible to the untrained eye. Vanessa and Dane knew the skill of finding them, having been shown by Lord Frederick several years ago.

Dismounting a few feet away, Vanessa tethered her horse among a clump of bushes, out of sight.

Approaching the cave, she stopped a couple of feet from the entrance.

A curious, rodent-like face appeared.

Vanessa took a cautious step forward and spoke quietly.

'Greetings. I am Princess Vanessa of Brindabeare.'

The scuttler came out of the cave, walking towards her.

'I'm friends with many scuttlers,' she said. 'Reuben lives in the Great Forest. He's a special friend of mine.'

The scuttler's eyes widened, and the face broke into a smile.

'My name is Audrey,' she said. 'Reuben is my friend too.'

Vanessa smiled, reaching out to shake Audrey's hand.

Like all scuttlers, Audrey stood about three feet tall, her light grey fur covered in a combination of rags and other materials she'd found in her foraging.

'Audrey,' said Vanessa. 'I need you to find Reuben. Tell him to find Lord Frederick and bring him here.'

Audrey nodded.

'Everyone is looking for you.'

'I escaped,' Vanessa replied. 'I need to get back to Brindabeare. Can you use your portal and find Reuben?'

Audrey nodded again.

'Stay here. I will find him.'

Relieved, Vanessa watched Audrey walk a short distance to her right, towards her portal, a hidden opening near her cave. All scuttlers had one, allowing them to travel to the portal of another, no matter how far away.

She couldn't believe it – she'd done it!

In a matter of moments, Reuben would be here with Lord Frederick, and she'd be safe.

Relaxing for the first time since her capture, she realised how tired she felt. She'd been riding a while; her first real activity since capture, and as her adrenaline slowed, there were aches in her arms and legs she hadn't felt before.

Raegan would be very angry now, she thought with a smile.

Lord Frederick and the Royal Knights will find him and end his crusade for power once and for all ...

'Did you really think you would escape?'

Vanessa snapped her head around.

Two Black Knights emerged in front of her.

Two more emerged from behind her.

Vanessa turned around on the spot.

The Black Knights walked their mounts forward, closing in around her.

'No,' she breathed. '*No!*'

A moment later she was trapped.

'You had no hope,' said the leader. 'You were in our sights the entire time. Having made what you thought was a valiant escape; you can now see it was nothing more than a fool's errand. And sitting here, in the middle of nowhere, with no help to call on? That is the greatest folly of all.'

Dismounting, he reached out, grabbing Vanessa by the throat.

'You will suffer for your transgressions.'

Releasing his grip for a moment, he slapped Vanessa hard across the face. With an anguished scream, she fell to the ground.

Once her hands were tied, her captors hauled her to her feet, lifting her onto the horse that had aided her escape.

With tears streaming down her cheeks, she could only watch helplessly as the grey mist encircled her once more.

Chapter 9
A SIGHTING AND A DEMAND

The meeting had taken the rest of the morning.

Away from the glare and drama of the courtroom, Dane had been giving the Brindabeare Council and General Silvers a full debrief of all that occurred since he and Harvey were sent to scout the campsite. Also present were Hindmarsh, Harvey and Will, adding their input where needed to ensure a complete and accurate recounting of everything that had transpired.

The King rose.

'A recess is in order,' he said. 'We will reconvene in an hour.'

The King, Lord Frederick and the councillors left the room.

Dane glared at Medhurst, who had sat silently during the debrief, avoiding direct eye contact throughout. He walked quickly from the chamber, diverting his gaze away from Dane.

'A moment,' said General Silvers, as Dane turned to leave.

His eyes blazing with fury, Dane stared at Silvers, Hindmarsh and Harvey.

Will watched anxiously.

'We were wrong to judge you,' said Silvers.

Hindmarsh and Harvey nodded their agreement.

'I apologise for doubting you,' said Hindmarsh.

Dane hesitated.

'Why should I believe you?' he said, trying to keep his temper in check. 'You thought me a traitor. All of you.'

'That was before we knew –'

'That's the whole point!' Dane yelled. 'I know what you're going to say. *That was before you realised it was a projected image.*' Before you realised it wasn't Thunder. Before Lord Frederick changed your minds with the truth!

'Despite all I said. Despite being Vanessa's best friend since I could walk. Despite everything you know of me. If none of those things had been revealed, you would have let me hang!'

'I'm sorry,' said Harvey weakly.

'Why should I believe you?' said Dane. 'Any of you?'

'Be careful,' said Silvers.

'Why?' said Dane. 'What could you possibly do to me that would be worse than these last few days? What I was subjected to because none of you believed me?'

'Be that as it may,' said Silvers, 'it is for Commander Hindmarsh and I to decide whether you remain with the Royal Knights.'

'No, it isn't!' said Dane. 'The King has restored my position.'

'That's true,' said Hindmarsh. 'But it is up to the General and I as to whether you stay there. The King will not act contrarily to the views of his Commander-in-Chief, or me.'

Dane stopped, momentarily floored.

'We understand you've been wronged,' said Hindmarsh. 'We understand you've been treated unfairly. We regret our actions towards you. I regret all I thought and said during the trial. But we need to move on and direct our efforts to finding the Princess.'

Despite the anger roiling through him, Dane took a couple of deep breaths as he considered what Hindmarsh had said.

'He's right,' Will said quietly.

Dane nodded, his anger fading.

To Silvers, Hindmarsh and Harvey, he said, 'I'm sorry I lost my temper. I'd like to be in the next party to search for her.'

Silvers and Hindmarsh looked at each other for a moment.

Silvers nodded.

'Very well,' said Hindmarsh.

Dane and Will left the chamber together, heading towards the main dining hall.

Will told Dane more about the rider with the projected image.

'I swear, he looked exactly like you. There was nothing anyone could see that gave a hint it was a duplication.'

'I still don't understand it,' Dane replied, some of his anger returning. 'We saw projected duplications the night Raegan tried to take the castle.'

'This was different,' said Will. 'It was projected onto something real; it moved, it attacked, it killed. It was more than a duplicated image.'

'I guess Raegan is getting better with his dark magic,' said Dane.

'Well, thankfully for you, Lord Frederick spoke to me and worked out Raegan had forgotten to duplicate Thunder.'

Dane nodded.

'There's a lot I have to thank Lord Frederick for. During the trial, he kept looking at me with this strange look, as though he wanted everyone to accuse me.'

'He needed to make sure there would be no suspicions when he found you innocent.'

'I see that now,' said Dane. 'But it would have been better to know earlier. At least I would have been prepared for it.'

'I think your reaction was as important as anything else that happened. Especially when you saw your mother.'

'The way Medhurst spoke to her; how he threatened her, I wanted to kill him right then and there. She's completely distraught about the whole situation, and he showed her no respect at all. His desire to find me guilty overrode any thoughts of decency and respect.'

'What did you do? To have him loathe you as he does?'

'I would like to know that myself,' said Dane.

Entering the dining hall, Dane felt every eye on him.

All talk ceased, the room silent and tense as he and Will made their way towards the food tables. Men and women, knights and others alike. Until this morning, they were all convinced he was guilty, ready to see him hang. Now, suddenly among them once more, no one seemed to know what to do.

Some, such as Harvey, looked on with shame and embarrassment. Lovell and others had looks of loathing on their faces, still convinced he was guilty. There were others who didn't look at him until he passed, and some who turned away if they thought he was looking in their direction.

'You'd think I'd been found guilty,' Dane said to Will as they gathered their food.

'Don't let it bother you,' said Will.

Several present were responsible for the treatment he'd endured before the trial; the cuts and bruises that were still fresh on his face and body, the aches he still felt in his ribs, arms and legs. Sitting with Lovell, he spotted Ernest Honeywood, Byron Southwell and some of the Royal Knights who'd arrested him and roughed him up all the way to Brindabeare; slapping, kicking and insulting him the whole time.

He saw Bowers shrinking into a corner.

He thought about all of it as he and Will made their way towards a couple of vacant benches.

Nodding to the others at the table, they sat down.

Turning away and picking up their trays, the others shifted to different seats.

'What? Now they don't want to be near me?' said Dane, tearing off a piece of bread. 'They do realise I'm innocent?'

'Don't let it bother you,' said Will. 'They'll get over it.'

'Over the fact I'm not dead?' said Dane. 'That's a comforting thought. How am I supposed to be able to do anything if no one trusts me?'

'They need time,' said Will. 'Give them a couple of days, and they will have forgotten about it.'

'I shouldn't have to give them *any* time,' Dane hissed. 'I'm innocent!'

Scanning the hall again, he saw faces ducking and turning away, others pointing and talking in hushed tones, fearful he might cast a spell on them if they made eye contact or heard what they were talking about.

Taking a piece of meat from his plate, Dane drained his goblet, slamming it on the table as he stood.

'Where are you going?' asked Will.

'Outside,' said Dane. 'I can't breathe in here.'

He felt every eye following him as he left his seat and stalked out a side entrance.

Cursing to himself as he crossed a courtyard, he tried to process and understand what had just happened.

I'm innocent – innocent!

And they're looking at me like I'm guilty!

Why?

What am I supposed to do?

Nearing the other side of the courtyard, he felt the soft air of the day's breeze on his face; his first real taste of freedom since he'd been arrested. Stopping and allowing himself to stand still for a moment, he took a full, deep breath, letting the air into every pore of his body.

Despite his experience in the dining hall, he felt some of the anger drifting away.

I never realised how much pleasure there is in the simple act of taking a breath of fresh air.

Hearing a noise to his left, he turned towards it.

Walking down a hill to the left of the courtyard, the squawks of Brindabeare's hunting, seeking, and messenger birds grew louder. Approaching the cages, Dane saw Angus Flitson, the Royal Falconer, walking to the middle of the field, carrying an eagle; slightly smaller, but equally imposing as Blaze, on his arm.

Standing still a moment, Angus gently raised his arm. With a flexing and flap of its wings, the bird took flight, heading towards the Great Forest.

'Hello Angus,' said Dane.

'Master Dane!' Angus exclaimed. 'How nice to see you!'

He shook Dane's hand long and hard, to the point where Dane had to gently pull away. Short and portly, with thick, bushy eyebrows over bulging green eyes that gave a look of someone in a constant state of wonder and surprise, most thought Angus to be somewhat mad, or at least, eccentric. To Dane, he was who he was; nothing more, nothing less.

'I had no doubt you were innocent,' said Angus. 'No doubt at all.'

'Thank you,' said Dane. 'Has Blaze come back?'

'Oh yes, Master Dane! Yes, yes, yes!'

Dane looked at Angus, a puzzled expression across his face.

'But ... how,' he began.

'Here she comes, Master Dane! If you want, you can land her!'

Looking to the sky, Dane saw a large bird of prey heading towards them.

Moving forward several feet, Dane stood still, holding out his arm.

'Remember, Master Dane, keep your arm very still.'

Dane waited.

As it came closer, Dane recognised Blaze, flying straight as an arrow, her wingspan filling his vision as she glided to a stop, stretching her talons and gently gripping his arm.

'Excellent, Master Dane!' said Angus. 'Excellent!'

Turning on the spot, Dane marveled at the eagle perched on his arm.

Handing her over, Dane looked towards the Great Forest.

'How did she find her way back? If I was in the dungeon, and Vanessa is missing, how did she know where to go?'

'Brindabeare is her haven, Master Dane. If she has nowhere to go, she finds her way here.'

Dane nodded.

'She found no trace of Vanessa?'

'No, Master Dane,' Angus replied. 'She had nothing with her that gave a sign she knew where the Princess might be.'

Dane gritted his teeth in frustration, stifling a curse. It had been a forlorn hope at best, and now it was gone.

'Thank you, Angus. I'll come back for her soon.'

'Very well, Master Dane,' said Angus, nodding several times in quick succession. 'Very well.'

'Royal Knight Thorburn,' said the King at the end of the debrief, which had stretched into the early evening. 'Your deeds were most commendable. I thank you for all you did and regret our treatment of you.'

'Thank you, Sire,' Dane replied. 'I'm sorry I wasn't there … when Vanessa was taken.'

All eyes looked to the chair immediately to the King's left – Vanessa's place – unoccupied, the empty space casting a dark cloud over all in the room.

'Lord Frederick,' said the King. 'Is there anything you would like to add?'

'Reports of more sightings have been received,' Lord Frederick replied. 'Messages arrived this morning, and during the day, with word the Princess has been seen in Kordeit, Feryndale, and Wandabyne.'

Dane couldn't believe what he was hearing.

'How can that be?' he asked aloud.

'It has been most frustrating,' said Lord Frederick. 'There is no doubt Raegan is sending images of the Princess to all parts of the land, to create as much confusion as possible. Our spies report nothing to collaborate any of them.'

'Additional search parties will be dispatched, commencing tomorrow,' said General Silvers. 'I expect messages from the party we sent to Feryndale by tomorrow evening.'

'Very well,' said the King. 'We are done here.'

Moving through the Great Forest, having completed its morning patrol, the group were on their return to Brindabeare; Dane and Will in the group of eight riders. Rounding a familiar bend, Dane saw something out of the corner of his eye. He slowed Thunder in an instant. The riders around him had to swerve to avoid bumping into him.

'What are you doing?' asked Will.

Dane waited at the side of the track.

'It's Reuben.'

Will's face drew a puzzled look.

'A scuttler. He wants to speak with me.'

'Where is he?'

'Over there, outside his cave.'

Will strained his eyes. He couldn't see anything.

'Thorburn!' said Robertson, leader of the patrol. 'What are you doing?'

'A scuttler wishes to talk to me,' Dane replied. 'He knows the Princess. It might be important.'

Robertson cast a suspicious eye.

'It will only be a moment,' said Dane.

A friend of Lovell's, he'd never dealt with Robertson before, and he wondered if Robertson's hesitation was due to genuine concern, or because of questions about his innocence and whether he could be trusted.

'We will wait for you at the edge of the forest,' Robertson replied. 'The patrol must report to the city as a complete party. Hevenshire, wait here, and see to it he returns by the time the sun crosses that tree over there. Understood?'

Will nodded, moving aside.

Robertson and the rest of the patrol rode away.

'He hasn't given you much time,' said Will. 'You'd better get going.'

'The cave's just over here,' said Dane, dismounting and walking away.

Will watched Dane walk into the foliage and disappear. He could only hope Dane would reappear just as mysteriously.

Ducking his head to fit through the small opening in the cave, Dane found Reuben seated at a small table, the walls around him bulging with his latest hoardings.

'Greetings, Reuben,' he said, handing over a piece of cloth from his clothing. 'What is it you wanted to tell me?'

Eyes widening with delight, Reuben reverently put the cloth on the table beside him.

'The Princess, Master Dane. She's been sighted.'

'I know, Reuben. There have been many sightings since she was kidnapped. None have amounted to anything.'

Reuben nodded.

'Audrey saw her. The Princess and a group of Black Knights.'

Dane's eyes went wide.

'Where? When?'

'Last night. She was fossicking and saw the Princess approach her cave. She was alone. She asked Audrey to find me, to get Lord Frederick.'

Dane's eyes went wide.

'*Vanessa spoke with her?!*'

'Yes,' Reuben replied. 'She escaped. But as Audrey was about to enter her portal, the Black Knights captured her again.'

'Where Reuben? Where is Audrey's portal?'

Scuttlers kept the location of their caves secretly to themselves, and Dane saw anxiety and panic in Reuben's face.

'I don't want to know the exact location,' Dane said quietly. 'Just where, so I can tell Lord Frederick.'

Reuben relaxed a little.

'Near Hezabar,' he said. 'In a small thicket of trees.'

'Hezabar,' Dane repeated, his mind racing. 'They're aligned with Candahorn, so it makes sense. Did she see where they went?'

Reuben shook his head.

'No, Master Dane. She said they disappeared into a cloud.'

'What does that mean?' Dane asked.

'I don't know,' said Reuben. 'Audrey said they disappeared into a cloud, and then they were gone. Like they vanished.'

'Vanished?' said Dane.

Thoughts spun quickly in his mind.

Another duplication?

Vanessa and a group of Black Knights?

Will said the image of Dane at the scene of the kidnapping had been real in every detail. But he'd also said the imposter hadn't said a word to anyone.

'Reuben, are you sure Vanessa spoke to her? Spoke directly to her?'

'Yes,' Reuben replied. 'The Princess spoke to her.'

'Is there anything else?' Dane asked.

Reuben shook his head.

'I have to report this. Thank you, Reuben. I will ask Lord Frederick to come and see you'

'I hope you find her.'

His mind swelling with hope, Dane left the cave.

To Will's relief, he saw Dane reappear from the side of the hill, sprinting towards him.

'What's wrong?' he asked.

'Vanessa's been sighted,' said Dane, leaping aboard Thunder. 'Not an image – she spoke to one of the scuttlers.'

Spurring their mounts, they took flight.

'This is outrageous!' Medhurst yelled. 'A scuttler allegedly sees the Princess, and we're sending a patrol out there?'

Dane took a deep breath, choking down the anger boiling inside.

'I'm reporting what I've been told,' he said. 'I trust Reuben.'

'If it pleases you, Sire,' said Lord Frederick. 'I will investigate immediately.'

The King nodded.

Lord Frederick rose, dematerialising a moment later in a flash of white light.

'Royal Knight Thorburn,' said the King, 'you say the scuttler heard the Princess speak.'

'Yes, Sire,' said Dane. 'That's what made me think it was real, and not a duplicated image. Reuben was adamant Vanessa spoke to Audrey. So, she escaped – even if it was only briefly.'

'But then,' interrupted Medhurst, 'they simply *disappeared into a cloud.*' And this scuttler couldn't tell us anything about where they went. Miserable, lying creatures. I can't believe we're wasting our time on this.'

Dane gave Medhurst a look of deep loathing.

If only we were outside … if only …

'That will do,' said the King. 'I agree with Royal Knight Thorburn. It is worth investigating.'

'The fact it's Hezabar makes it possible,' said Fairbrother.

'Yes,' said Dane, shifting his attention away from Medhurst. 'I thought the same thing. They're aligned with Candahorn. It's where they could be holding her.'

The King clicked his fingers.

A clerk of the court approached.

'Summon General Silvers.'

The clerk left the chamber.

In a flash of light, Lord Frederick reappeared.

'It's true, Sire,' he said. 'Reuben brought the scuttler, Audrey, to me, and she has recounted everything Royal Knight Thorburn has told you.'

'Sire?' asked Medhurst desperately.

'Yes?'

'What about the cloud? How they disappeared?'

'A good question,' said Lord Frederick. 'What Audrey recounted is consistent with a cloaking spell.'

Dane listened intently as Lord Frederick continued.

'Audrey said some of the Black Knights carried torches. After they recaptured the Princess, the light and smoke from the torches changed; a cloud formed around them, and they disappeared.

'This is consistent with a cloaking spell. The smoke from the torches merges with the air; the combined effect creating an illusion there is nothing there. While you can see the surroundings, you can't see inside the perimeter of the torches.'

Dane thought for a moment.

'But if they're hidden from everyone outside the range of the torches,' he said, 'how can they see where they're going?'

'The spell is quite versatile,' said Lord Frederick. 'In the same way a wizard uses the elements of nature in a manner that is unique to each, the same is true for a cloaking spell.

'Depending on its objectives, it can allow you to see normally, with full, uninterrupted vision. At other times, it can impede the vision of those inside the perimeter of the torches. In some instances, it can do both at the same time.

'I expect they will be using the torches to limit what the Princess can see, so she does not know where she is. With an effective cloaking spell, they could be travelling in circles and she would have no knowledge of it.'

The chamber doors opened, and General Silvers and another knight came striding into the room.

'You sent for me, Sire?' Silvers asked.

'Yes,' the King replied. 'We have a confirmed sighting of the Princess. I want a party ready to depart at first light.'

Silvers nodded.

'Carruthers,' said the King, 'what brings you here?'

The Head of the Royal Guard stepped forward, handing over a note. Reading its contents, the King showed no emotion

'When and how did this arrive?' asked the King.

'A short time ago, Sire,' Carruthers replied. 'The envoy is still here. We have detained them in the outer-east courtyard.'

'Very well,' said the King, handing the note to Lord Frederick. 'Please share the contents with everyone present.'

Lord Frederick read aloud:

'Lord Raegan advises Vanessa Meriwether is his prisoner and captive.

Vanessa Meriwether at this time is safe and well and will remain unharmed until further notice.

Vanessa Meriwether will be returned unharmed, subject to the following conditions:

Winston Meriwether is to make a full and unconditional surrender of all title and claims to the throne of Valentaland.

Winston Meriwether is to irrevocably pass all titles of rule to Lord Raegan.

Such surrender and passing of titles of rule is to be made at a Leader's Convention and recorded in the official records of Valentaland.

Winston Meriwether is to execute the wizard Frederick at the Leader's Convention and present Lord Raegan with Scarafuse, the sword of wizard Frederick as evidence such execution has occurred.

Winston Meriwether is to execute Dane Thorburn, son of Gil Thorburn, at the Leader's Convention; such execution to be verified by Governor Randall Mortensen of Candahorn.

Winston Meriwether and his family will withdraw from Brindabeare and live in exile in the Highland Mountains.

If Winston Meriwether or any of his family are seen anywhere other than the Highland Mountains after exile, such action will be seen as a breach of the terms of unconditional surrender and punishable by execution.

A hush fell over the room.

The councillors were aghast, none daring to speak, struggling to digest what they'd heard.

Dane couldn't believe his ears.

Unconditional surrender?

Execute Lord Frederick?

Permanent exile in the Highland Mountains?

Execute Me!

Dying for the King wasn't the issue, but hearing his death read out as a condition of surrender churned his stomach.

In the next moment, the King spoke.

'Bring the envoy here,' he said. 'Now.'

'But, Sire,' Carruthers began, 'envoys aren't brought to chamber. We see them outside, where we ...'

'Carruthers,' said the King, *'Now.'*

Carruthers left the room.

Dane looked at the King, then to Lord Frederick.

They were controlling their thoughts better than he was. Neither showed any emotion. The note had to have affected them; but if it were so, they were keeping it to themselves.

'Sire,' Fairbrother began, 'what do you intend to do?'

A glance from the King silenced him.

General Silvers moved to the entrance, ready to assist Carruthers when he returned with the envoy.

All were quiet, each digesting what they'd heard; wondering what the King was about to do.

Moments later, the doors burst open.

First Carruthers, then the envoy made their way into the room, four Royal Knights flanking them.

Two Black Knights stood before the King.

One held a staff with two flags – a signature flag and a smaller, plain flag, identifying the bearer as an envoy.

Dane noticed the colours on the signature flag – a combination of those of Candahorn and its rebel allies – Pardosta, Rhondo, Mundool and Hezabar – another sign of arrogance and contempt for the rule of the King; its purpose, no doubt, to provoke those who saw it.

Reacting on instinct, Dane drew his sword.

'Sheathe your sword, Royal Knight Thorburn,' said Lord Frederick. 'Envoys are not to be harmed.'

Envoy?

Dane seethed.

Envoy or not, they're Black Knights, and they deserve to die - every last one of them.

Straining against his burning desire to cut them down, Dane did as asked.

The King stepped to the front of the dais.

'You are the bearers of this note?' he asked.

One of the Black Knights nodded.

'The note was written by Raegan?'

The Black Knights made no response.

'The note was written by Raegan?' the King asked a second time.

Again, there was no response.

'I will ask a final time, and if you choose not to answer, you revoke your rights as envoys, and I will have you imprisoned and executed.'

Dane and the other Royal Knights drew their swords.

'The note was written by Raegan?'

One of the Black Knights shook his head.

Dane was floored.

The Royal Knights seized the Black Knights.

'Release them!' said the King. 'They answered the question.'

Reluctantly, the Royal Knights did as they were told.

'Very well,' the King said to the Black Knights. 'Who wrote the note?'

One of the Black Knights answered.

'The note was written by Lord Raegan, Supreme Ruler of Valentaland.'

Dane bristled with anger – *how dare they speak that way to the King!*

Envoy or not, it took every ounce of Dane's self-control to stay calm.

Ignoring the insult, the King held out his hand.

Lord Frederick handed back the note.

'Please pass my response to Raegan,' said the King, tearing up the note and allowing the pieces to fall to the floor. 'Now, get out of my sight.'

Chapter 10
INSPECTIONS COMMENCE

Talking quietly among themselves as they finished their meal, the knights considered the task in front of them. Council had ordered an additional party to search for Vanessa, and they were to leave before sunrise.

Twenty-five strong, a mixture of Royal Knights and knights from the Advance Regiment, the strongest of Brindabeare's regular armies, had been chosen.

Dane and Will were among the group, as well as a few of their fellow cadets who'd trained with them the previous year. Donovan Braidwood and Albert Webster had graduated to the Advance Regiment, along with Fenwick, who sat a few tables away.

Others in their cohort were deployed elsewhere in the army – Henry Featherstone to the 2nd Regiment; Hamish Ingham in one of the patrols searching for Vanessa, and Winslow to the Reserve Regiment. Harrop had failed his training, and as Dane had found out first-hand, had been assigned to the dungeons. Morgan Hainsley was dead – revealed as a traitor and slain by Vanessa during Raegan's failed invasion of the castle.

'Raegan demanded the King execute *you*?' Will asked again.

'Yes,' said Dane. 'Lord Frederick and me.'

'You're very calm about it,' said Donovan.

'It sure would have shaken me,' said Albert. 'Raegan wants the King to hand all rights to the throne to him, and execute Lord Frederick, *and* you?'

'It's a hollow demand,' said Dane.

'What's more important, is the King didn't flinch. Vanessa – the Princess – his daughter, is being held captive and the first time he receives real information, he stood like a rock.

'He asked nothing about where she was and made no demands of the envoy. If I were in his position, I would have killed them both and sent their heads to Candahorn.'

'Yes,' said Will. 'And Raegan may have responded to that by sending part of the Princess back to the King.'

Dane recoiled, his mouth agape.

'He wouldn't *dare* kill her!' he said strongly.

A couple of faces at other tables turned to look at him.

'I agree with you,' Will said quietly, 'what I meant to say, is while the Princess is Raegan's prisoner, we can't provoke him out of blind rage.'

Dane nodded, sitting lower in his seat, waiting for the others to turn away.

'You're right,' he said. 'It's just as well I'm not the King.'

Hindmarsh approached the group.

'Time to leave,' he said. 'Thorburn, retrieve your eagle.'

Rising as one, the group headed for the main hall.

'If Raegan wants you executed, it will quiet anyone who still doubts you being involved with him,' said Will.

'Maybe,' Dane replied, picturing the suspicious faces of those who continued to doubt him in his mind. 'No matter what happens, there will be some, like Lovell who will always think I'm a traitor.'

Reaching an exit on his left, Dane broke away from the others, heading to a courtyard.

'*Dane!*'

Turning towards the voice, he saw Marilena running towards him, panic and despair on her face.

'Find her,' she pleaded, catching up to him, tears running down her face. '*Please.*'

Looking into the desperate eyes of his mother; apart from the trial, he couldn't remember seeing her so distraught.

Gently placing a hand on her shoulder, he replied in a quiet, yet firm tone.

'We will. Whatever it takes.'

Marilena nodded.

'Somehow,' she said, 'while you were gone – it certainly wasn't easy; but I had a sense you'd find a way to take care of yourself. And despite everything that happened, you did. But … she's … well, she's not you. She's … she's …'

Marilena burst into tears.

'Mother,' said Dane, hugging her gently, 'we will find her. She's stronger than you think. Raegan wouldn't dare to harm her; she's his bargaining tool.'

Marilena continued to sob.

'Mother, look at me.'

Dane released her, and Marilena looked into the deep, strong eyes of her son.

'Vanessa is my best friend. She's the Princess and future ruler of the land; and I am a Royal Knight, sworn to protect her.'

Dane's face turned hard, locking into a look of steely determination.

'I will find her.'

Marilena nodded.

'Very well,' she said softly. 'I don't know what I would do without her … I don't know what I would do.'

'Don't let yourself think that way,' said Dane. 'We will find her, and we will bring her back.'

With a last grasp of her arm, Dane nodded a farewell, continuing to cut his way across the courtyard towards the falconry.

'She's ready, Master Dane,' said Angus, emerging with Blaze.

'Thank you,' Dane replied, allowing Angus to gently place Blaze on his left shoulder.

'Some food?' asked Angus.

'Yes. I don't know how long we will be gone. If it runs out, she will have to hunt.'

'Very well, Master Dane. Find the Princess, won't you?'

Standing before the King and Lord Frederick, the party watched Hindmarsh cut the battle ribbon and hand it to the King, placing the other half inside his gauntlet.

'You know what you have to do,' said the King. 'Find the Princess and return her to me.'

Raising his sword in the air, the remaining ribbon tied to the tip, the King looked to the sky.

'For the people of our city!' he yelled.

As one voice, everyone replied, 'in the name of the King!'

The party turned away from the tower, heading out of the castle and down Main Street.

Despite the early hour, a few people were gathered along the roadside, watching them leave.

Word of Raegan's demands had spread, and everyone looked on, hope and longing on their faces.

'Dane Thorburn is with them,' said one, loud enough for Dane to hear.

'Raegan wants the King to execute him!' said another.

Dane ignored them; his eyes locked on the road.

Crossing the Borsan River Bridge, the party headed into the Great Forest.

'Another patrol has been sent, My Lord,' said the man. 'With orders to search all provinces along the Astuvius River.'

'As we knew would happen,' Raegan replied.

'When they reach us, do we allow them in?'

Raegan thought a moment.

'Indeed, but don't make it easy. You will have nothing to hide when they get here, so let them see what they want to see.'

'Very well,' said the man. 'If I may ask, what are you going to do with her?'

An evil smile crossed Raegan's face.

'Winston Meriwether will either agree to my demands, or his precious daughter will perish in a city created by the gods themselves.'

The sound of the cell door broke the night's silence.

A body was thrown inside, landing on the floor with a dull thump.

Too tired and broken from their own beatings, none but one tried to help their colleague.

Shuffling over to the stricken knight, the Junior Knight kneeled next to him, carefully feeling the contours of his face. Blood ran freely in several places.

After gently working his way over the rest of the body, with all the broken bones he found, the Junior Knight knew the man wouldn't survive the night.

With this latest victim, it would mean more than half the party that left Brindabeare would be dead, the torture longer and worse by the day.

Cradling the knight's head in his lap, the Junior Knight offered a small cup of water. Seemingly too weak to swallow, the knight made no move to take it. The Junior Knight held his hand near the knight's face, letting the water drip off his fingers.

After a few drops, the knight opened his mouth.

With laboured breath, every word a struggle, he said, 'You … don't … need … to worry … about me. Save it … for … yourself.'

'I won't let you die alone,' said the Junior Knight, squeezing the man's hand.

The Junior Knight felt the man's gentle squeeze in response.

'May … the … gods … bless … you.'

The Junior Knight stayed with his friend until his last breath.

The journey had been an uneventful seven days so far. The Great Forest lay well behind them, and they would arrive in Grelfan tomorrow. Once evening camp had been established, the perimeter secured and the horses tethered, Hindmarsh addressed the group.

'Remember,' he said, 'we are not invading anyone. I have papers from the King, with authority to conduct an inspection.

'On arrival, we enter under the King's authority and conduct our search. Our spies will discreetly assist where they can. Anything you find is to be reported immediately. We move at first light. Dismissed.'

Dane and Will made their way to their bedrolls, considering the possibilities that lay ahead.

'I think it will prove a pointless exercise,' said Will.

'What makes you say that?' asked Dane.

'Raegan is not a fool,' said Will. 'It's not like they won't see us coming. The Princess will be nowhere near any province we search. Even if, by some incredible piece of luck, we stumble on the province where she is being held, there's no way we'll find her.'

'We have to try,' said Dane. 'Anything is better than doing nothing. Sooner or later, something will turn up.'

'I hope you're right. Otherwise we're chasing shadows.'

Grelfan revealed nothing.

A small farming province, it had only a token defence - little more than a perimeter fence and a small armoured force.

They searched every inch of the province - houses, including the Governor's residence with its small dungeon, stables and pens, forges, stalls, and markets.

Nothing.

'Despite the rumours, we've seen no trace of her,' said Governor Levensworth. 'I don't know why anyone would think we'd be holding her here. Grelfan has always been loyal to Brindabeare and the King. We share the same outrage and concern about the kidnapping. We hope with all our hearts she is found safe and well.'

'Thank you,' said Hindmarsh, shaking a stronger hand than he expected from the old, weather-beaten man it belonged to. 'If you see or hear anything, send word to Brindabeare immediately.'

'I will, Commander. I will.'

Dane, Will, Donovan, and Albert talked through the events of the inspection that evening.

'Nothing,' said Donovan. 'Not a single clue.'

'Don't lose heart,' said Dane. 'It's the first province, and they're loyal to the King. We can't expect to find her immediately.'

'Dane's right,' said Will. 'Raegan will be aware we're searching for her and take more precautions. I'm sure images will be reported in many other places, and I think images will suddenly appear in provinces immediately after we inspect them.'

Albert rolled his eyes.

'That doesn't give me any confidence,' he said.

'We'll find something,' said Dane. 'Soon.'

'How can you be sure?' asked Albert. 'If Raegan does what Will said, we may never find her.'

'We're going to find her,' Dane said, anger rising in his voice.

'But ...'

'Enough!' Dane yelled. 'We are *going* to find her!'

'Calm down,' said Will.

'I will not calm down!' said Dane. 'If you think this is such a bad idea, go back to Brindabeare and moan about how hopeless it all is; and let those of us who want to do something, do what we need to do to find her!'

Will raised a placating hand.

'Don't say another word!' said Dane, storming off, the others gaping in his wake.

Dane was still seething as he saddled Thunder the next morning.

Does everyone think it's a waste of time?

What are we supposed to do – nothing?

Do nothing and wait for Raegan's next demand?

What will happen to Vanessa in the meantime?

Focusing those thoughts on his saddle, he pulled the strap tight. Thunder whinnied in protest, jerking sideways.

Snapping out of his thoughts, Dane instinctively loosened his grip on the strap.

'Easy,' he said, patting Thunder gently.

Thunder relaxed, letting Dane get close, nuzzling against him.

Will approached, Donovan and Albert with him; cautious and unsure who would greet then.

'About last night,' said Will.

'It was my fault,' said Dane. 'I overreacted

'We all want to find her,' said Will.

The others nodded

'I know,' said Dane. 'I let my feelings get the better of me. I'm as frustrated as you that we found nothing at Grelfan.'

The journey to Pardosta uncovered their first clue.

Separated from Grelfan by the Astuvius River, it would take the better part of two days to get there, and after a solid morning of travel, the group stopped for a rest.

Stretching their legs, Dane and Will walked around the clearing, before resting against a large rock. Dane had called Blaze to him, before releasing her once more, watching her take flight, circling higher and higher in the sky.

A voice nearby distracted them.

'Why don't you just tell us where she is, Thorburn?'

Fenwick stood there, leering at them.

'What are you talking about?' said Dane.

'You know where she is. Where Raegan's holding her. Stop playing games and tell us where.'

'What are you trying to say?' asked Will. 'You still think Dane's in league with Raegan?'

'That's exactly what I'm saying,' Fenwick replied.

'Really?' said Dane, pushing down the anger he felt stirring within.

'You're a traitor,' Fenwick retorted.

Dane let out a deep breath, shaking his head.

'I'm not interested in your opinion,' he said, walking away.

'I'm not the only one who thinks so,' said Fenwick.

Dane ignored him.

'If you don't answer me, you're nothing but a coward,' said Fenwick.

Dane and Will kept walking.

'You're a traitor and a coward.'

In the next moment they heard a loud screech, followed by another, and another.

Looking skyward, Dane saw Blaze zooming in, landing on the rock Dane and Will had been leaning on.

Hopping from foot to foot, she continued to screech.

Brushing past Fenwick, Dane ran to her.

Blaze continued hopping and screeching, bobbing her head up and down at the same time. Dane couldn't see anything wrong with her. What did it mean?

He hadn't seen Blaze act like this before; he couldn't understand it – then he noticed the rock. Blaze was looking right at it, hopping and bobbing and screeching all the while.

Suddenly, he saw it.

'Well done, Blaze!' he exclaimed.

Will looked at Dane.

'What's going on? Why is she screeching and jumping around like that?'

'Look at this!' said Dane pointing.

Will noticed a scratch on the rock.

'What am I looking at?' he asked.

'Here!' Dane exclaimed. 'Can't you see it!?'

'Yes,' said Will. 'It's ... a scratch.'

'Vanessa did it!' Dane shouted. '*Vanessa did it!*'

'What? How do you know?'

'It's our mark! I taught it to her!'

'What?'

'It's our mark!' Dane yelled again. 'It's our mark!'

Others came over, bewildered by all the commotion.

'What's going on?' asked Hindmarsh.

'This mark!' said Dane. 'It's Vanessa's – I mean, it's the Princess's mark!'

Hindmarsh looked at the scratch in the rock.

Others looked doubtful.

Dane couldn't believe the suspicion on a couple of faces.

We have a clue!

Now is not the time to doubt me!

'Explain yourself,' said Hindmarsh. 'Now.'

'Blaze found it,' said Dane, allowing her to settle on his shoulder. 'The Princess made this mark. It's something we created when we were young. It's a secret way for us to talk to each other. Angus has trained Blaze to recognise it.'

'What do you mean? How can you be sure she made this mark?'

'It's new. When you look at the other scratches and marks – this one is fresher.'

Hindmarsh nodded.

'It's her mark,' said Dane. 'The 'V' is her signature. The smaller markings next to it show how many days since an event that it was made.'

Those around him leaned closer, studying the markings while Dane completed his explanation.

'There are two crosses and two single marks. The crosses equal five days; the other marks are single days.'

'That means twelve days,' said Will, catching on. 'But twelve days since what?'

'Since she was captured!' said Dane. 'Vanessa made these marks on this rock, twelve days after she was captured.'

'How?' asked Hindmarsh. 'And without being seen?'

'A hairpin!' said Dane. 'She came over here, saw no one was watching her, and used the point of a hairpin!'

'You're sure about this?'

'Without a doubt!' said Dane.

'And so,' said Hindmarsh, 'if these markings were made twelve days after she was captured, then that means they were made – nearly thirty days ago.'

The realisation sobered everyone.

Thirty days – she could be anywhere by now.

'It's a start,' said Dane.

'Yes, it is,' said Hindmarsh. 'We'll send word to Lord Frederick.'

A couple of minutes later, Blaze was in the sky, clutching a note in her claws.

Arriving at Pardosta, the group waited for the envoy to return. Larger than Grelfan, they'd increased their defences since defecting to the Candahorn alliance. Pardosta had a solid stone wall around it, and an army considerably larger than they'd seen at Grelfan. Entry was via a single gatehouse; currently closed, with guards blocking entry.

The Brindabeare party remained a safe distance away, waiting patiently. The envoy returned, stopping a few feet from the Brindabeare party.

'Pardosta has declared its allegiance to Candahorn,' said one of the envoy, 'and no longer recognises the authority of Winston Meriwether. Entry is refused.'

Dane's blood boiled as he heard this.

How dare they!

If they didn't allow them in peacefully, they would get in by force. About to reply, Hindmarsh hesitated when he saw a puff of smoke rise from the ground, followed by a loud *BANG!* as Lord Frederick appeared with Blaze perching on his shoulder.

'Is everything all right here?' he asked. 'I see we are about to enter Pardosta for an inspection.'

'I'm afraid not,' said Hindmarsh, turning to the Pardosta envoy. 'Please, repeat your message to Lord Frederick.'

The envoy did as asked.

Lord Frederick raised an eyebrow.

'I see,' he said. 'Very well. Gentlemen, allow me to make you aware of your position.

'Under the decrees of the Valentaland Charter, signed at the conclusion of the Great War, the city of Brindabeare, ruled by King Winston Meriwether, is the ruling city of Valentaland.

'This applies regardless of your allegiance to any other city or province. Accordingly, any orders sent under the seal of King Winston, unless an act of war, are to be obeyed without question.

'Failure to do is considered an act of treason, punishable by imprisonment and execution.

'This party has orders to conduct an inspection, which does not fall under anyone's definition of an act of war.

'I suggest you relay this to Governor Maynard, with the message that unless he wishes to be executed for treason against the King, he allows the party to inspect his province in accordance with the orders received.'

The envoy hesitated for a moment, before turning and heading back to the gatehouse.

Lord Frederick addressed Hindmarsh and the party.

'I have seen the markings on the rock recognised by Royal Knight Thorburn,' he said. 'And I agree with what has been reported. They are indeed markings made by the Princess herself. I suggest everyone familiarise themselves with what they represent and report anything of a similar nature.'

'Very well,' said Hindmarsh. 'Can you show us what these markings are?'

With a wave of his hand, a large, smoky image appeared in the air above Lord Frederick, matching the markings Dane found on the rock. After a short explanation, everyone understood.

A short time later, the envoy returned.

'You are granted access to conduct your inspection,' said one of the group.

'Thank you,' said Lord Frederick.

The envoy departed.

Once they were out of earshot, Lord Frederick spoke to the group.

'I suggest we take extra time here. Aligned with Candahorn, and by association, with Raegan, it is more likely the Princess may have been here.'

Once inside the outer walls, Dane, Will, Lord Frederick and Hindmarsh went straight to the dungeon. Located at the bottom of a dark, winding stairway, it contained five holding cells.

Ordering the Pardostan guardsman out, Lord Frederick placed a sentry at the top of the stairwell. With a flick of his hand, the wall torches were alight.

'Let's take our time in here,' he said, entering the first cell.

Starting in the four corners, each looked carefully at the stones in front of them. Dane had just started to look when he saw it.

'Over here!' he said, pointing into a corner.

Crowding around, the others nodded.

Among the scratches and dents in the wall, they saw one newer and fresher than the others – with the same markings they'd seen on the rock the day before.

Dane did the calculations quickly.

'One cross and four single marks,' he said. 'Nine days after she was captured. That means she was here before the rocksite.'

Dane dropped his head.

'She's long gone.'

A torch flickering torch caught Will's attention.

'Not necessarily,' he said, walking towards it.

Everyone turned towards him.

'Here's another one,' he said.

Dane rushed over.

Yes!

Working the calculations, Dane's body surged with adrenaline.

Six crosses and a single mark – equaled thirty-one days – which meant Vanessa was here ...

'Yesterday!' he exclaimed. 'She was here yesterday!'

'It would appear so,' said Lord Frederick.

'We need a full regiment!' Dane yelled. 'We need to lock this place down and force them to talk!'

Hindmarsh looked at Lord Frederick.

'What are we waiting for?!' Dane yelled. 'We need to arrest the Governor and force him to tell us where Vanessa is!'

'I suggest we remain quiet for the moment,' said Lord Frederick. 'We don't want to play our hand too early. We will speak with Governor Maynard; but it might be better not to reveal everything we know.'

Dane couldn't believe it.

Had he heard Lord Frederick correctly?

'W-why?' he stammered.

'Because,' said Lord Frederick, 'based on what we now know, it appears they may be moving the Princess in a pattern around Pardosta. The markings are twenty-two days apart. If we retain a presence here; somewhere near the gatehouse, perhaps, where we can see everyone entering and leaving, it may disrupt Raegan's plans, forcing him to keep her in another location longer than planned.

'If, at the same time, we conduct searches of other provinces and find markings in those dungeons; we increase our presence there as well.

'If a clear pattern emerges, we will soon know which province she is likely to be held in, or better still, find her there.'

Dane pondered it a few moments.

'Very well,' he said.

Will and Hindmarsh nodded.

'Let's see if there are any more markings here,' said Hindmarsh.

Checking the walls twice more, they came up empty.

'Let's move to the next cell,' said Lord Frederick.

Chapter 11

A HIDDEN PASSAGE

The sun sat high in the sky, its heat bearing down as he approached the lake. Nothing moved or stirred, the air itself seemed to be still.

Plenty of time remained in the day for what needed to be done.

Standing still, he let his breathing slow, his muscles relaxing in time with each breath. Reaching into his mind, he sought the warmth of the flame, the source of his power.

Breathing deeper, he felt it stir from the depths of his consciousness. At first a soft, faint pulse, it increased in time with his breathing, like a heartbeat growing stronger and stronger as it rose, filling his body with its energy.

Careful to remain calm as it pulsed harder still, he felt another surge as it consumed him completely, the sheer force knocking the wind out of him.

On hands and knees now, he struggled, his face contorting in pain as the power surged again, threatening to tear him apart from the inside. Raising his head, he looked to the sky as a final burst of energy surged through him, a flash of light bursting from every pore, every piece of him.

All sensation, all feeling disappeared as a ripple of liquid fire travelled through his body.

The light faded. Its pulse slowed and its breathing returned to normal, before it sat silent within the depths of its own consciousness once more.

Adjusting to its surroundings, it found the scent immediately.

Without hesitation, the Gargaun wolf walked towards the lake and disappeared.

Arriving at the end of another long day's travel, the party slowed to a halt.

As always, they were sure to arrive after sunset, with nothing but the cover of darkness around them.

'Hold still, if you know what's good for you,' a voice commanded.

Vanessa offered no resistance.

Hands tied, the hood in place, she allowed her captor to drag her from her horse. Apart from the sound of the rest of the party dismounting, everything else around them lay silent.

Hands gripped each arm, leading her towards the dungeon.

Darkness enveloped her, the hood blocking the light of the torches around them.

The cells were underground, well away from all other life and noise. Walking down a stairway, she heard a door opening in front of her. Stopping a moment later, her hands were untied, and with a shove from behind, she stumbled into the cell, crashing against the rear wall.

The door slammed shut, locking from the outside. A moment later, her captors were gone.

Grimacing from the pain in her shoulder, she took a moment to steady herself. Removing the blindfold, she slumped to the floor, staring helplessly at the door opposite.

Another day.

The same routine as the day before.

No doubting tomorrow would be the same.

It was part of the plan – the standard procedure for breaking a prisoner. Make every day the same as the one before; keep interactions to a minimum, the boredom sapping more and more of her spirit, driving her mad with the sheer repetition of it.

If only they knew.

The monotony of the day was their weapon – the solitary confinement of the night was hers. They'd expect her to be exhausted from the day's travel, ready to collapse into her cell, eventually falling asleep; woken before sunrise to start the routine again.

What happened during the night was the opposite.

Steeling herself, Vanessa started her evening routine.

Pacing the cell, she counted the steps from front to back – three, about the size of other cells she'd been in; from one side to the other – six. A plate of stale bread and cheese, and a cup of water sat to one side – nothing different about that; she'd eat what she could stomach later.

Smoothing her dress; ruffled, dirty, torn in places where she'd tripped and fallen, she splashed some water from a small bowl onto her face, waking up her tired eyes and mind.

Untying her hair, she walked to a stone under the torch, about waist high. Carefully, she scratched out her marks – the 'V', followed by seven crosses and two single marks.

Thirty-seven.

Thirty-seven days since she'd been captured.

She leaned against the wall, sliding her marker back into place, letting her thoughts drift for a moment.

Will Dane remember them?

Is he in the party searching for me?

One of the few times she'd overheard her captors talking, she'd found out Dane had been cleared of all the charges against him. She allowed herself to smile at the memory – the wave of relief that swept through her.

Had he told others about the marks and how to read them?

He'd know the event was her capture – the rest would be easy.

Studying her latest etchings, they were exactly as they needed to be. She'd been careful to make them blend with the rest of the stone, so they wouldn't attract attention. They were clear enough if you knew what you were looking for; innocuous enough not to be noticed otherwise.

'At least it's something,' she whispered to herself.

There were many markings now – one in every cell she'd been in; others where she'd been able to make them without being seen when stopping for breaks.

Walking the room, stretching her legs as best she could, something in one of the corners caught her eye.

My mark!

Leaning in, she saw she'd made it twenty-one days earlier.

She'd been in this cell before – not just in this dungeon – this very cell!

Was there something – anything that might give a clue?

Twenty-one days ... twenty-one days ...

Wait ...

Yes!

Twenty-one days – *when I escaped!*

It was at the time I escaped!

Knowing there were two marks in this cell, she'd make sure to check the cells carefully from now on. Maybe she could work out a pattern, something that might help her understand where she was being held, where she was going from day to day.

Taking her time, she checked the cell thoroughly.

Despite her new hope, her shoulders sagged a little when she found no further markings.

'*Look forward, not back,*' she thought to herself.

Being in the same cell meant her captors had been careless. And if they'd been careless about this, what else may they have been careless about that could be used to advantage? What might they be careless about in the future?

Pacing the cell, she let the hope swell within her; a part of what she needed to do each night, and started her mental exercises. In a cell tonight, she could speak softly; better than when she slept in the open, where others may hear.

A routine she'd rehearsed with Lord Frederick, Marilena and Lindstrom; it had one purpose - to keep her mind sharp. Stimulating her mind during the night helped offset the dullness and boredom of the day.

She started reciting the line of kings since the Great War, 'Malcolm, Reginald, Walter,' and the others, right through to her father.

Next, the queens - 'Alwynne, Natasha, Jacqueline,' and the rest, ending with her mother.

Allowing herself a quick respite, she hoped her mother and Marilena were all right. She knew her father would be strong; he wouldn't bend to Raegan's demands - not with Lord Frederick, the Royal Knights and might of the Brindabeare Army at his disposal.

Her mother and Marilena on the other hand, would be frantic with worry.

Back to her exercises, she named all the cities and provinces in the land – 'Delgan, Feryndale, Hezabar,' followed by, 'Grelfan, Pardosta, Candahorn, Rhondo,' and so on.

Naming them all, working her way north to south, from the west to the east, she paused a moment after each, wondering whether she'd been held in any of them; which one she might be in right now.

It had been two years since Candahorn and its group of rebels walked out of the Leader's Convention; rejecting Brindabeare's rule and declaring their independence; and later, aligning with Raegan in his failed invasion of the castle. At last count, the other rebels were Hezabar, Mundool, Rhondo and Pardosta.

They would be the first places searched. She knew it would be unlikely she'd be held in Candahorn – they would deny all knowledge of involvement, making sure nothing would point to them being part of it.

Though she'd neither seen nor heard anything to give the slightest clue as to where she might be, where she may have been, or she may be going, the others were certainly a possibility.

Her memories were vague at best. She hadn't been to any of them for several years, never set foot near their dungeons.

She hadn't seen Audrey's portal before, and hadn't thought to ask where they were during the excitement of her near escape.

How close had it been?

Did I really break free, or were they toying with me?

Snapping out of her regrets about that day, she pushed those thoughts from her mind, picking up a piece of bread, continuing to pace the room.

The wizards were next; starting with those at the very beginning of time – 'Masterlord Aldred, Airlord Bavol, Earthlord

Eldon, Waterlord Keera, and Firelord Adan,' – those who wrote the Annals of Creation, the governing rules of the whole land, written to ensure all in the land lived in harmony with the Ruling Elements of Nature.

She moved to the wizards who served on the Nadensa Council, the ancient wizard city, the ruling city of the entire land, until its destruction during the Great War.

Since the beginning of time there had only been a small number, but she named them all, all the way to those serving at the time of the Great War.

'Masterlord Halbert, Airlord Andras, Earthlord Terrran, Waterlord Delmar and Firelord Edan,' she said to herself.

Stopping at the thought of Edan's name, she pondered the most defining time in the history of the entire land.

In his bid to seize power from the council, Edan had triggered the Great War through an alliance with Candahorn, and created the firewalkers – devastating, utterly wretched creatures, from the very core of the fire element itself. Under his command, the firewalkers had wrought unfathomable destruction on Nadensa and the whole land.

No wizard had ever penetrated so far to the core of a ruling element, and the disruption it caused to the balance of the ruling elements threatened to destroy everything.

All seemed lost, until a devastating force, said to have been unleashed by Vrenin, the God of Fire himself, destroyed the firewalkers and reduced the entire city of Nadensa to ruins. With the exception of Lord Frederick and Raegan, all wizards in the land, including Edan, perished that day.

King Malcolm, Lord Frederick and Raegan led Brindabeare to victory over Candahorn, establishing Brindabeare as the ruling city of the land. From that time on, apart from occasional flashpoints of trouble, a period of enduring peace had been maintained, until Raegan's attempts to seize power for himself.

Vanessa wondered how far Raegan's quest would go.

Could it result in similar consequences to the Great War?

Lord Frederick had shared his suspicions about Raegan exploring the dark sides of the fire element. His ability to transform ordinary knights into his stronger and more powerful Black Knights came from within the fire element, but could he penetrate to its very core, the way Edan had done?

Surely not.

A sound interrupted her line of thought.

Footsteps?

Coming towards her?

Straining her ears, leaning hard against the cell door, she listened again.

No – there was nothing outside the door.

She heard a scratching, scraping sound, as though someone was trying to get in ... from ... behind the wall!

In the next instant, with a giant heave, part of the wall at the rear of her cell opened away from her.

Shrinking to the opposite wall, Vanessa crouched down, shaking, trying to make herself as small as she could.

Had Raegan come for her at last?

Were they going to kill her in this cell?

Kill her and hide her body on the other side of the wall, where she'd never be found?

The wall continued to open, revealing a gap large enough for a person to fit through.

Two men stepped out, one holding a torch.

The other reached down to her.

'Hurry,' he said, dragging Vanessa to her feet.

Unarmed and dressed in common clothes, both with the same average height and build; they didn't appear to be dangerous or sinister as they looked at Vanessa with anxious, urgent expressions.

Nevertheless, unsure what to do, Vanessa resisted, struggling against the man's grip.

'Princess, we're here to help you,' the man said quietly. 'Come with us. We'll get you out of here.'

Seeing the pleading, nervous looks on the faces of both men, Vanessa felt herself tingle with excitement, her mood shifting from fear to hope in a heartbeat.

With a surge of adrenaline, she rushed into the gap in the wall. Resisting the urge to take flight into the darkness, she waited while the two men pushed the wall back into place.

Grunting under the strain, they pushed hard against the hidden door, easing it into position.

'Let's go,' said the man with the torch, leaping ahead into the darkness.

Vanessa and the other man followed.

'Who are you?' she asked, the first time she'd spoken to anyone in days, her voice croaking.

'Everley and Hooper,' said the man with the torch.

Shuffling behind him, Vanessa strained to see ahead.

'Where are we going?' she asked.

'We're getting you out of here,' Hooper replied behind her. 'This passageway leads past the perimeter wall, on the other side of the province, away from the main gate.'

'Where are we?'

'Hezabar,' said Hooper.

Hezabar.

She was right – one of the provinces aligned with Candahorn!

'Why are you helping me?'

'We work for the King,' said Hooper.

Vanessa felt another wave of hope surge through her.

Spies!

The Hezabar spies had found out she was here and were getting her out.

'This passage,' she said. 'How did you know about it?'

They'd been walking a couple minutes now, and Vanessa saw no end, nothing but darkness beyond Everley's torch.

'It was built as an escape for the Governor, in the event of invasion,' Hooper replied. 'It's also used for smuggling.'

'How far does it go?'

'We're almost there,' said Everley in front of her.

The ground started to slope upwards.

An opening lay ahead, the light of the moon visible in the distant sky, the cool breeze of the night drifting into the passageway.

Vanessa took a deep breath, allowing the fresh air to fill her lungs, the breath of freedom filling every part of her.

Everley clambered out, hoisting himself up, turning and reaching down with his free hand.

Vanessa grabbed onto him, allowing him to pull her up and out.

Hooper emerged a moment later.

Vanessa couldn't believe it – she was free!

'Thank you!' she said, hugging them in turn.

'Just a moment, while we get this back in place,' said Everley, motioning to the large boulder next to the opening.

Hooper joined him, straining as they heaved against the boulder.

Vanessa saw horses waiting a short distance away.

In the next instant, two flashes of red light pierced the air, striking Everley and Hooper in the back.

The lifeless bodies of both men slumped to the ground.

Vanessa screamed, running for the horses.

An invisible hand grabbed her throat, tightening around her.

Stopped in her tracks, Vanessa raised her hands to her neck, gasping for breath.

'Are you going somewhere?' Raegan growled from behind her.

Struggling in vain against the choker-hold, Vanessa's face contorted with pain.

Raegan released his grip.

Vanessa slumped to the ground, gasping for breath, sucking in gulps of air.

Walking into Vanessa's line of sight, Raegan, surrounded by a cadre of four Black Knights, the leader among them, leered down at her.

'It appears, despite our best efforts, there are those who remain determined to help you,' he said. 'I wonder how many of these worthless tramps have to die before they realise it's a fruitless task.'

Vanessa rose to her feet, gulping deep breaths of air, locking her eyes on Raegan.

'They are not worthless tramps,' she said. 'They are men devoted to the King; to me; willing to do anything to serve. People like them, like most people in this land, will follow those who rule with compassion and fairness; like my father and those before him – like me; as opposed to a usurper who wants to rule by force.'

Raegan didn't flinch.

Stepping closer, his face inches from Vanessa's, he spoke quietly, with a venom, a malicious hate that chilled Vanessa to her core.

'My preparations for what lie ahead will soon be complete,' he said. 'Enjoy your last taste of freedom while you can. Where you'll be going, only madness and death awaits.'

Chapter 12

AMBUSH AND ULTIMATUM

Tension hung in the air.

Riders glanced nervously at each other, sweat dripping into their eyes as they waited in the midday sun. Horses shifted uneasily, snorting dry, humid air through their nostrils, anxious to charge ahead.

The parties stood about a hundred yards apart, eyeing each other, waiting for someone to make a move.

Dane had one eye on the enemy; the other on Hindmarsh, waiting to see what the Commander would do.

They were well and truly outnumbered – Lord Frederick had returned to Brindabeare; and with five, including Albert, remaining at Pardosta, they were now a party of twenty – against what looked like at least a hundred.

'Thorburn, Pendelford,' said Hindmarsh. 'Step forward.'

Dane and another Royal Knight moved out of the line.

'We will act as envoy.'

Both nodded.

'What are we going to do?' asked Dane.

'We ask the reason for denying entry,' Hindmarsh replied. 'Nothing more.'

'Will they attack us?'

'Not an envoy,' said Hindmarsh. 'This is a show of defiance, nothing more. We will hear what they have to say, and retreat.'

'We're not going to do our inspection?'

'Outnumbered as we are, we are not.'

Dane nodded.

'I will do the talking,' said Hindmarsh. 'Understood?'

'Yes, Commander,' Dane and Pendelford replied.

'No matter what is said, either by me, or the other party, you are not to say a word. You are not to make any threatening movements, and you are not to draw your sword unless instructed.'

'Yes, Commander.'

Looking across the void between himself and the enemy, Dane saw their envoy had also stepped forward.

With Dane and Pendelford on either side, Hindmarsh nodded, and the three of them strode forward, Pendelford bearing the Brindabeare staff.

At a walking pace, they covered the ground between themselves and the enemy. They would meet about halfway.

The three riders of the enemy envoy showed no emotion as they approached.

They stopped a pace apart.

Nothing was said for a moment; each sizing up the other.

Hindmarsh broke the silence.

'I am Commander Aidan Hindmarsh,' he said. 'We come on orders of King Winston Meriwether, ruler of Valentaland. We have papers allowing us to search this province.'

The other party said nothing for a moment, before their leader spoke.

'I am Kenrick Meyer,' he said. 'We represent Governor Mortensen of Candahorn, and we do not recognise the authority of your so-called King.'

Dane felt his anger rising inside him, ready to explode.

Despite Hindmarsh's instructions, Dane felt his hand instinctively slide towards his sword.

'I see,' Hindmarsh said to Meyer. 'And, may I ask, why a Candahorn regiment is stationed at Mundool?'

'Mundool is but a small province,' said Meyer. 'They received word from abroad that forces from Brindabeare were spreading across the land, unlawfully invading provinces under the guise of conducting inspections. Mundool has asked Candahorn for its protection.'

Mustering every ounce of his self-control, Dane steadied himself, trying to remain calm.

'You are aware Princess Vanessa has been kidnapped?' asked Hindmarsh.

'We are aware the daughter of Winston Meriwether has been reported as missing,' Meyer replied.

Dane grit his teeth, biting down on his tongue, struggling against every urge to strike Meyer down.

Hindmarsh ignored the insult.

'Under the authority of the King, we are a group of twenty, conducting inspections of provinces to ascertain her whereabouts, in the hope of returning her to Brindabeare unharmed.'

'The disappearance of Winston Meriwether's daughter is unfortunate,' said Meyer. 'But, as I have informed you, we do not recognise the authority of your so-called King to invade this peaceful and defenseless province.'

'Very well,' said Hindmarsh. 'Inform your superiors, who-ever they may be, that Brindabeare finds Mundool and Candahorn guilty of aiding and abetting the abduction of Princess Vanessa.'

Meyer spat on the ground.

'I will do no such thing,' he said; he and his party turning their mounts towards Mundool and galloping away.

Reaching for a knife in his gauntlet, Dane felt Hindmarsh grab his hand.

'Don't.'

'But how can we let ...'

'We will not attack an envoy,' said Hindmarsh. 'No matter the provocation.'

Taking a couple of deep breaths, Dane relaxed his hands.

With a reassuring tap on Dane's arm, Hindmarsh smiled.

'It took all my control not to want to strike them down too.'

Turning away from Mundool and the Candahorn regiment, they made their way back towards the rest of their party.

They were about ten yards away when a group of about thirty Black Knights emerged from the rear of the rest of the Brindabeare party, charging straight for them. With Black Knights in front of him, and the Candahorn guard at the entrance to Mundool behind, Dane and the entire Brindabeare force were trapped.

In an instant, chaos reigned.

The strength gained during their transformation gave the Black Knights one advantage; the element of surprise provided another.

Flat-footed and caught completely off guard, the Brindabeare party swerved and dodged the attack as best they could, trying to avoid the first blows. Some were struck down before they could react.

Spurring Thunder hard, Dane had his sword drawn in an instant, swinging at the first Black Knight he encountered. Ducking and slashing at the last instant before contact, he avoided the blow of his attacker, striking with his own blow across the ribs, in the exposed area under his attacker's raised arm. With a roar of pain, his attacker slumped in the saddle.

Dane surged forward, looking for his next opponent.

There was no way to know if the Candahorn regiment were coming at them from behind, but he knew the only escape lay ahead – directly through the Black Knights.

Another Black Knight came at him.

Dane fended the blow, striking fast and hard with a couple of his own, high, then low, slashing across his opponent. Boring Thunder into the flanks of the opposing horse, Dane continued to swing, the force and number of blows telling.

With a final thrust forward, he cut through his opponent, the body slumping forward and collapsing to the ground, disappearing a moment later.

'Away!' Hindmarsh yelled.

The order to flee – for those who could.

Whirling Thunder around, Dane quickly surveyed the scene.

At least half the Brindabeare Knights were dead.

A couple around him had made it through and were taking flight. He saw Will make a final thrust into his opponent, then head straight towards him.

There were a few Brindabeare Knights left, battling gamely against ten to fifteen Black Knights.

'We need to get out of here,' said Will.

In the next instant Dane noticed Fenwick, struggling against his attacker.

Drawing a knife on reflex, it spun through the air, lodging in the throat of the enemy rider.

Stunned at his good fortune, Fenwick turned away from the battle. Spurring their mounts, the three of them raced to safety.

Weary riders tethered and tended their horses.

Unsure if there were more enemy waiting for them, they'd been riding for several hours; finally stopping to set up camp when night set in.

Dane counted six – less than half their number.

Will, Hindmarsh, Fenwick, Donovan, and a Knight named Gribbens had survived.

'Injuries?' asked Hindmarsh.

'I'm fine,' said Dane.

The others nodded.

Apart from a couple of cuts and scratches, the group were unscathed.

'What did we walk into?' asked Will.

'An ambush,' Fenwick spat, staring daggers at Dane. 'A well-planned ambush.'

Dane felt his anger rising. If Fenwick dared ...

'It was as though they knew we'd be there,' said Fenwick, keeping his eyes on Dane. 'The *exact time* we would be there. As it was when the Princess was attacked. Someone must have told them. A traitor, in league with Raegan, who, not surprisingly, stands among us now.'

Dane snapped.

Unbeknown to him, Will and Donovan, sensing what was unfolding, had grabbed hold of his arms at the same time and held him tightly, preventing him from getting loose.

Looking at both, his anguished face begged to be let go, his body straining for a split second, before he stopped under their combined restraint.

'I saved your life,' he snarled at Fenwick. 'Your miserable, *stinking* life!'

'Enough,' said Hindmarsh. 'It's no secret Brindabeare has parties searching for the Princess. The Candahorn regiment were there for two purposes – to stop the inspection going ahead and to force us to engage when the Black Knights attacked.'

Dane relaxed, nodding to Will and Donovan, who let go of his arms.

Fenwick took a step back.

'What will happen now?' asked Will.

'We won't know until we get to Brindabeare,' said Hindmarsh. 'We will be on our own until then.'

Dane thought to himself – *not necessarily.*

Standing, he started walking away from the group.

'Thorburn?' asked Hindmarsh.

Dane turned, touching his arm and pointing to the sky.

Hindmarsh nodded.

Walking a few paces further, Dane held his arm out, turning in a circle, whistling as he did so.

After a few moments, he pointed, beckoning Will to join him.

Using a burning branch from their fire as a torch, Will made his way towards Dane, stopping a couple of feet away.

A minute passed before he heard it, the flapping of wings through the darkness. A moment later, Blaze emerged, dropping from the night sky, landing on Dane's arm.

Walking to the rest of the group, Dane eased Blaze onto his shoulder.

'We can get word to Brindabeare well before we arrive,' he said. 'I will send her at first light.'

Rough hands dragged the Junior Knight and the four remaining prisoners to their feet.

Without explanation, they were marched across a small field, towards a heavily wooded room.

Through his battered eyes, the Junior Knight saw fresh cuts of timber, other debris and tools lying around.

Together with the isolation of this hut, room, or whatever it may be, relative to the other buildings and structures around him, he understood – it had been built for whatever lay in store for him and his colleagues.

'Lord Raegan has a final punishment waiting for you,' said one of the guards. 'Unless you give us the information we have been seeking, you will die in there.'

'Please,' said the Junior Knight, squinting out of blackened eyes, 'we've told you. We don't know anything.'

The guard shook his head.

'Stubborn to the end,' he said, reaching into his pocket and pulling out two small pieces of what looked like hard wax, which he pushed into his ears.

The Junior Knight couldn't understand what the man was doing.

'Very well,' said the guard. 'While it doesn't compare with what lies in store for your so-called Princess, Lord Raegan says it will be the end of anyone who enters.'

Grabbed roughly by the shoulders, the guards thrust the Junior Knight inside with the others. A strong, thick plank slid into place, locking the door from the outside.

A moment later, it started.

'Everything is ready,' said Raegan. 'They are to leave at dawn.'

'Very good, My Lord,' said his companion.

'I will arrive ahead of them and guide them the last few miles.'

'Very well.'

With a flash of red and a *BANG!* Raegan dematerialised and disappeared.

Governor Mortensen of Candahorn considered his position.

With the girl dead, Brindabeare would either surrender, or wilt under the combined power of Raegan and the might of the army he led on Raegan's behalf.

Writing a short note, he clicked his fingers, and an aide entered the room. With thoughts of his future surging through him, he stood proudly, feeling taller than his already large frame, towering over the other man.

'Send this immediately,' he said.

Smiling again after the man departed, Mortensen absorbed himself in his thoughts once more.

'I'm glad you're safe,' said Marilena.

Dane nodded.

He and the others had returned late the night before.

Dane and Marilena were in the main dining hall. Dane had a full plate in front of him, ravenous after the little he'd eaten the last few days. Marilena; withered, tired and pale, hadn't touched a thing.

'We ran out of supplies when we were attacked,' said Dane. 'We hunted for whatever we could find.'

Marilena nodded.

'We found a couple of markings,' Dane offered. 'That means she's alive.'

'What do you mean?'

As Dane explained himself, he saw Marilena's eyes brighten with hope for a moment, before drifting away, back down her path of despair.

'Mother,' said Dane, 'we will find her. We'll search Mundool – Candahorn force or no Candahorn force – and anywhere else we have to.'

'It's been so long,' she said.

'But she's alive,' said Dane. 'We know she's alive.'

'Yes,' said Marilena softly. 'Yes.'

Dane rose from his seat as the Queen entered, accompanied by Patrice Whiltshire, her aide. Resplendent in a long sandy-gold dress, she shuffled towards him. Apart from her auburn hair and grey-green eyes, her features were like her daughter's in every way.

At the moment, however, she didn't look herself at all. Dane could see she'd been crying; her cheeks flushed, her usual beauty and radiance nothing like the tousled, anxious lady approaching him.

'My Queen,' said Dane, bowing and gently kissing her offered hand.

The Queen inclined her head towards Dane.

'I'm grateful for what you're doing in search of my daughter,' she said softly, holding back tears. 'I hope you find her. Soon.'

'We will,' said Dane. 'We will.'

Placing a shaking hand on Dane's arm, the Queen looked at him, pleading and desperation on her face.

'Thank you,' she said, turning and leaving the hall.

Dane saw Will approaching from the other end of the hall.

'Council wants to see you,' he said.

Dane nodded.

'Give me a moment.'

Gently leading Marilena away from Will, he said, 'Mother, I know this is hard for you; but you have to remain strong.'

Marilena nodded, doing her best to look calm.

'For the Queen,' Dane added. 'You saw her just now. She's not dealing with this well at all. You're not either; but you have to be strong – or at least appear strong – for her sake.'

Marilena looked at Dane, a hint of understanding on her face he hadn't seen before now.

'You're right,' she whispered.

Dane nodded his goodbye, leaving the room with Will.

'Why do they want us before Council?' he asked.

'I'm not going,' said Will. 'They want you and Commander Hindmarsh. You were in the envoy and survived the attack. They don't need me.'

'Very well,' Dane replied. 'Has anything else happened since we got back?'

'Not a lot,' said Will. 'Apart from Fenwick trying to take credit for saving everyone.'

Dane looked at Will, stunned.

'Yes,' Will replied. 'Are you sure you did the right thing in saving him?'

The day had moved from morning to early afternoon, and Council was still deliberating.

Hindmarsh and Dane had given full accounts of everything – what they found at Pardosta, and the entire episode at Mundool.

Plans were being discussed for Brindabeare's next movements.

Three parties were preparing to continue the search.

One would go further south, towards Haspoth, ultimately meeting up with Wandabyne, the largest city in the south of the land. There, they would join Wandabyne forces and continue to search the deep south.

The others would resume searches of the provinces along the Astuvius River.

'If I may say,' Dane offered, 'given the ambush at Mundool, perhaps we should send a regiment. While it would be slower, the numbers involved would make the searches more thorough. It would reduce the likelihood of a repeat.'

'Well spoken,' said General Silvers. 'I agree with Royal Knight Thorburn.'

'We are missing one point,' said Fairbrother. 'How do you justify sending a regiment to conduct an inspection? A party that size may be seen as an act of war.'

'It's possible,' said Lord Frederick. 'The inspection party will be the same number as those sent previously. The rest will stand down and wait at a safe distance. They can then be called ...'

Before Lord Frederick could finish, a cloud of smoke filled the chamber. A light gules in colour, it came out of the far wall, billowing towards the centre of the room.

A moment later there was a *BANG!* and a foggy image of Raegan appeared.

'Greetings,' he said.

Lord Frederick pointed at the image in front of him, an azure light shooting from his fingers. The bolt passed harmlessly through the red cloud before crashing into the wall behind it.

'Where is she Raegan?' he said. 'What have you done with her?'

The smoky image smiled.

'She is quite safe,' it said.

'Raegan,' said the King. 'I want her returned unharmed. If you so much as lay a hand on her ...'

'You are in no position to make demands,' said Raegan. 'If you wish to see your daughter again, you will listen very carefully, and do exactly as I say.'

No one in the room moved a muscle.

Dane watched on, enraged, yet drawn to the smoky image.

'Now I have your attention,' said Raegan, 'here is what will happen. If you wish to see your daughter again, you will honour the terms offered by my envoy within the next thirty days.'

The King stood, looking straight at the smoky image of Raegan.

'The answer is no,' he said.

Raegan raised an eyebrow.

'Your daughter's life means nothing?'

'My daughter's life means everything,' said the King. 'I also have a duty to my people and to Valentaland. I will not be held to ransom.'

Dane felt his heart swell with pride and admiration for the King, a surge of adrenalin rippling through him.

The smoky face of Raegan showed no emotion at the King's response.

'Perhaps you need more convincing,' he said.

A second column of smoke appeared from the wall at the far end of the room, filling the space next to the first. After a moment, an image began to appear, dim at first, before becoming clear to all in the room.

Vanessa sat alone, slumped against a rock, sobbing.

A wave of despair rolled across the room.

Dane rocked back; a mixture of pain and desperation spreading across his face.

Vanessa!

Helpless – isolated and alone in some ungodly place.

His stomach churned with pangs of guilt at her predicament, mixed with the anger and shame he felt at not being able to help her. A surge of anger ripped through him.

'Where is she Raegan!?' he yelled. '*Where is she!?*'

Raegan's image turned towards Dane.

'You're not dead after all,' he said. 'But you soon will be, if she is to be returned. Her life, or yours? The choice is obvious to me.'

'We'll find her Raegan,' said Dane. 'We'll find her, and we'll find you.'

'Where is she Raegan?' asked Lord Frederick; his eyes glued on the image of Vanessa.

'At the present time, she is unharmed and in no immediate danger,' Raegan replied. 'If my demands are not met, that will change.'

'Where is she?' Lord Frederick asked again.

'On her way to where the most savage prisoners in all the land are held. Those whose evil and cunning cannot be contained within the walls of a dungeon. A place where even the greatest minds go mad.'

Lord Frederick shuddered.

'Impossible,' he breathed.

'Impossible?' said Raegan. 'Why no, dear brother. Very possible indeed.'

Lord Frederick sat stone still, his face aghast.

No one else in the room had a clue what the two wizards were talking about.

'How could you?' Lord Frederick stammered. 'It's been dormant for centuries.'

'I suggest you stop worrying about that and consider my demands,' said Raegan. 'If I don't see a full, unconditional surrender within thirty days, I will place her inside, where only misery and death awaits.'

The smoky images vanished.

The room erupted in conversation.

'Where is she?' asked Medhurst.

'Can we find her?' asked Lindstrom.

Place her inside,' said Fairbrother. 'What does he mean?'

Lord Frederick sat down, oblivious to the questions.

Dane had never seen him like this – defeated – at a loss as to what to do next.

'Lord Frederick,' said the King. 'You know where Raegan is taking her?'

Lord Frederick nodded.

'Where is it?'

Lord Frederick drew a deep breath.

'The Princess is being taken to the City of Lost Souls.'

Chapter 13
AN ANCIENT PRISON

The chamber erupted.

'What is this, '*City of Lost Souls*'?' asked Medhurst.

'Where is it?' said Fairbrother.

'Can we find it in time to save her?' asked Lindstrom.

Dane ignored the questions, continuing to watch Lord Frederick. The great wizard didn't appear to be listening either. Head tilted, eyes distant, staring into the space where Raegan had spoken to them – from what Dane could see, he appeared in some kind of trance.

'*Silence!*' said the King.

The room calmed for a moment.

'Lord Frederick. What do you know of this place?'

Standing before all in the chamber, Lord Frederick spoke in a calm, steady voice.

'As Raegan said, the City of Lost Souls is indeed a place for, '*the most savage prisoners,*' in the land. A place for, '*those whose evil and cunning cannot be contained within the walls of a dungeon.*' And a place where, '*even the greatest minds go mad.*''

Dane's mouth and eyes were wide with disbelief, his mind a babble of thoughts.

The most savage prisoners in the land?

A place where they 'go mad'?

Where is this place?

Why haven't we heard of it before?

Lord Frederick continued.

'The City of Lost Souls is a prison for banished wizards. It is located somewhere in the Gargaun Ranges. Its origin dates to the beginning of all time.'

Several voices spoke at once.

'An ancient prison?'

'In the Gargaun Ranges?'

'Where in the Gargaun Ranges?'

'Not another word until Lord Frederick has finished,' said the King.

The room fell silent.

'Throughout history,' said Lord Frederick, 'there were wizards whose deeds were so foul, so evil and despicable; and whose power was so strong, they could not be imprisoned in a dungeon – they would simply escape.

'Executing them was not possible – the strength of their power neutralised all attempts to kill them; the counter-abilities of other wizards ineffective.

'The solution was to construct a more secure prison, a place from which escape would be impossible. It needed to be a place so terrible, so forbidding, that no wizard would ever want to be put there – to serve as a suitable deterrent for those contemplating such evil deeds to warrant sentencing there.

'The last known wizard sentenced to the City of Lost Souls was Valonia, and she was sentenced a hundred and fifty years before the Great War.

'Raegan and I barely knew of its existence when Nadensa was destroyed. I am at a loss to understand how he has found it.'

'Why is that?' asked the King.

'It lies somewhere within the Gargaun Ranges,' said Lord Frederick. 'But its exact location is unknown. A condemned wizard would be brought to a meeting point, from which Gargaun wolves would appear. Larger than other wolves; prisoners were bound to these creatures, who led them through a void and into the city.'

'What do you mean?' said the King.

'An invisible barrier,' said Lord Frederick. 'A crossing point that none but the wolves could see, and through which no one, unless accompanied by a Gargaun wolf, could enter. To those outside the city, the wolves and the prisoners walked forward and disappeared, right before their eyes.'

Dane felt his heart racing.

Gaping mouths and wide eyes filled the chamber. The King shook his head slowly, stunned and bewildered, trying to make sense of it all.

Lord Frederick continued.

'The void was essential to the mystique and fear of the city. Since its inception, no wizard entering the City of Lost Souls had ever been seen again.

'Unless you cross the void and enter the city, you can walk the Gargaun Ranges and find no trace of it. Unless you are escorted by a Gargaun wolf, there is no way to find it.

'Those within the city are contained within, cannot escape, and cannot see anything beyond the void. Once they enter, the wolves break the bond, and the prisoners find themselves abandoned and alone.'

'This is the fate that awaits my daughter?' said the King.

'I'm afraid so,' said Lord Frederick. 'And I regret to say, that is not the worst of it.'

'What could possibly be worse than that!?' Dane yelled, losing all control of his emotions.

Others turned towards him, stunned at the outburst; yet so overcome by what Lord Frederick had told them, they were unable to summon the words to admonish him.

'The city is a series of endless, shifting tunnels,' said Lord Frederick, 'from which any ability to know where you are, or where you have been, is impossible.'

'Explain,' said the King.

'It's perhaps the greatest reason prisoners never escape,' said Lord Frederick. 'The city consists of an endless, shifting, tunnel system. Creatures known as otterlings; so small they cannot be seen, are constantly digging tunnels and caves in the city. Some are digging to create the tunnels; others are collapsing them.

'A prisoner finds themselves in a tunnel, in which they can only follow it forward; they can never go back the way they came. The reason for this is the otterlings are constantly digging, creating and collapsing the tunnels, shifting them all the time.

'It's designed to confuse the prisoner, to ensure they have no idea where they are at any time; no idea where they have come from, no idea where they are going.

'Occasionally they emerge into daylight, but they can only go into another tunnel; never back into the one they exited – because the tunnel they came from would be gone – caved in by an otterling.'

Dane's mind whirled – *if Vanessa ends up in there, we'll never find her.*

'And there is one more thing,' said Lord Frederick, 'possibly the most sinister of all.'

Faces in the room contorted in disbelief and despair – they'd heard enough already. What could be worse than what they'd already heard?

'The sound of otterlings digging is constant and unceasing. It's everywhere. They can hear it; yet cannot see it. It sounds like a sword scraping on stone. The sound has a pulse; invisible, but there just the same, moving the prisoners through the tunnels.

'In addition to everything else in the city, it is this pulsing sound that is said to send prisoners mad – breaking their minds and destroying them – rumoured to even drain them of their power – to the point they lose their very soul.'

No one in the chamber spoke, too stunned to reply, as they digested what Lord Frederick had told them.

Medhurst broke the silence.

'That has to be the most barbaric, inhumane system of justice I have ever heard of,' he said.

'You would be quite right,' said Lord Frederick, 'if it were for mortal prisoners. But remember, the City of Lost Souls is a prison for wizards who had committed the most despicable deeds. We needed such a system of justice, such a forbidding, unforgiving place, in order to prevent them escaping and continuing their evil ways.'

'What hope is there if the Princess is put in there?' asked Fairbrother.

Lord Frederick shook his head slowly.

'I don't know. As I've told you, none who entered the city ever escaped.'

'How can you be sure Raegan isn't lying?' said Fairbrother. 'How do we know he's found it?'

'We have to stop him,' said Dane. 'Before they get to the Gargaun Ranges – before they put Vanessa in there.'

'Thorburn,' said General Silvers. 'Mind your place.'

Dane turned to the General; twin looks of understanding and loathing in his eyes.

'Forgive me, General,' he said. 'Van – the Princess,' he corrected, 'she's not just the Princess to me. She's my friend – my best friend.'

'That may be ...'

The King stood, raising his hand.

'I don't particularly care for protocol at this time,' he said.

Silvers nodded his assent.

Despite the King's words, Dane felt no satisfaction. Nothing mattered apart from finding Vanessa.

'Royal Knight Thorburn has said what we all know,' said the King. 'We must do whatever we can to ensure my daughter is not placed inside this city. It would appear our only hope of saving her.'

'You won't consider Raegan's demands?' asked Lindstrom.

Despite all they had heard in these last few minutes, the King turned to Lindstrom, staring him down as though he were talking to Raegan himself.

'I will not,' he growled.

Lindstrom shrank back in his seat.

'I apologise, Sire,' he said.

The King waved him away.

'The time it will take to reach the Gargaun Ranges will take most of the thirty-day period. We haven't a moment to lose.'

Everyone in the chamber nodded their agreement.

'We abandon the search parties,' said the King. 'I want men from the Advance Regiment and Royal Knights ready to leave at first light. All remaining forces are to be on alert; ready to respond to further orders.

'We will send word to Wandabyne and the surrounding provinces in the south. Cramden and Wedlan are the closest to the ranges; but even then, they are on the other side of the Storsh River and are at least a week away.'

'I am sure they will assist in any way they can, Sire,' said Fairbrother.

'I will consult the Annals of Creation; and go to the Gargaun Ranges and see what I can find,' said Lord Frederick.

'Very well,' said the King. 'General Silvers, Commander Hindmarsh; prepare your men for departure.'

'Yes, Sire,' both replied.

'You are not to brief anyone about where you are going, or what we are facing, until you clear the Great Forest. I want no panic to spread within the city, and no word to spread beyond. Is that clear?'

'Yes, Sire.'

'The official reason we are sending a larger force is to increase the scope and breadth of our search, by sending one force that will disperse to various locations, once it clears the Great Forest.'

'Yes, Sire.'

'Dismissed.'

'Make it stop! Make it stop!'

Stumbling blindly, the Junior Knight bumped into a wall, lurching away from it as though it had attacked him.

A dull buzzing sound, like a giant swarm of bees, filled the room. Constant and unrelenting, it followed them, seeming to come from one side, then the other as they stumbled around. They found themselves swatting and dodging invisible flying creatures they thought were attacking them, all the while trying to keep their hands in their ears to combat the noise.

Some of his companions had already died; taking their own lives, rather than contend with the noise a moment longer. The other knight staggered around in the same manner, trying in vain to quiet the noise, knowing all the while it made no difference.

The Junior Knight felt another jolt; not from the wall – he'd collided with his companion. For a moment each looked at the other, stunned, unsure what had happened.

The other knight removed a hand from his ear.

Both looked at it at the same time.

It was covered in blood.

In a daze, the Junior Knight looked at his companion, and saw the blood running freely down his face.

In the next instant, his companion let out a blood-curdling scream, running head first into a wall. Collapsing to the ground, he breathed no more.

Early night appeared outside, and the torches were casting their evening glow along the corridors. Dane had been told to wait for Lord Frederick outside Vanessa's chambers.

'Why are we meeting here?' he asked when Lord Frederick joined him.

'We need to be discreet,' Lord Frederick replied. 'I don't want others stumbling on the location of the Annals of Creation.'

Dane's eyes widened.

Lord Frederick nodded.

They headed down a couple of hallways, rounding a corner on the other side of the castle. Dane knew this place. Memories flashed through his mind. The first as a five-year-old; it was here he'd fallen over a dead Knight and split his chin open on the night Raegan killed his father.

It was also here he'd fought during Raegan's last invasion. He and Will had fought with Royal Knights to defeat the Black Knights Raegan had sent to the castle disguised as envoys.

Their friend and fellow cadet Morgan Hainsley had been among the Black Knights that day. He'd betrayed his friends and tried to kill Vanessa. In the ensuing battle, Vanessa managed to defeat Morgan herself, before Dane hid her in a secret room – one very few knew about.

Lord Frederick stopped at the torch rack that opened the entrance to that very room.

Dane's heart skipped a beat.

Their secret room held the Annals of Creation?

Lord Frederick pulled down on the torch rack and the entrance slid open. Making their way to the empty room at the end of the passage, Lord Frederick waved his hand, lighting the torches around them.

'The Annals of Creation are in here?' said Dane.

'Indeed,' said Lord Frederick. 'I revealed it to the Princess in the days before she departed for Feryndale.

By decree, two are required whenever the Annals are consulted. Apart from the King, Princess and yourself, Will and your mother are the only others who know of this chamber. The King is preoccupied and consented to you accompanying me.'

'What about Raegan?'

'No,' said Lord Frederick. 'He knows the annals exist and has indeed read from them. We moved them to this room after his first attempt to seize power.'

Dane nodded, cringing at the memory.

Lord Frederick moved to his left, stopping next to a ledge about six feet off the ground. Guiding Dane to a spot a couple of feet to his right, he placed his hand on a stone next to the ledge.

Dane watched the ledge detach from the wall, floating towards the centre of the room, before stopping and hovering in mid-air, dropping slowly to the floor. A hole opened in the floor and the room filled with the sound of a soft hum from below. Finally, on a dais slightly smaller than the size of the open hole, a huge, dust-covered, leather-bound book emerged.

Dane stood still, spellbound at what he saw.

In front of him sat the Annals of Creation – the ancient book, said to have been written at the very dawn of time. In it were the governing rules of Valentaland; everything from the origin of the elements of nature, to the Wizard's Creed; from the creation and operation of the ruling council of Nadensa, to the original Valentaland Charter.

For a few moments he could do no more than stare wide-eyed at the great book.

Lord Frederick approached the dais and started turning the pages over. He beckoned Dane to join him.

'It's only a book,' he said.

For a moment Dane found himself lost for words.

'It's ... incredible. I never thought I'd get to see it.'

Standing beside Lord Frederick, Dane glanced at the page in front of him. He'd never seen anything so elaborate and immaculate.

Said to be written by Eldon himself, every letter, every mark had been painstakingly handcrafted.

They were on a page dealing with crime and punishment; how trials were set up; the need for the accused to be tried by the ruling council, the giving of evidence, the method of deliberation.

Lord Frederick thumbed through more pages, stopping for a cursory read here and there, not staying on any one page for too long.

'What are you looking for?' Dane asked. 'Is there something in here about the City of Lost Souls?'

'There is something about the need for a prison,' said Lord Frederick. 'I'm not sure how much there is about the City of Lost Souls. The City of Lost Souls came into being after the initial Annals were written. I can only hope Eldon added to them. If they followed the protocol decreed in the Annals, something as significant as the City would have been added. Ah, here it is.'

'What does it say?' asked Dane.

'Unfortunately, very little,' said Lord Frederick, 'but it will have to do.'

Carefully closing the ancient book, Lord Frederick and Dane walked to their places near the back wall. Lord Frederick touched a stone next to the one he touched earlier, and with the same slow hum, the dais started descending towards the hole in the floor, carrying the Annals of Creation with it.

'Dane,' said Lord Frederick. 'A word before you go.'

Dane waited.

'I'm told there are those among us, including knights, who doubt your loyalty.'

'A few,' Dane replied with a nod.

'And what do you think about that?' asked Lord Frederick.

'Well,' said Dane, 'I don't like it, but there doesn't seem to be a lot I can do about it.'

Stroking his beard, Lord Frederick considered the response before asking, 'and how do you feel about it?'

'I just told you,' said Dane.

'No,' said Lord Frederick. 'You told me what you thought about it – I asked how you felt about it.'

'Is there a difference?'

Lord Frederick raised an eyebrow.

Dane considered for a moment, picturing the suspicious looks of Lovell and others in his mind, hearing Fenwick's snide remarks, feeling his heart beating faster.

'It makes me angry,' he said, his emotions continuing to stir. 'I don't understand why they think I'm a traitor, that I had anything to do with Vanessa's kidnapping. Even now, well after the trial, they still don't want to believe I'm innocent.'

He didn't notice he'd clenched his fists as he continued.

'I was so glad when I was cleared, so relieved to be – free. But with those who think I'm guilty, it feels like part of me is trapped. I shouldn't have to worry about whether people think I'm guilty – whether the next person I speak to is going to trust me.'

'Why do you have to worry about it?' said Lord Frederick.

'What ...'

'Why do the opinions of others matter? Why *should* they matter?'

'Well ...'

'What is more important – what others think of you? Or what you think of yourself?'

Dane stopped mid-thought.

Lord Frederick had a point – something he hadn't considered until now.

Seeing Dane relax a little as he pondered the questions, Lord Frederick smiled. Resting a hand on Dane's shoulder, he said, 'no matter what you do, there will always be those who will question you; who won't want to believe you, no matter what you place before them.

'But if you can look at yourself in the mirror and know you have done right in everything, that you have given your best in all you have done, that's all that matters – what others think is irrelevant.'

Dane felt a wave of relief wash through him, as though a curtain weighing on his soul had been thrown back, letting the light shine from within. In the next moment, a tingle of pride ran down his spine, and he felt himself standing a little taller.

'You're right,' he said. 'You're absolutely right.'

Lord Frederick smiled again.

'Thank you,' said Dane. 'Thank you, for everything.'

'They leave at first light,' said the Black Knight.

'Very well,' said Raegan. 'It appears the Princess will be sacrificed to the city.'

'You intend to go through with it?' replied the Black Knight. 'You will lose your bargaining power; your leverage.'

'If Meriwether is so disinclined to acquiesce to my demands in order to save his daughter, I have no leverage,' said Raegan.

'Once she dies, I will retrieve her body, and show all how his desire for power was more important than his daughter's life. Perhaps that will give me the leverage I need.'

'Indeed,' said the Black Knight. 'I will return before they realise I've been away.'

Raegan nodded, dematerialising and disappearing with a flash of light and a *BANG!*

Dismounting, the Black Knight stood with his arms outstretched, turning on the spot while the black war paint on his face disappeared, his armour changing to its Brindabeare form. Satisfied, he climbed back into his saddle, spurring his mount towards the castle.

The trumpets sounding earlier in the afternoon had placed the city on full alert.

A year ago it would have sent everyone into panic, but after the events leading up to Raegan's failed coup, the tightening of city security and protocols, and Vanessa's kidnapping; the sound of war trumpets were as much a part of city life as the rising and setting sun.

Preparations for the departing knights continued. Their armour, swords and knives were being sorted and collated in the cadet training quarters. Some were dining in the main hall.

His rendezvous with Lord Frederick over, Dane joined them, ignoring any suspicious stares as he entered and gathered his food, making his way to a bench where Will and an attractive maid he recognised were sitting. Tall and slim, her hair hidden under a bonnet, she looked pained and upset, her eyes glancing nervously up and down as Will carried the conversation.

'Hello Genevieve,' he said, taking a seat opposite, next to Will.

'Hello Dane,' she replied, smiling weakly. 'I hear you're both in the search party.'

Dane nodded.

'Yes, we are.'

Genevieve fiddled with the food on her plate. A junior maid of the north wing, one of her tasks included tending to Vanessa's chambers; a somewhat empty task at the moment. She and Will had become close since the Tournament of Knights the previous year.

Dane reached over, placing a reassuring hand on her arm.

'We'll find her,' he said. 'We're sending a larger force and widening the search. We're taking no risks this time. We'll be ready for anything. And we'll find her.'

Will nodded his agreement.

'I was saying the same thing,' he said.

Genevieve nodded.

'I just want her back. We're so worried. We miss her terribly.'

'Dane's right,' said Will. 'We're going to find her or die trying.'

Genevieve cringed, continuing to stare at her food.

Another maid approached, wiping her hands on her apron, striding straight towards them.

Dane rose to greet the Chief Maid of the castle's north wing.

Older and shorter than Genevieve, dressed in light blue instead of grey, everything in her demeanor projected punctuality, tidiness and order.

'Hello, Lady Madeline,' he said.

'Hello, Master D ... I mean, Royal Knight Thorburn,' she replied.

'Don't bother with formalities,' said Dane, seeing her discomfort. Dane had known Lady Madeline from a young age, creating all sorts of mischief with Vanessa in the north wing.

'Very well,' said Lady Madeline, relaxing a little.

'Just don't threaten me with a bucket of water,' said Dane.

Despite their predicament, it lightened the mood for a moment; all remembering the incident at the Royal Baths during the previous year's Tournament of Knights.

'I came to retrieve Genevieve,' said Lady Madeline, 'and Commander Hindmarsh asked I send you to barracks to prepare for your departure.'

A couple of kitchen hands appeared, clearing the table of plates and goblets.

Genevieve reached over, grabbing Will by the hand. Dane saw her mouth a silent, *'be careful,'* before turning and leaving with Lady Madeline.

Heading out of the hall together; Dane and Will came to Fenwick; seated with Harrop and Winslow. Seeing Dane for the first time since their encounter in the dungeon, Harrop glanced nervously at them; taking comfort in knowing nothing would happen in the dining hall.

'Don't you have somewhere to be?' asked Will, glaring at him.

'Maybe,' Harrop replied.

'What about you?' Will said to Winslow.

Winslow shrugged.

'Fenwick,' said Dane. 'We have to go.'

Fenwick remained seated, making no move to indicate he'd heard what Dane said.

'Now,' said Will.

Standing, Fenwick stared them down.

'I don't take orders from you,' he snarled.

'They're Commander Hindmarsh's orders, not ours,' said Dane.

'I don't take orders from him either,' said Fenwick.

Before Dane and Will could reply, another voice entered the conversation.

'Really?' it said.

Everyone turned to see Noel Hawthorne, Commander of the Advance Regiment, walking towards them, accompanied by Hindmarsh. Several years older and a touch taller than his companion, Hawthorne leaned his square, ginger-bearded jaw at Fenwick as he spoke.

'You don't take orders from a Commander of the Royal Knights?' he asked.

'Commander,' Fenwick stammered. 'I …

Hawthorne raised a hand.

'Enough. I heard your exchange with Royal Knight Thorburn.'

'But, Commander …'

'I said, enough. You say you don't take orders from Commander Hindmarsh. It appears you don't wish to take orders from me either. I will not tolerate dissension or disobedience. Resume your seat and continue your meal with your cohorts. You are no longer part of the Advance Regiment.'

Fenwick's jaw dropped.

'But …'

'Perhaps one of the other regiments can find a place for you, but you are no longer a member of mine.'

Fenwick slumped into his seat.

With a nod from Hindmarsh toward Dane and Will, Hawthorne and Hindmarsh strode away.

Dane and Will cast a fleeting glance at Fenwick, before beating a hasty retreat.

'You saved his life and had him removed from the Advance Regiment,' Will whispered with a grin. 'I don't know how much more he can hate you than he does now.'

'His own pigheadedness got him removed from the regiment,' said Dane.

'I wasn't serious,' said Will. 'I thought you'd be pleased.'

'I couldn't care less about Fenwick,' said Dane. 'All that concerns me is what lies ahead.'

Chapter 14

TOWARDS THE END

Stopping for their morning rest, Vanessa was hauled awkwardly from her saddle. Holding her hands out, the bindings were removed. They'd been tight; cutting into her skin, but she said nothing, rubbing each wrist in turn; showing no other signs of stress or strain.

'Over there,' said one of her captors, motioning to a shaded area.

Slumping under a tree, she looked around; what she could see, as always, limited by what lay within the torch perimeter. Yet as she took it all in, it somehow felt different.

The air was hot and humid, sucking the moisture out of everything around her. By itself this wasn't unusual, yet she felt they were in a more open, desolate place than any they'd been before. It seemed more isolated; as though they were many days from the nearest settlement.

Wiping a sweaty arm over her forehead, she noticed her hands, like her clothes, were covered in a mixture of sweat, dirt and grime. Glancing at her rations, she saw the bread and cheese; as always, barely edible; and if not for the water, she knew she'd struggle to get it down.

Drinking slowly, allowing the water to soothe her dry, aching throat, she noticed the group had grown in number from the day before.

There were at least three or four more; the horses loaded with extra supplies. Why would that be necessary?

Unless …

'W-where are you taking me?' she said, looking at the two Black Knights guarding her.

Neither offered a response.

'Where are you taking me?' she asked again. 'It's not as though I can do anything about it. I can't inform anyone.'

'Keep quiet,' said the Black Knight to her left.

'It's a reasonable question – to civilised people. I should have expected such a benign response from people like you – cowards who hide behind masks, masquerading as knights.'

Both captors reached for her at once, hauling her to her feet.

One grabbed both arms, pinning them tightly behind her back.

The other reached across his body with his right arm, swiping it fast and hard across her face.

Screaming, Vanessa slumped against the Black Knight who held her.

'Let that be a lesson to you,' said her assailant.

'Tinton!' a voice boomed. 'Rotherwall! What's going on?'

The leader arrived.

'She was getting a little too …'

'Be that as it may,' said the leader, 'if I see you lay another hand on her, I will kill you where you stand. She is to arrive at the meeting point unharmed. What lies ahead is difficult enough, without you manhandling her. Is that clear?'

'Yes, General.'

Vanessa's arms were released from behind her.

'I was asking where we were going,' Vanessa offered.

'That is not your concern,' said the leader.

Sitting under the tree once more, Vanessa rubbed her face.

Despite the sting she felt from the blow, the information she gained had been worth the pain.

They *were* going somewhere new; somewhere difficult and dangerous, somewhere her captors hadn't been before. A sliver of hope – a place they didn't know; and where, despite their best precautions, they'd be vulnerable – more than all the other places and stops in her travels so far.

Mountains and forests sprang to mind – the Osa River? Wherever it may be, there were risks and dangers for those who weren't careful.

Last of all, two of her captors had been revealed – Tinton and Rotherwall. Although she could do little with that information right now, she'd remember it when she made it back to Brindabeare.

The afternoon ride had gone without incident. The setting sun and a light, dry breeze gave them some comfort at the end of a long and arduous day.

Vanessa watched the evening routine closely – looking for a weakness, something out of place.

They set the torch perimeter in the same manner as every other night they'd slept in the open.

Bedrolls were laid, a small fire lit.

The horses were tethered a short distance away.

Once her captors had eaten, she was given her rations.

'Here is how we are going to proceed,' said the leader, after she'd finished. 'You will be watched at all times by at least two of my men.

You will be allowed to spend the night unbound, as long as you obey us, do exactly as you are told, and make no move to escape.'

Vanessa listened, offering nothing to indicate she understood.

'Should you in any way disobey these orders, your nights will be spent with your wrists and ankles bound. Is that clear?'

Vanessa nodded.

'Finally, you are not to speak to any of my men; unless you wish to spend your remaining time gagged at the mouth.'

Vanessa nodded again.

'Very well. And you can forget about Tinton and Rotherwall. You didn't think I would use their real names, did you?'

With a smile, the leader stood and walked away, leaving her by the fire with two others.

Vanessa said nothing, keeping her face neutral, giving nothing away.

In his efforts to show her how clever he'd been, he'd just given her another piece of information.

'Your remaining time with us,' she thought.

At some point – possibly soon, they were going to be separated.

When, and under what circumstances, she had no idea; but they were going to be separated just the same.

Thoughts flowed like a torrent through her mind.

Are they going to kill me? I've been their prisoner for … nearly sixty days? If this group was going to kill me, they'd have done it by now.

Are they taking me somewhere and leaving me – with no food and water, to starve to death?

Raegan had said, 'where only misery and death awaits.'

What did that mean?

Where did that mean?

The Strivett Mountains? – nothing but wild animals – bats, sar-koe, razor-boars, panther and bears. I won't last there for very long.

The Gargaun Ranges? No settlements there. I'd be hopelessly lost, with nothing around for miles.

The Osa River?

One after the other, the possibilities came to her, each seeming to be worse than the one before.

Although she knew the geography of the entire land; the mountains, rivers and forests; she'd never been to any of them; never set foot near them, and she knew her chances of surviving in any of those places would be slim at best.

Perhaps it would have been better not to have heard all that information.

Burying her face in her hands, new waves of helplessness rolled over her.

Where are they taking me?

What are they going to do with me?

Where is Dane?

Where is Lord Frederick?

Where is Father?

Where is – ... anyone?

Another long day had come to an end; yet despite her exhaustion, Vanessa twisted and turned, finding it hard to get settled. In the open as they were, she had little protection against the elements. Pebbles and stones under her bedroll were digging into her back, the cold of night filling the air and seeping out of the ground.

Closing her eyes, she started her mental exercises, doing her best to maintain the routine. If it worked as planned, it would allow her to relax and regain some mental strength; allowing the renewed sharpness in her mind to pull her out of her current state, helping her to find a positive way to think and deal with whatever lay ahead.

Whispering to herself, she began.

'Malcolm, Reginald ...'

Who was next?

'Walter.'

The rest flowed easily, 'Hayden, Alistair, Zachary,' and all the way to her father.

The queens rattled through her mind with ease.

The cities and provinces – 'Delgan, Feryndale, Hezabar, Grelfan, Pardosta, Candahorn, Rhondo, Mundool and ... Mundool and ...'

Which province came after Mundool?

A province aligned with Candahorn?

It's in order – 'Candahorn, Rhondo, Mundool and ...?'

She could see Lindstrom and Marilena standing in front of her.

'Which province is next?' they asked.

Which province is next?

'Which province is next!?' she screamed.

Sitting up with a start, gasping for breath; she saw the entire party of captors looking at her.

Confused and disorientated, she took a few deep, calming breaths, looking around, trying to understand where she was. She heard the crackling sound of the fire, she noticed the night sky, the horses tethered in the distance.

Lindstrom and Marilena were gone.

The Black Knights continued to stare, bemused looks on their faces.

The leader kneeled in front of her.

'Do you not remember our bargain?' he said.

'Y-yes,' said Vanessa, with pleading eyes; hoping he wasn't about to shove a gag in her mouth. 'I'm s-sorry. It was … a bad dream.'

'Bad dream or not,' said the leader, 'it had better not happen again.'

Vanessa nodded.

'I'm sorry,' she whispered.

The leader walked away.

Lying down again, she closed her eyes, trying to resume her exercises. Which province is next? Which province is next …?

Night had fallen, but it made no difference to the noise in the room.

Unbeknown to the Junior Knight, the sound had stopped a couple of minutes ago. It had been so loud and constant; his mind and ears didn't register the silence around him.

It would only be a brief pause, enough for the guards to open the door, place some food and water, and leave.

For the first time since capture, the Junior Knight caught a break on this evening.

Seeing, yet not quite seeing, he saw the open door.

The night air flowed into the room, grazing his face.

Despite his failing senses, he felt the change around him – and for a fleeting moment, saw a way out.

With a surge of adrenaline, arms flailing, he ran.

'Gggg-ettttting out!' he screamed.

Taken by surprise, the first guard had no time to react when the Junior Knight ran straight over him, bumping past the other, into the open night.

Travel the next day was difficult; the day after, harder again; the following day, harder still. Real or imagined, each day felt worse than the one before – some passing slowly; others in what felt like a blur; all of it meshing into one long grind.

The only change was the weather – some days it rained, slowing them at one time or another. Her captors offered her nothing to protect her from it – when it rained during the night she had nothing but her bedroll to cover her.

Wreaked with worry, Vanessa rode in a daze, oblivious to everything around her. She could think of nothing but what lay ahead; where and when her captors would leave her to whatever fate, whatever misery, Raegan had planned.

Unable to get through her evening routine that first night, and not wanting to risk the consequences of a repeat, she'd stopped altogether; losing touch with her inner strength.

Making it through the day meant nothing; it only served to bring her another day closer to the end.

The afternoon rest arrived.

Slumping out of the saddle, she nearly collapsed.

'Get up!' said one of the Black Knights. 'Do you think we're foolish enough to fall for that again?'

Struggling to her feet, Vanessa held out her wrists, tightly bound as always, as if to say, *'how can I do anything with my hands tied?'*

Once her hands were free, she made her way to her resting place, leaving the food alone and taking the waterskin. Pouring a little over her head, she felt the back of her hair, touching the hairpin at its tip, momentarily pricking her finger.

With a wince, she pulled her hand away.

'Only one more day,' she heard someone say.

Which of her captors had said it, she had no idea.

One more day!!!

Rooted to the spot, the realisation dawned on her a moment, before she started sobbing uncontrollably, her body trembling from head to foot.

There was nothing more to do; nothing left – it was hopeless.

The two guarding her watched in silence – they'd known she would break sooner or later.

In the next instant, she was on them, taking them both by surprise.

'No!' she screamed. 'No! No! No!'

Over and over she screamed, each louder than the last, slashing and stabbing at them with her hairpin each time.

The first slash cut one face, the next cut the other.

In an instant both were bleeding freely, blood running over the war paint on their faces.

One fell to the ground, grabbing at his face; the other stumbled backwards.

With a will and strength she didn't know she had, Vanessa attacked the staggering guard, pounding his face and neck with the hairpin in her fist; slashing, scratching and scraping all the while.

With a final swipe across the neck, her stricken opponent collapsed in a heap, his body disappearing.

Continuing to scream, Vanessa whirled towards the other Black Knight.

With one hand over his face, he could offer little in resistance, other than raise his free hand.

Reaching down, Vanessa ripped the sword from her opponent's sheath, kneeing him hard in the chest, sending him sprawling onto his back. Raising the sword in the air, she pointed the blade straight down, and with an almighty scream, plunged it into his chest.

A moment later, the body disappeared.

Others rushed over; one clamping his hand around her from behind, lifting her off the ground.

'No!' Vanessa screamed. 'No! No!'

Pulling her away from the empty armour, her latest assailant tightened his grip.

The sword fell from Vanessa's hand.

Writhing under the grip of her assailant, she continued to scream. Another stood in front of her, and with a back-handed slap that sounded like the snapping of a tree branch, she slumped to the ground, unconscious.

A dull, throbbing ache made its way into her mind.

It pulsed louder, increasing with each beat.

Unable to bear it a moment longer, she forced her eyes open.

Night had fallen.

She felt cold – as cold as the nights it had rained. Had she had more of her senses, she would have realised they were at the foot of a mountain range, where the evening air was much cooler.

At present, she could make little sense of anything other than the pickaxe pounding against the inside of her forehead.

Through the pain, she felt her hands tied in front of her; realising in the next moment her feet were also restrained.

'She wakes at last,' said a voice above her.

The leader entered her vision, towering down at her.

Two others grabbed hold of her, hauling her to her feet. The pain in her head grew worse, her wrists and feet burning into the ropes that bound them.

'You killed two of my men,' said the leader. 'And I did say, if you did as instructed, you would be able to rest freely. After what you have done, that is no longer possible. Thankfully, we will soon be rid of you, and you will be left to whatever fate Lord Raegan has in store for you.'

Vanessa cringed through the pain, tears welling in her eyes.

'While your tears may be real,' said the leader, 'you can understand why I am disinclined to do anything about them.'

'Food,' said Vanessa. 'You have to give me food.'

'I have to do no such thing,' said the leader. 'Our orders were to keep you alive until Lord Raegan was ready to proceed. He gave your father thirty days to carry out his requests, and he has failed to do so.'

Hearing this, Vanessa stiffened, standing as straight as she could.

'He'll never bow to Raegan's demands,' she said through her tears. 'Never.'

'With where you are going tomorrow, I think you will quickly come to wish that he had.'

Vanessa stood straighter still.

'My father will spend every ounce of energy,' she sobbed desperately, 'every breath he has to find me. If he finds me dead, you can be sure he and Lord Frederick will not rest until they have killed every one of you.'

The leader laughed out loud.

'Your father's energy and resources have failed you. Here you are, in a place you don't know, far away from your father, and whatever he and that other wizard have been able to muster.'

'You still have to give me food,' said Vanessa, struggling with the pain in her head, wrists and feet. 'And water.'

The leader shook his head.

'I do not,' he said. 'You will still be alive by tomorrow; food or no food; water or no water.'

Vanessa stood in the grip of the other Black Knights, continuing to sob.

'However,' said the leader, 'to show I have some compassion, you can have whatever you can gather.'

He walked away, returning after a few moments; bread in one hand, a waterskin. in the other. Dropping the bread to the ground, he pulled the stopper out of the skin, letting it fall, emptying next to the bread.

'Better hurry, before it's all gone,' he said.

The other Black Knights released their grip; Vanessa slumping to the ground as they did so.

Struggling as best she could, she twisted herself over and over, squirming towards the bread and the ever-diminishing waterskin.

The leader laughed again.

'Lord Raegan said, it would only be a matter of time before the Meriwethers were groveling before us.'

Chapter 15
THE OSA RIVER

The regiment were on the outskirts of the Great Forest, three days into their journey, when Dane, glancing to his left, saw a familiar friend in an unfamiliar place.

'Commander,' he said urgently. 'Can we pause a moment? There's a scuttler's portal nearby, and one of them wishes to speak with me. It would only be for a minute or two – three at most.'

'I'm not going to stop the entire regiment,' said Hindmarsh. 'Make it quick.'

Dane and Will turned off the track, heading east about fifty yards.

'How can you see it from so far away?' asked Will.

'Once you know where to look, they're quite easy to find,' said Dane.

Stopping at the edge of a clearing, Dane dismounted and walked away, leaving Thunder with Will.

Straining his eyes, Will had no clue where Dane was going, and, just like the last time; as he watched, Dane disappeared into the foliage.

Reuben was waiting.

'Greetings, Reuben,' said Dane, handing over a small piece of leather from his uniform.

Reuben took the gift reverently.

'What are you doing here?' asked Dane. 'This isn't your portal.'

'This is Horace's portal,' said Reuben, beckoning Dane inside.

'This is Horace. And this is Oswald.'

Dane nodded to both.

'What do you wish to tell me?' asked Dane.

'The Princess has been seen,' said Reuben. 'I haven't been able to find Lord Frederick and inform him.'

Dane said nothing, knowing Lord Frederick was searching the Gargaun Ranges at this very moment.

Reuben nodded to Oswald.

'Oswald saw her, perhaps seven or eight days ago now. They stopped in the midday heat, some way past Hezabar.'

'Did you see her?' asked Dane.

'Yes,' said Oswald. 'She rested under a tree, with her back to me.'

'Hezabar,' Dane repeated.

'Yes,' said Oswald. 'I could see outline of the walls in the distance.'

'And, there's one more thing you should know,' said Reuben.

'Yes?'

'They were mistreating her.'

Dane felt a wave of heat surge through him.

'*What!?*'

Nodding glumly, Oswald said quietly, 'One held her, and another struck her.'

'*I will kill them all!*' Dane yelled.

Reuben took a cautious step back.

'Apologies, Reuben,' said Dane, seeing the anxious looks on the faces around him. 'I didn't mean to be angry at you. Thank you. All of you; for what you've told me.'

Emerging from the cave, running to where Will and Thunder were waiting, Dane seized the reins, climbing back into his saddle.

'What's wrong?' asked Will, seeing the tension and anger on Dane's face.

'She's been sighted,' Dane replied.

'That's a good thing. Isn't it?'

'Not really. Somewhere past Hezabar. It confirms just how far ahead of us they are.'

'Well, it may not be great news,' said Will, 'but it's something. Perhaps Lord Frederick will find her before we get there.'

'And,' said Dane, continuing as though he hadn't heard what Will had said, his anger rising with every word, 'the scuttler said they struck her.'

'They *what!?*'

'They struck her,' said Dane. 'And when we catch up with them, I will find the one who did it and cut his hand off!!'

Spurring Thunder hard, he took flight, allowing his anger to leak out as they sought to catch up to the rest of the regiment.

Lord Frederick walked forward, his senses soaking into the surroundings. Despite the fullness of the night, he could see clearly. He could feel the wind rippling its way across the lake about a hundred yards to his left.

There!

At last – a trace of what he'd been searching for.

Reaching into his mind, he sought the connection he'd studied from the Annals of Creation.

After about a minute, he saw it; much larger than he expected; more the size of a panther than a wolf; grey-black, with emerald green eyes, walking slowly towards him.

Holding his arms submissively, he waited.

Closer and closer it came.

Suddenly, there were others; about a dozen, appearing from the shadows, falling into line, either side of the first.

They were a couple of feet away when they stopped; the alpha wolf, first; the others in a semicircle behind.

'From the Nadensa Council,' said Lord Frederick. 'I offer bounty, and a prisoner for the City of Lost Souls.'

For a few moments, nothing happened.

Looking at the alpha wolf, Lord Frederick saw its head tilt upwards, as though it was wanting to look directly at him.

The pack did the same.

All took a step forward.

The alpha wolf let out a slow, deep, guttural growl.

The pack did the same.

The growl grew louder; the entire pack as one.

Raising their heads to the sky, the pack let out a loud, mournful howl, echoing in the night, before turning on their heels and running away.

Glancing at the figure next to him for a moment, Lord Frederick clicked his fingers and it disappeared.

'Not good,' he said.

It had taken days of searching; and now he'd found them, his fears were confirmed. They weren't going to fall for a projected image – it had to be the real thing.

With flick of his hand and a loud *BANG!* he disappeared.

'What range does the eagle have?' asked Hindmarsh.

'I can't say exactly,' said Dane. 'Angus says she could spot prey as small as a rabbit from about three miles away, maybe more.'

'Very well,' said Hindmarsh. 'So, she should have no trouble seeing them?'

'Seeing what?' asked Dane.

'She can hunt, and she can track – both you and the Princess,' said Hawthorne. 'But, can she warn of attack?'

'It depends,' said Dane. 'Why do you ask?'

Walking further away from the rest of the group, where they were sure to be out of earshot, the two commanders looked at each other. Hawthorne nodded, and Hindmarsh spoke.

'As you know, we're coming up on the Osa River. It lies directly between us and the Gargaun Ranges.'

'And it's full of sarkoe,' said Dane.

Giant crocodilian creatures, sarkoe range from thirty to forty feet in length; their deadly jaws full of razor-sharp teeth that closed shut with such force, they could snap through their prey in a single bite. The right thing to do would be to give them as wide a berth as possible.

'We are aware of that,' said Hawthorne. 'At the peak of their season, that's true. What has never been clear, is exactly when the peak of their season is. Some reports have said it is now, while others say it is later, in the warmer weather.'

Putting the pieces together, Dane saw what they were thinking.

'If we avoid it and cross the Penton River, it will take longer,' he said. 'But if we cross the Osa River ...'

'Exactly,' said Hindmarsh. 'We wouldn't risk the entire regiment. Perhaps a group of ten, maybe as many as twenty, would cross the river, and make a start on the rest of us. If it goes well, we may get more across.'

'Or, if the sarkoe attack, they may not make it out of the river at all, and we lose ten to twenty men' said Hawthorne.

'And you're thinking,' said Dane, 'if Blaze could see them, she could warn us?'

Hindmarsh and Hawthorne nodded.

'I don't think Blaze knows what a sarkoe is.'

'But,' said Hawthorne, 'if she tracked you, she would find you. If she can see you from as far as you say, she could sense if you were in danger.'

'I'm not sure,' said Dane. 'She would be able to find me ...'

'And if she saw something moving towards you ...'

'Perhaps,' said Dane.

'It may not matter,' said Hindmarsh. 'It's more a precaution. We'll have lookouts up and down the river. Those that cross will look from the other side.'

'She won't be any benefit to anyone but me,' said Dane.

'You would enter the river first, wait while the others cross, and exit with the last group.'

Dane followed the line of thought.

'You're asking me to stay in the river, where I could be attacked at any time?'

'It should be over in as little as thirty minutes,' said Hindmarsh.

Dane held up his hand.

'If you think I don't want to do it, you're mistaken. If it saves us a day, it's worth the risk. Once Vanessa – the Princess, is in the City of Lost Souls, she's as good as dead. We need as much as time as we can to find her.'

Dane hesitated; realising what he'd just said – something he hadn't wanted to say out loud. As bad as it sounded, he felt better for having said it – setting the reality of the situation in stone; hardening his resolve to succeed.

'There's no point reaching the ranges safe and well if she's already in the city.

'We have to take a few risks to try and turn the situation more in our favour – any way we can. It doesn't matter whether I'm the only one foolish enough to try – I'll do it.'

It had been days – how many, he had no idea.

Alone, he hadn't seen a single soul since running from the room with all the noise.

The noise …

The ever-present, never-ending noise.

Even now, in the middle of nowhere, wherever nowhere happened to be, it continued to scream in his ears, inside his head.

It filled the air around him. It came up from the ground beneath him. It didn't matter where he was, it never left him – it would never leave him.

Stumbling like a drunkard, he struggled over the next rise.

Exposed to the elements, he felt the cold; and with the cold, he realised he was hungry – desperately hungry – and *thirsty* – he'd do anything for a drink of water.

From the edge of his vision he saw it – *a well!*

He found himself running, energy in his legs he hadn't felt for days. Despite his aching chest and lungs, he willed himself to run faster – *how great the water will feel!*

It didn't matter if he drowned in it – perhaps it would stop the noise once and for all.

Down the hill, to the left, he could see it clearly, he could even see the bucket swinging gently from its rope.

It was going to be so *good!*

Leaning over the wall, he reached for the bucket …

He reached for the bucket …

Reached for …

Slumping to the ground, the well disappeared.

'No,' he said. '*Noooo!*'

On his knees, spent from his effort to get here, he slumped helplessly over the broken fence, the noise in his ears as loud as ever.

Including Dane, there were ten in the first group.

Hawthorne was to lead.

If they made it across without incident, more would follow.

'Are you sure we're not mad?' Will whispered to Dane.

Looking across the river, Dane saw nothing to give him pause at what they were about to do.

'We'll be across before we have time to think,' he said.

About two hundred yards wide; at the deepest point, the water would be lapping at their horse's girth. Any deeper and they would have to wait for the water to drop with the tide; time they could ill afford to waste.

'The quickest way is straight across,' said Hawthorne. 'Do not hesitate; do not change course.'

The others nodded.

'Two at a time. Do not enter until the group in front is halfway across.'

Dane went first.

Thunder didn't hesitate, walking straight into the water.

Dane felt safe and sure – the water rising gently while he made his way to the middle, the bottom firm beneath him.

Hawthorne and Officer Kerringvale followed, crossing without incident.

The next two groups travelled safely across.

Officers Deverall and Fernbeck were the last pair ahead of Will. Glancing at Will after they had passed, Dane saw him entering the river, unfazed, striding towards him.

Ahead, Dane saw the others on the opposite bank; Deverall and Fernbeck were making good progress, about twenty yards ahead of him ...

In a split second it happened.

With a sudden jolt, Deverall was struck from the side; the force knocking his mount off balance. A moment later he was struck again – an enormous head rising from the water, jaws open for a moment, before snapping shut, biting down hard on his leg.

Screaming in agony, Deverall could do nothing; trapped in the clutches of a thirty-foot sarkoe. Pushing past Deverall's horse, the sarkoe maintained its grip, contorting its prey wickedly as it continued its path downriver.

After a moment or two, the strength of the croc's grip simply tore Deverall out of the saddle.

In the next moment he was underwater, carried away.

Dane and Will watched, horrified for a moment, before turning their eyes back to the river, looking for more sarkoe.

Upriver, they saw nothing that gave them immediate cause for alarm. On both banks, Knights were running desperately up and downriver.

'Here!' shouted one.

'There!' shouted another.

'There!' shouted one on the other bank.

'There!' shouted another.

Stranded in the middle of the river, Dane and Will were unsure what to do, which way to go.

'We have to get out of here!' Dane yelled, spurring Thunder hard.

It was difficult where they were – the water at its deepest, where the going was hardest.

More screams broke out from the shore.

Hawthorne, Kerringvale, and the others who'd made it across the river were scrambling into their saddles.

Dane and Thunder kept pounding forward; Will to their right, slightly ahead. Blaze swooped across Dane's line of sight, gliding low over the water, rising upriver and hovering a couple of feet above the surface about forty yards away, screeching all the while.

Dane watched for a moment, wondering what she was doing.

In the midst of his panic, he saw it; a large, dark snout on the surface of the water, angling its way towards him – and Blaze; hovering above, dipping and rising, offering herself as bait.

The Commanders were right ...

Veering to the right, trying to increase the distance between himself and the sarkoe, he bumped into Will.

'There's one over there!' he yelled.

Will turned sharply away.

Now in shallower water, Dane and Will edged closer and closer to the shore. Glancing at Blaze for a moment, Dane would not have believed what he saw next, had he not seen it with his own eyes.

With a swish of its massive tail, the sarkoe lifted a full third of its body out of the water, its massive jaws opening to their full width; trying to catch the eagle hovering tantalisingly out of reach.

With a *CRACK!* as loud as a thunderclap, the jaws snapped shut, inches from its prey; before the sarkoe landed in the water with a splash.

Switching his eyes to the shore, Dane gasped.

On the sand, several yards up the bank, blocking his path to freedom, another sarkoe, closer to forty feet long, waited; swishing its tail, snarling at him. Keeping its eyes on Dane, it made no move towards Will when he made it to shore, urging his mount up the bank. Dane could see he wasn't going to make it out before he'd be attacked.

With a mixture of adrenaline and desperation surging through him, he drew a knife from his gauntlet, hurling it at the sarkoe.

Dane swore as the knife bounced harmlessly off its hard skin.

Emerging from the water, the sarkoe moved towards him.

In the next moment, two things happened at once.

Blaze swooped; as fast as an arrow; screeching all the while; her talons grazing the top jaw of the sarkoe, distracting it for a moment. At the same time, Thunder reared, stamping his front feet hard on the sand, landing right next to the giant croc.

The sarkoe swiped its head away, snarling.

Dane reacted instantly, turning Thunder in the opposite direction, and with a quick kick, they took flight, racing away.

For a moment he rode blindly, making sure there were no other predators waiting for him.

After a couple of minutes, he slowed down, letting his adrenaline and breathing normalise.

Taking in his surroundings, he looked to his left, searching for the others.

'Dane!'

Looking around, he saw Will making his way towards him.

'Over there,' he said, motioning to a place about a hundred yards or so ahead of them.

Making their way towards the others, neither said a word, recovering from what had just befallen them.

Hawthorne nodded as they reigned in.

'How did you get out of the river?'

Dane shook his head.

'With a lot of help from Blaze,' he said. 'She baited one in the river; then swooped another waiting on shore.'

'Deverall was taken,' said Will.

'We know,' said Hawthorne. 'But it could have been worse. Apart from Deverall and Epper, we all made it.'

'Where's Epper?' said Dane. 'He made it across.'

'Yes, he did,' said Hawthorne. 'Unfortunately, he didn't make it past the sarkoe on shore. As soon as they emerged, we had to flee. Epper wasn't fast enough.'

'I didn't know they attack on shore,' said Dane. 'They're supposed to be water creatures.'

'True,' said Hawthorne, 'but they do attack on land, and they're quite fast, despite their size.'

'I hope I never see another one again,' said Will. 'That was enough to last a lifetime.'

'I think we can all agree on that,' said Hawthorne. 'However, we've saved ourselves a lot of time. We won't see the others again until we are in the ranges, if at all.'

'There's plenty of daylight left,' said Dane. 'Let's go.'

Chapter 16
A LOST FRIEND

Torches cast an eerie glow around the clearing.

The first man looked around anxiously.

'I can't afford to linger,' he said to his companion.

'There is no need for concern,' said his cohort.

'I'm risking a lot being here,' the first replied. 'If my absence is noticed, it will lead to suspicion.'

Before either could react, there was a cloud of gules-red smoke, followed by a *BANG!*

Stepping forward, Raegan nodded to the two men.

'Report,' he said to the first.

'Some of the regiment crossed the Osa River.'

'Hardly worth the risk you have taken to inform me,' said Raegan.

'I thought it was important. We didn't think they would take the risk. It means some are closer than we thought.'

'How many?' asked Raegan.

'Nine.'

'Nine?'

'One was taken by a sarkoe.'

Raegan managed a smile.

'Dane Thorburn is among them,' said the informant.

Raegan considered the information for a moment.

'That explains everything,' he said. 'A daring move, triggered no doubt by his higher sense of duty to find the girl. In the end it means little. None will survive what I have planned for them.'

He looked at the other man.

'When will the girl reach the ranges?'

'In two days,' replied the informant. 'The journey has been uneventful. There is nothing to suggest she will not arrive as planned.'

'Very well,' said Raegan. 'Is there anything else we need to know?'

'As expected, all Brindabeare efforts are directed to the Gargaun Ranges.'

'Yes,' said Raegan. 'And what a worthless and costly exercise that will prove to be.'

'There is no way they can rescue her?'

'None,' said Raegan. 'No matter how many they send, there is no way in without the assistance of the wolves. First, you must find them. Then you must persuade them to help you. Neither is easy.'

'And there is no escape?'

'None,' said Raegan.

'My Lord,' said the first man. 'Forgive me. If there is no escape, how have you been able to enter and exit the city?'

Raegan smiled.

'Never you mind.'

Dane, Will, Hawthorne and the rest of the party saw the ruins ahead.

Another remote settlement, burnt out like the others.

This was the third they'd seen in the last two days.

The huts were destroyed, all trace of life gone.

Hawthorne signaled to stop.

Cursing under his breath, Dane reigned Thunder in with the others.

They were losing any gain from crossing the Osa River in the heavy rain they'd encountered over the last few days. Tracks were muddy, the going slow and tedious; the rain so unyielding at times, they simply had to stop and wait for it to ease.

Dane couldn't help himself.

'How long are we going to wait?' he asked.

'Patience,' Hawthorne replied. 'We will take our rest here, and ride through to the end of the day.'

Looking into the distance, Dane felt his anger roiling inside him.

'It still seems so far away,' he said. 'And every time we stop, it seems our chances of finding the Princess get smaller and smaller.'

'We can only arrive as quickly as circumstances allow,' said Hawthorne.

'But ...'

'That will do,' said Hawthorne. 'It gives me no pleasure to encounter delays either.'

Defeated for the moment, Dane saw Will leaning against the remains of what had once been a wall, looking into the distance.

'We're wasting our time here,' he said.

Will nodded.

'If we don't linger too long, it may be all right. The tracks are a mess.'

'And the longer we stop, the messier they become,' said Dane. 'And the harder for us to navigate.'

'At least we're under shelter,' said Will, glancing around. 'Or what's left of it.'

'I didn't know these places even existed,' said Dane. 'It's supposed to be desolate out here.'

'There are always small groups who choose to live alone,' said Will. 'As long as they have what they need to survive.'

'But it's clear they didn't. This is a massacre. They had nothing to defend themselves.'

'Perhaps,' said Will. 'When they chose to live out here like this; they would have thought they'd be left alone.'

'This looks like something Black Knights do for recreation,' said Dane. 'Let's hope there are no more.'

Blaze returned in the afternoon.

'What of the regiment?' asked Hawthorne.

'They're delayed more than we are,' said Dane. 'Commander Hindmarsh reports they travelled only six miles in the last day.'

Hawthorne considered the information.

'Commander, I know we spoke earlier, but we need to keep moving. We have to ride through the night. The regiment has little hope of arriving in time to offer anything before the Princess is put in the city. If she is to be saved, it has to be us. We need to get there as soon as we can.'

'That may be ...' said Hawthorne.

'I agree with Dane – Royal Knight Thorburn,' said Will. 'We should keep going.'

'We will ride later into the day, and see where we are at nightfall,' said Hawthorne. 'If the weather has improved, I will consider it. If it has not, there is even less to be gained by riding in driving rain in darkness than there is in daylight.'

Releasing Blaze once more, the ride resumed.

Apart from Dane, Will and Hawthorne, the others were Kerringvale, Fernbeck, Witheridge, Cotterall and Dorsley.

The rain had eased, but it continued to slow them down. Supplies were low; they'd taken minimal loads with them when they crossed the river. At least the rain allowed them to keep their waterskins full.

Harlanwood lay in the distance to their right, with the ranges looming on the distant horizon. Apart from the burnt-out settlements, since crossing the Osa River, the land had been hilly and empty, with occasional clumps of trees dotting the landscape.

Despite the close company, few words were said. Like the others, Dane found himself in his own space, concentrating on the wet tracks; willing everyone to be able to go faster. In better weather, they would have covered this ground easily.

A larger clump of trees came into view, near what looked like the remains of a fence. The first of the group had passed when Dane saw it.

Something moved.

Something that looked like ...

An arm!

'*Stop!*' Dane yelled. 'Stop! There's someone over here!'

Dismounting, sword drawn, Dane ran to the fence.

He could see the arm, dangling helplessly over the fence.

What he saw when he arrived shocked him.

Kneeling against the other side of the fence; his head lolling to one side, one arm slumped over to support himself, was a Brindabeare Knight.

Dane recognised him immediately.

By now, others were running towards him.

'Over here!' he yelled desperately, spotting Will. 'It's Hamish!'

Dane looked at his friend.

While he had no weapons or armour, and there were cuts and bruises all over his body; it was the look on his face that worried Dane the most – completely devoid of expression – eyes wide and listless, mouth hanging open.

Lifting Hamish's arm over the fence and easing him backwards, Dane allowed Hamish to rest against him.

'Hamish!' said Dane. 'Hamish! It's me. Dane Thorburn.'

No response.

'Hamish! Are you all right?'

Nothing.

'Get me some water,' said Dane.

'Who is it?' asked Hawthorne.

'Hamish Ingham,' said Dane.

'I remember him,' said Fernbeck. 'He was the Junior Knight in the first search party – the one that never made it back.'

Dorsley handed Dane a waterskin.

Gently supporting Hamish's head, Dane offered some water.

At first it dribbled down Hamish's face, but after a moment he responded, slowly swallowing.

'Good,' said Dane. 'Easy.'

Gradually, Hamish responded, taking more and more of the water.

'Hamish, are you all right?' asked Dane, handing back the waterskin.

'Rrrr,' said Hamish.

'What's his condition?' asked Hawthorne.

Although he'd taken the water, the look on Hamish's face hadn't changed.

'I don't know,' said Dane. 'He's wounded. He's been badly beaten, but there's something else. Something ... wrong ... with him.'

'Rrrr–aa,' said Hamish.

'What is he saying?'

'I don't know,' said Dane.

'Raegan?' said Will.

'Rae ... gan,' said Hamish quietly.

'Very good,' said Dane. 'What about Raegan?'

Hamish's eyes blinked, perhaps for the first time since Dane found him.

'Rae ... gan,' he said again.

Dane could see every word; every movement was a struggle.

'Raegan,' said Dane. 'What did he do, Hamish? What did he do?'

Trying to speak, Hamish took several gulps.

Rae ... gan,' he said. 'C-c-c-apt-ur-ur-urd.'

'Capture,' said Dane. 'Capture. You were captured by Raegan?'

'O-th-th-ers ... d-d-dead.'

'How did you end up here?' asked Dane.

Hamish said nothing, breathing heavily, looking wide-eyed into the distance.

'Let him get to it,' said Will. 'Don't rush him.'

'What did Raegan do?' asked Dane. 'What did Raegan do to you?'

'N-n-n-oi-se,' said Hamish.

No one in the group understood what he meant.

'Noise?' said Dane.

'N-n-n-oi-se,' said Hamish again. 'D-d-d-dun-dun-geon.'

'Noise in a dungeon?' Will suggested.

'Could be,' said Dane. 'It's not making any sense. Captured by Raegan? Noise in a dungeon?'

None in the group could figure it out.

'K-k-k,' said Hamish, his head lolling from side to side.

'Where's the water?' said Dane.

Hawthorne passed him another skin.

'Drink some more,' Dane said to Hamish.

Hamish made no sound or movement other than swallowing the water.

'Hamish,' said Will. 'Raegan captured you, and put you in a dungeon? With a noise?'

For the first time, Hamish moved, feebly raising his hands towards his head.

'A dungeon with a noise?' said Hawthorne. 'What does that mean?

'I don't know,' said Dane.

'Neither do I,' said Will.

Dane looked at Hamish again. He'd never seen anyone with such a distant, helpless expression. Hamish seemed to have no sense of where he was, or what he was saying. It was as though he was in a trance, captured under some kind of spell.

'Hamish,' said Dane. 'What was the noise?'

Squirming against Dane, Hamish tried to move his hands to his face.

'Is he trying to cover his ears?' asked Hawthorne.

'Maybe,' said Dane.

'Ask a different question,' said Hawthorne.

'Hamish,' said Dane, 'what happened to the others.'

'N-n-n-oi-se.'

'Noise?' said Dane.

Nobody had any ideas.

'Hamish, what happened to the others?' Dane asked again.

Hamish's head rolled back.

Struggling to help, Dane adjusted his arm on the back of Hamish's neck, lifting his head up.

'N-n-n-oi-se ... d-d-d-ead.'

'It makes no sense,' said Hawthorne. 'Noise dead?'

'Wait,' said Dane. 'Wait. Maybe it's ...'

He trailed off, thinking.

'Hamish,' said Dane. 'Did the noise kill them? The rest of them? Was it the noise?'

Everyone looked at Dane, wondering what he was talking about. Hamish squirmed again, seeming to convulse against some unknown, invisible force. His head swung viciously from side to side; his arms flailing, tearing against his face, hair and body; his legs were kicking out, and he started screaming.

'Aaaaaarrrrgggghhh! Aaaaaarrrrgggghhh!'

With a final convulsion, Hamish rolled himself over, completely out from under the support Dane had offered him. Raising his head, his eyes wide, possessed by some unknown, uncontrollable demon inside him, he swished from side to side, and with a final, brutal thrust, slammed himself head first into the ground.

Nobody moved for a moment.

All were rooted to the spot; shocked at what they'd seen.

Dane reached over, turning Hamish onto his back.

He was dead.

Dane bowed his head.

Hamish had been his friend; apart from a brief time in training, when he'd allowed himself to get caught up in silly rumours about

Dane; he'd been loyal, dutiful, trustworthy, and a joy to have in his company.

To see him like this, to see him end like this, was more than Dane could bear.

Will kneeled beside him.

Looking at each other for a moment, neither said a word; consumed by their own grief.

Placing his hand on Dane's shoulder, Will waited, allowing Dane to gather himself while he did the same. Both stood together, wiping their faces as they did so.

'He needs to be buried,' said Will.

'He deserves it,' Dane said to Hawthorne. 'It won't take long, and we'll make up the time. We can ride into the night if we have to.'

Hawthorne considered for a moment, then nodded.

'Very well,' he said. 'But, we still don't know what he was talking about.'

'I do,' said Dane. 'I think I know *exactly* what he was talking about.'

'What ...'

'After he's buried,' said Dane.

'Cotterall and Dorsley can take care of that,' said Hawthorne.

'Will and I will do it,' said Dane. 'He was our friend.'

Seeing the determination and pleading on Dane's face, Hawthorne relented.

Dane and Will said nothing to each other while they dug the grave. Others found what stones they could to mark it for them.

'Thank you, Commander,' said Dane.

Hawthorne nodded.

'You said you knew what he was talking about,' said Hawthorne.

'I do,' said Dane. 'Some of it I don't completely understand, but I know most of it.'

'Tell us.'

'It's to do with Raegan and the City of Lost Souls,' said Dane. Puzzled faces greeted his response.

'What do you mean?' said Hawthorne.

'Lord Frederick told me about it in a council meeting.'

'Very well,' said Hawthorne. 'Go on.'

'There's a sound in the City of Lost Souls,' said Dane. 'A constant, never-ending pulse; a scraping sound that breaks the mind of everyone and sends them mad.'

'But he wasn't in the City of Lost Souls,' said Hawthorne.

'I know,' said Dane. 'But it wouldn't be going too far to suggest Raegan created something similar and used it on others; like the party Fernbeck mentioned.'

'How would he be able to create that sound if he's never been in the City of Lost Souls?' said Will. 'How could he know what it is?'

'I don't know,' said Dane. 'Lord Frederick says no prisoner ever put in the city has been able to escape. But he knew exactly what the forces in the city do; how they eventually drive those inside completely mad, and he said the scraping sound was the worst of it.

'If Lord Frederick knows about it, we can be sure Raegan knows it too. The City of Lost Souls was created for wizards – a similar sound, no matter how small, would drive anyone else mad in a very short time.'

'That's all very well,' said Hawthorne, 'but how do you explain a knight – here; where there's not even a settlement, affected by this sound – whether it be from the City of Lost Souls, or something else?'

'You could see he was possessed…lost…mad,' said Dane. 'How he reacted once we pieced what little of the story together we could.

'Once we asked him about the noise, whether it killed the rest of his party; he sank even further into whatever had possessed him.'

'I'm still not convinced,' said Hawthorne. 'There are still some pieces that don't make sense.'

'I know,' said Dane. 'I don't know how Hamish ended up here. I can only think he escaped from wherever he and the others were captured. Maybe Candahorn, Rhondo, or Mundool. Or maybe they were abandoned here, and he was the only one left when we arrived.'

'It wasn't enough that they were captured,' said Dorsley. 'He was tortured.'

'Candahorn's been waiting a long time for something like this,' said Kerringvale. 'They want Brindabeare, and every Brindabeare Knight to suffer.'

Looking into the distance, Hawthorne considered everything he'd heard.

'The ranges are still days away,' he said.

'The City of Lost Souls sounds like a horrible place,' said Will.

'It is,' said Dane. 'That's why we *have* to get there before Raegan puts Vanessa inside. Once she's in there, there's no hope. Even if we're able to find it, we'd be too late to save her.'

✦

Chapter 17

ARRIVAL

L ocated on the south-west coast, the Gargaun Ranges are considerably smaller than the Highland Mountains, where Fire God Vrenin and the Highland Dragon are said to reside; the Strivett Mountains on the north-west coast, and the Xerin Mountains to the east.

Apart from a small forest at its base, the Gargaun Ranges have none of the habitation of the others; it is devoid of animal life; there are no settlements; there is no need to pass through them when travelling from one place to another. It is empty and isolated – which made it the perfect location for the ancient wizarding prison known as The City of Lost Souls.

The new morning filled Vanessa with dread.

Whatever lay in store would finally be revealed, and the Black Knights made little effort to hide what they believed lay ahead.

'If you think the past days have been difficult, the worst is yet to come,' said one of her captors.

'I wouldn't want to end up where you're going,' said another.

'You'll be lucky to survive more than a couple of days,' sneered another.

Seeing the rising panic on Vanessa's face, the three laughed out loud.

'You're not so strong now, are you?'

'Where's that arrogance you're so fond of displaying?'

Turning away, Vanessa looked helplessly into the distance.

Now she was finally here – wherever 'here' happened to be – new, stronger waves of panic were sweeping over her.

Despite the cooler weather, she felt hot and cold at the same time; sweat dripping down her face, seeping through her tattered clothes; causing her to shiver as she considered the many possibilities once more.

'You'll be lucky to survive more than a couple of days.'

What does that mean?

What are they going to do?

All the possibilities she'd thought the last few days were right in front of her – one was *about* to happen.

What am I going to face?

Bats?

Sarkoe?

Razor boars?

Panthers?

Beringei?

Bears?

Something worse?

'Trembling like a leaf,' said the first Black Knight.

Hearing him say it made her shiver even more; tears were rolling down her cheeks, turning into sobs, her body shaking uncontrollably. Others noticed, laughing and pointing.

Closing her eyes and lowering her head, she tried to shut it all out – the laughter, the thoughts of what might happen, the utter helplessness of her predicament.

As the ride into the ranges continued, a couple of Black Knights reached over, prodding her with a hand or sword in turn; making her jump uncomfortably, extracting as much discomfort and suffering as they could on this final leg of the journey.

Riding up behind her, one reached forward, hitting her across the back of the head.

Already shifting around in the saddle; this latest blow threw her completely off balance. With an anguished scream, she fell forward and sideways, before tumbling out of her saddle and hitting the ground with a thud.

The Black Knights around her stopped. Those ahead, unaware of what had happened, continued about fifty yards, before shouts brought them trotting back to the group.

None made an effort to assist Vanessa.

Lying on the ground, spitting the dirt from her mouth, she made no effort to stand.

'On your feet, Meriwether,' said a Black Knights to her left.

Vanessa made no movement.

'I won't say it again.'

Vanessa remained motionless.

'Very well.'

She heard feet dropping to the ground.

In the next moment, a rough hand grabbed her by the hair from behind, hauling her to her feet.

'Aaarrgh!' she screamed.

The leader came to stand in front of her.

'Would you mind explaining what is going on here?' he asked.

'Threw herself out of the saddle,' said the Black Knight holding her, still pulling her by the hair.

'Is that so?' said the leader. 'Well then ...'

'That is *not* so!' said Vanessa. 'One of them struck me from behind and I slipped and fell! My hands are tied, and I had no way to prevent it!'

The leader looked calmly at Vanessa, his face displaying no hint of emotion. Speaking to the one who held her, he asked simply, 'Is this true?'

'Absolutely not,' the Black Knight replied. 'Ask all who saw it.'

Others in the group were nodding.

'Not true,' said a couple.

'Very well,' said the leader. 'So, *Your Highness*. It appears, despite everything we do to restrain you, you appear determined to thwart us. I must say, despite the considerable inconvenience you continue to cause me, you possess either a remarkable spirit, or an arrogance beyond belief.

'Even now, with the outcome of your inevitable fate so near, you continue to make life for us as difficult as possible. Well, let me tell you, in the event you were not already aware. What is in store for you is a fate I would not wish on anyone; and it would have been wise for you to have made this journey as pleasant as possible – for your own sake.

'Given you have proven time and time again that you cannot follow orders, no matter how simple they may be, I now have no choice but to take steps to ensure that you will.'

Nodding to a couple of others, he waited.

Vanessa struggled and squirmed against the Black Knight holding her, who reached around her with his other arm, gripping her tightly.

'*You will all die!*' she screamed. '*All of you! Every last ...*'

Before she could finish, a gag was shoved in her mouth.

Vanessa continued screaming – the gag turning it into a muffled squeal.

Handed a length of rope by another of his cohorts, the leader tied one end to the bindings around Vanessa's wrists.

Finally, a hood was placed over her head.

The leader leaned in, talking with a quiet, dripping venom in his voice.

'Our orders are to get you to the meeting point alive,' he said. 'Alive has many meanings. It can mean well fed and in one piece. It can also mean on the brink of death, and the many stages in between.'

Vanessa struggled against the rope tied to her, now pulling tight, causing her to walk.

The leader continued.

'As you have shown you are no longer capable of travelling this last distance on horseback without causing disruption, you will make it on foot. Should you so much as stumble, I will start cutting off your fingers, one by one, until we arrive. It does not matter to me whether you arrive with all of them, or none.'

Rumour and gossip swept through Brindabeare like wildfire.

'They haven't found her! They had thirty days. Raegan said if the King didn't surrender, he'd kill her.'

'They tried to cross the Osa River and were attacked by sarkoe. Only half of them survived.'

'They're torturing her in a dungeon somewhere.'

'They're going to declare war on Candahorn. That's where Raegan's holding her.'

'I hear she's being taken to the Gargaun Ranges. Why would they take her there?'

'No, it's the Strivett Mountains.'

'Well, I heard they're going to leave her to die in Harlanwood.'

'Raegan has her in some kind of spell, and Lord Frederick can't find her.'

'But Lord Frederick is supposed to be more powerful than Raegan. How can that be true?'

On and on it went, each rumour more speculative than the one before. In the council chambers, others with far more knowledge of what was happening were also discussing matters ...

'Our sources say the group that crossed the Osa River will arrive the day after tomorrow,' said General Silvers. 'The rest of the regiment has been delayed further than last reported, and will arrive, at best, two days later.'

'That will be too late,' said the King. 'Our best hope is for the few who crossed the river to get there as quickly as possible and search as quickly and thoroughly as they can.'

'Forgive me for saying so, Sire,' said Medhurst. 'Unless they are incredibly fortunate, that is a very slim hope.'

'That may be,' said the King. 'But at this time, it may be the only hope we have.'

Lord Frederick addressed the Council.

'I have searched the ranges several times, and I found only one pack. And after offering the bounty, the wolves looked at the projected image and refused to accept it.'

'All instructions from the Annals were followed?' asked the King.

Lord Frederick nodded. 'Apart from the duplication; yes, they were.'

'And yet,' said Medhurst, 'Raegan has not only been able to find the entrance, but he has also been able to engage the Gargaun wolves to help him.'

'Raegan must offer real subjects,' said Lord Frederick. 'From ... well, I'd rather not speculate. However, we know an entire search party sent from Brindabeare has never returned.'

'If you found a pack, at least you know where the entrance to the city lies,' said Fairbrother.

'Not necessarily,' said Lord Frederick. 'Despite finding only one pack, there were traces of many. None of the trails lead anywhere in either direction. They give no sign as to where the entrance may be.'

'So, we've found nothing,' said Medhurst. 'The Princess is due to be put in this 'city' tomorrow, and we are no closer to knowing where it is.'

Lord Frederick nodded.

'Unfortunately, that is correct. Once we are done here, I will return to the ranges and continue my search.'

'We will be too late!' said Medhurst. 'The thirty-day period expires tonight! There's nothing more we ...'

With a penetrating look from the King, Medhurst stopped mid-sentence.

'Sire, forgive me. I didn't mean ...'

The King waved him away.

'Did you see anything else?' the King asked Lord Frederick. 'Anything that might identify the fail-safe measure mentioned in the Annals?'

'I did not,' said Lord Frederick. 'I dare say, without knowing exactly what this measure is, it is all but impossible.'

The King nodded.

'Is it possible,' offered Lindstrom, somewhat weakly, 'that the City of Lost Souls is not where the Princess is being taken?'

'I doubt that very much,' said Lord Frederick.

'It could be a diversion,' said Lindstrom. 'A ploy to draw us away from where he is really holding her. Perhaps a ploy to trap our knights in the ranges?'

'Raegan would not make such a claim about the City of Lost Souls unless it were true,' said Lord Frederick. 'His arrogance and combative nature drives his desire to do things others cannot – to the point of obsession.'

'Has any trace of an enemy force near the ranges been reported?' asked the King.

'No, Sire,' said Silvers. 'And though no one from Wandabyne, Cramden or Wedlan has seen an enemy presence, I have no doubt our men will defeat any enemy who may confront them.'

'I have found no traces of an enemy force either,' said Lord Frederick. 'Whoever is with the Princess is using a cloaking spell I have been unable to penetrate.'

The King nodded gravely.

'I don't believe there is any more to be done here,' he said. 'Dismissed.'

All bar the King and Salsbury made their exit without a word.

Slumping in his seat, exhausted, the King let out a deep breath.

'Sire, are you all right?' asked Salsbury.

'We have to save her,' the King said softly. '*We have to save her.*'

Thankfully, the track and terrain were not treacherous.

Forced into a slow jog to maintain the required pace, Vanessa had been running nearly an hour.

With her hands and arms stretched in front, the only way to ease the pain from the ropes biting into her wrists had been to run at a pace that kept slack in the rope tying her to the horse. Keeping that pace meant her legs were now begging for mercy.

With the hood blinding her eyes, and the gag and hood constraining her ability to breathe normally; it was torturous in every way.

Several times she stumbled, nearly falling; but with the threats of the leader hanging over her, she doggedly refused to go down. The way he had spoken to her, she had no doubt he would make good on his threat if she did.

Her captors continued taunting and teasing, yelling in hope each time she staggered. Forced to give every ounce of herself to the task of staying upright, she heard nothing.

Rounding a corner, the pace quickened; forcing her into a full run to keep up. Struggling even more to stay upright, her arms stretched to their full length, threatening to tear themselves from her shoulders. Her legs were screaming in agony, the muscles burning like fire. Her breathing was short and raspy, the hood blowing hot air around her face every time she exhaled.

After two hundred yards at this pace, the horse slowed to a halt. Feeling the tension in the rope go slack, Vanessa blundered to a stop, tripping over herself and collapsing in a heap.

'Grovelling before us once again,' said a Black Knight.

Laughter burst from the rest of the group.

Gasping for breath, Vanessa remained on the ground where she'd fallen.

One of her captors hauled her up, removing the hood and gag.

Sucking in her first full breath in over an hour, reflexes took over. Thankfully, with little food and water in her stomach, it was more of a dry retching. Several spasms in a row forced her to her knees, coughing and spitting while her body shook uncontrollably.

When it finished, she wobbled herself upright; her legs now aching with stiffness.

The leader stood in front of her.

'I see you have finally understood what it means to obey orders,' he said.

Vanessa said nothing, continuing to pant deep breaths.

'And here we are; where we will make our final goodbyes.'

Vanessa cast her eyes around her.

With all her energy absorbed in her latest ordeal, she hadn't had time to think about anything other than getting through it unscathed. Still recovering, her breaths deep and heavy; the fact she was finally at the place she would meet her fate had little effect on her.

The torches hiding her surroundings had been discarded, and she saw they were in a clearing of sorts, about fifty yards from what appeared to be a large lake, surrounded by mountains on all sides. Neither the lake nor the mountains gave an indication of danger.

The lake was a clear, shiny azure blue; a couple of miles long, about half a mile wide; the surface flat, calm and tranquil. The mountains were full of dead trees and scrub.

The area around her lay silent. There were no sounds of nature, no animals to be seen.

Scanning the area again, she felt her adrenaline re-start; new panic and fear starting to overwhelm her.

Her entire ordeal since being captured had led to this point – the days, nights, weeks and months; all of it blurring into a single moment – and she could see nothing but a peaceful paradise around her.

What's going on?

Her lower lip started to tremble as the fear took hold.

'W-what is this place?' she said.

'It's not at all what it seems,' said the leader. 'You will know soon enough.'

Looking desperately around herself again, she searched for a sign, anything that would give a hint.

Nothing.

Utterly beside herself now, she started hyperventilating, her aching legs ready to give out from underneath her.

She heard a sound to her right, and, glancing in that direction, saw Raegan emerge from behind a thicket about twenty yards away, walking slowly towards her, accompanied by a large animal she'd never seen before.

In the next instant another emerged, then another, and another. One after the other they came, until she counted twelve of them. At a slow pace, seemingly under Raegan's control, they looked at ease; and yet she could see strength and power in their bodies; a simmering, predatory fury in their eyes.

Raegan raised his hand and they stopped, fanning in a semi-circle behind him. He continued walking, stopping when he stood before her.

'My dear,' he said calmly. 'I trust you had a pleasant journey?'

Vanessa said nothing, continuing to stare at what looked to be the giant wolfish creatures standing behind him.

'I asked you a question,' said Raegan. 'Now is the worst time you could choose to defy me.'

'These men are nothing more than bullies and cowards,' she said, not taking her eyes off the wolf creatures.

Raegan shrugged.

'They were instructed to get you here alive, and here you are.'

Vanessa said nothing.

Raegan continued.

'I appeared before your father and gave him thirty days to meet my demands,' he said. 'Had he done so, I would have returned you to him, safe and unharmed. It is by his will, and his will alone, that you find yourself here.'

'He and Lord Frederick will find you and kill you,' Vanessa replied.

'Charming, to the last breath,' said Raegan.

The Black Knights laughed as one.

Raegan took a step back, opening his stance, gesturing towards the lake and the creatures he had brought with him.

'You are at the entrance of the City of Lost Souls,' he said. 'I'm sure you know nothing about that, so let me enlighten you a little. You recall, the last time we met, what I said to you?'

Raegan waited for Vanessa to react.

Vanessa knew exactly what he'd said – with widening eyes, she wondered; was he going to set the giant wolf creatures on her?

'In case your memory fails you,' said Raegan, 'I said where you were going, *only death and misery awaits.*' And the City of Lost Souls is such a place. It is an ancient place – a prison; where, once, a long time ago, the most evil wizards were placed; a place from which no escape has ever been possible.'

'W-where is it?' Vanessa asked. 'And what are those, those – *things?*' she added, pointing to the creatures standing patiently to her right.

'These are Gargaun wolves,' said Raegan, gently scratching the nearest behind its ears. 'Larger and far more destructive than other wolves; capable of tearing through flesh and bone in a single bite.'

Seemingly under Raegan's control, the wolves waited patiently.

Vanessa began trembling.

'Oh no,' said Raegan. 'You don't have to worry about them. Fierce meat eaters though they are, these particular wolves have a liking for *dead* meat.'

Vanessa was in full meltdown now, shaking uncontrollably, her mind a gaggle of thoughts.

If they were here to do away with her after she died, then what was Raegan going to do to her now?

Raegan smiled at her discomfort.

'What you need to be concerned about is the City of Lost Souls, which lies before you.'

Despite everything churning through her mind, Vanessa looked again at the lake and mountains, trying to understand what Raegan was saying.

'Once you are inside, you will lose whatever mind and wit you have, and you will become so desperate for everything to cease, you will end your own life.'

Vanessa shuddered, struggling to keep herself from collapsing.

'The wolves are your escort,' said Raegan. 'They will ensure you go in, and once you die in there, make sure there is no trace of you left behind.'

Raegan nodded, and two Black Knights grabbed hold of her.

Raegan waved his hand, and two short pieces of material appeared. With another wave, the rope binding Vanessa's wrist fell to the ground.

Vanessa started squirming against the grip of the Black Knights. 'No!' she said.

Raegan waved a hand towards Vanessa's wrists; a piece of material wrapping around each in turn.

Raegan and the Black Knights led her towards the wolves.

'No!' she screamed.

Struggling against her new bindings and her captors, barely able to walk, she offered little in the way of resistance, continuing to scream all the while.

Stopping in front of the first wolf, Raegan reached down, stroking its head.

'Very docile creatures,' he said, against the noise of Vanessa's screaming. 'Except when they smell food.'

Nodding to the wolves and signaling with his hand, four of them closed in around her – one in front, one behind, one on each side.

With a wave of Raegan's hand, another, much longer binding appeared. Looping around Vanessa's waist, it had four different ends. Raegan extended the first end to the wolf directly in front of her, tying it around a collar hidden in its fur.

'No!' Vanessa screamed desperately. 'No!'

Repeating the exercise with the other three, Vanessa was now tied to the four wolves.

Satisfied, and tiring of Vanessa's screaming, Raegan smacked her hard across the face.

With a yelp of pain, Vanessa stopped yelling; her face stinging, tears rolling down her cheeks.

'Here is where I leave you,' said Raegan. 'The best you can hope for is for a quick and painless death.'

With a nod and a tap on the head of the first wolf, the four started walking towards the lake, surrounded by the rest of the pack.

Staring helplessly ahead, Vanessa could do nothing to stop the wolves. Maintaining a slow, deliberate pace, the lake came closer and closer.

Were they going to drown her?

Was it that simple – after all Raegan's talk about the City of Lost Souls, the wolves were simply going to drown her?

'*No!*' she screamed.

It was only a matter of feet now.

The pack maintained its pace.

They were about to enter the lake.

Vanessa screamed again

She didn't see the first wolf step into the lake ...

Her eyes glazed over; she could see nothing ...

Her body felt limp, pins and needles rippling up and down her arms and legs ...

A wave of cold swept over her ...

Her eyes came back into focus; she could see again...

The bindings were gone ...

The wolves were running again...

Looking around, she had no idea where she was ...

In the next instant she raised her hands to her face, trying in vain to block out the sound of a loud, high-pitched scraping noise that seemed to be coursing through her entire body.

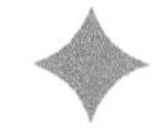

Chapter 18

SEARCHING THE RANGES

Raegan approached, sword drawn ...

Vanessa screamed ...

'Dane!' ...

Running as fast as he could, he saw Raegan raise his sword ...

'Dane!' Vanessa screamed. 'Dane!' ...

He ran faster, but they were moving further and further away ...

'Dane!' she screamed again. 'Why didn't you save me?'

Dane woke with a start, breathing heavily, a lather of sweat on his brow. Looking around, all lay calm and still, the earliest signs of dawn light creeping over the trees. Finally in the Gargaun Ranges, and with his adrenaline full of nervous tension, he'd only been able to snatch small slices of sleep.

Vanessa's in here somewhere.

Is she already in the city?

How do we find the entrance?

How do we get in?

Will we find her?

If we get in, how do we get out?

With all these thoughts racing through his mind, Dane stood, shaking the soreness out of his limbs, walking slowly among the others.

The forest they were in; or, to be more accurate – the cluster of trees at the entrance to the ranges, where they had taken shelter for the night, made no sound. He'd noticed something unusual when they'd first arrived – nothing of the life and noise you would normally hear in a forest. The only sounds were their own – it felt as though there was no life anywhere.

Slowly the others roused.

'De-camp and be ready to move as quickly as possible,' said Hawthorne. 'We have no time to waste.'

With a gentle pat as he moved along Thunder's flanks, Dane nuzzled into him, the closeness between them steadying his nerves.

'We need to do this,' he said quietly. 'Whatever it takes to find her; even if it's just the two of us.'

Thunder responded with a slight tug, letting out a gentle snort, as though he understood.

Checking the saddle and bindings; running his hands over his armour and weapons, he found all in order except a knife; remembering with a grunt he'd used it at the Osa River.

Moving to a small tree nearby, he held out his arm. Blaze stepped onto his gauntlet. Drawing her close, he held her up to his eyes.

'I don't want you to rest until you find her. I know you can do it. Find her and come back to me.'

With a flutter of her wings, Dane extended his arm again, lowering it for an instant, before thrusting it towards the sky. Launching into the air, Blaze rose above the trees, higher and higher, before disappearing out of sight.

'Are you ready?' asked Will.

Dane nodded.

'Absolutely. We have to find her – whatever it takes.'

Untying their mounts and saddling up, Dane and Will joined the others.

'Here is how we will proceed,' said Hawthorne. 'We will break into pairs, fanning out within the ranges. This will allow us to cover as much area as possible. As you know, our allies from Wandabyne, Cramden and Wedlan went no further than the outskirts; so, nothing beyond here has been searched.

'Make your arcs in the usual manner, and we will rendezvous at sunset – unless we are called together earlier. Despite our lack of numbers, we should be able to make good progress.'

'What are we looking for?' asked Witheridge.

'*The Princess!*' Dane yelled.

'That will do,' said Hawthorne, glaring at Dane. 'Given we know nothing of this City of Lost Souls, or what its surroundings looks like, it's a reasonable question. We look for any signs of the Princess's presence.

'She is likely to be heavily guarded; and may be in the company of Raegan himself. We will deal with whatever confronts us.

'You are all expert trackers – if you see anything to indicate the party may be within your search arc, use your call; and if the situation allows, wait in the usual manner. If you see the Princess in some way being led towards what may be the entrance of the city, you may not have time to wait – you will need to assess the situation and do whatever is necessary to save her.'

Dane and Will looked at each other.

The plan had its good and bad points. Covering as much territory as possible made it necessary to split up; but if one group found her, it would be only two against whatever number were guarding her. If everyone heard the call and made it in time, their total would be eight – would it be enough?

'Commander?' said Dane.

'Yes?'

'Blaze is in the air. If she finds the Princess, she will start circling and squawking.'

'Very well,' said Hawthorne. 'You know your search points. Let's move!'

As one, the group spurred their mounts, charging into the ranges, together for about a mile, before splitting into pairs and heading in different directions.

Dane and Will headed south-east, riding another mile, before turning to their right and starting their search arc. In the same way they would scout a camping site when part of Vanessa's entourage, they would circle the area in widening arcs, making their way further and further to the south-east.

Looking around, Dane saw nothing in the terrain that would impede them. The ground lay relatively flat and even; covered in short, dense grass. Trees of varying shapes and sizes dotted the space around them.

'It looks as though no one has been here for a long time, if ever,' he said.

'You may be right,' said Will. 'There's usually no reason for any-one to come here.'

The mountains around them were sheer and steep; no way horses would be able to climb. That narrowed the search area to the base.

Coming together at the end of their first arc, both scanned the area around them.

'It's as though there's no life at all,' said Will.

'I noticed that too,' said Dane. 'But we know the wolves are here – somewhere.'

'Let's keep going.'

Completing their first arc, Cotterall and Dorsley had seen nothing unusual or out of place. The second arc would take them into a cluster of trees, close to the base of the mountain on their left.

'We'll circle over to there,' said Dorsley, pointing ahead. 'Then we'll make our way around and see if there's anything on the other side.'

'Agreed,' said Cotterall, looking at the face of the mountain. 'There's no way up from here. Perhaps we'll find a way from the other side.'

It took several minutes for them to make their way around. Nothing they saw gave reason to think there might be anything wrong …

In an instant they were under attack.

Emerging from behind the trees, four Black Knights quickly surrounded them; swords drawn, cutting them down before they had a chance to react.

'Tether the horses and put the bodies out of sight,' said one of the Black Knights. 'Leave no traces.'

Dismounting, the other three did as instructed.

'That was far too easy,' said the Black Knight dragging Cotterall's body out of sight. 'Brindabeare's famous Advance Regiment,' he added, shaking his head and smirking. 'If that's the best they have to offer, we have little to worry about.'

Dane and Will found nothing on the second circuit.

'This is pointless,' said Dane.

'We have to be thorough,' said Will.

'But it's taking too long,' said Dane. 'We can see enough without having to do a full arc.'

'You never know what we could miss if we don't do it properly,' said Will. 'I agree it's taking time, but we have to be thorough.'

'Nothing's here,' said Dane. 'There's no trails, no sign of anything. The grass is too dense. We should keep going and move further east.'

'Let's do one more circuit and ...'

Will stopped mid-sentence, holding up his hand.

'What?' said Dane.

Will raised a finger to his lips, signaling Dane to be quiet. Leaning in, he said softly, 'I heard a horse. I'm sure of it.'

Dane's eyes widened.

'Where?' he whispered.

Gesturing to his left, Will silently drew his sword.

Dane followed suit.

Talking to each other with their hands, both nodded.

'Let's make our arc,' said Will in his normal voice.

'Agreed,' said Dane.

Swords ready, they worked their way towards the base of the mountain.

Nearing their target point, they looked at each other one more time.

Nodding, they spurred their mounts hard, swinging away from the outcrop hiding their attackers.

Instead of being pounced on by the four Black Knights behind it, Dane and Will became the attackers; pinning them against the base of the mountain, giving them nowhere to go.

Slashing hard, they struck their first opponents, who, taken aback by the sudden turn of events, feebly raised their swords. With another swipe from Dane, his opponent collapsed, the body disappearing a moment later. In the next instant, Will's opponent met the same fate.

The two remaining Black Knights surged forward, taking advantage of Dane and Will's inability to fight more than one opponent at a time, breaking free of the mountain wall and slashing at them as they fought their way free.

Knowing what was coming, Dane had his sword in a defensive position immediately; and by turning Thunder side-on at the same time, he put his mount between himself and his attacker, making it harder to be struck.

Recovering, he turned Thunder head-on, allowing himself to attack directly. Boring forward, he swung at his opponent, moving from defense to attack.

Swinging high and low, blow after blow in quick succession, his assailant couldn't understand his misfortune; how it had gone wrong so quickly.

Dane continued his onslaught; his sword, arm and body moving in one fluid motion: his whole sense of being coursing with adrenaline, a ruthless fighting force.

Again, and again, the blows struck, several in quick succession.

With a final burst, a couple of blows cut through his assailant's armour and finished him. Without waiting for his vanquished enemy to fall to the ground, he swung Thunder towards Will.

With Dane's arrival creating enough of a distraction, Will finished his foe with a final strike. Four empty suits of armour were all that remained.

'Well found,' said Dane, sheathing his sword.

'Well fought,' said Will, with a smile.

'What do you think this means?' Dane asked. 'They were waiting for us; wanting to pick us off. Why do you think they would do that?'

'I'm not entirely sure,' said Will. 'It might mean we're close. Close to the entrance to the city.'

'Yes,' said Dane. 'Maybe they were guarding it; making sure no one finds it. Vanessa might be nearby!'

With renewed hope, Dane scanned their surroundings.

'Let's make our way around the base,' he said. 'There's nothing here; maybe there's something further around.'

At a slow walk, they continued their search, eyes and ears alert for any sight or sound out of place.

It took half an hour to reach the other side of the mountain.

'Nothing,' said Dane. 'Not a trace. And we already know there's nothing back over the other side.'

'It's unusual,' said Will. 'Why else would those Black Knights be here?'

'I wasn't expecting it to be easy,' said Dane. 'Lord Frederick said the city is something you can only find with the wolves. But there's no trace of anything. The whole area shows no sign of a disturbance.'

'It may still be here,' said Will. 'We just have to look harder.'

Another circuit found nothing new.

'I don't know what we do now,' said Dane. 'There's no trace of horse or wolf tracks anywhere.'

'Maybe, we just wait,' said Will. 'She may not be here yet. They may have been scouts; sent to make sure there were none of us around when she gets here.'

'Yes!' said Dane. 'Yes! That's possible! She's not here – they were scouts! We might have arrived in time to save her!'

'Do we call the others?'

'I'm not sure.'

Before they could ponder it further, a high-pitched whistling sound reached their ears; faint, but enough for them to know another pair were signaling for help.

Will beckoned to his left.

'What?' said Dane.

'We have to go,' said Will.

'But ... we might be at the entrance.'

'We've fought four Black Knights,' said Will. 'With nothing to indicate why, except our own guesses. The other group may have found something more.'

'Very well,' said Dane. 'But we need to be able to find our way back quickly. Let's mark it as we go.'

Will nodded.

They heard the call again.

'South-west,' said Dane.

Heading towards the call, Dane and Will rode hard for a good half-hour. After hearing the call twice in that time, it had now gone silent. Thinking they'd lost the trail; they were about to change course when they saw Hawthorne and Kerringvale emerge from their right.

Reigning in, the two groups came together.

'Who made the call?' said Hawthorne.

'It wasn't us,' said Dane.

'Fernbeck and Witheridge, or Cotterall and Dorsley,' said Hawthorne. 'Did you find anything?'

'Four Black Knights were waiting for us,' said Will.

'The same happened to us,' said Kerringvale.

Dane and Will looked at each other.

'We thought they may have been guarding the entrance to the city,' said Dane. 'But we didn't find anything.'

Hawthorne motioned ahead, where they saw Fernbeck approaching them. Dane could see he'd also been in a fight.

'We were attacked,' he said, panting as he joined them. 'Four of them. Declan didn't make it.'

'It seems all our groups were attacked,' said Hawthorne. 'And we can only assume the same for Cotterall and Dorsley. Did you make the call?'

Fernbeck nodded.

'We found fresh horse tracks,' he said. 'It looked to be a group of twenty or more.'

'Where?' said Hawthorne.

'I'll show you,' said Fernbeck.

'We need to be cautious,' said Hawthorne. 'If we've been attacked in pairs, there may be something waiting for us.'

'Follow me,' said Fernbeck.

Setting off as one, they rode into the midday sun. After a few minutes, the way ahead dipped gently.

Looking around, Dane guessed they were heading for a valley floor of sorts.

'Just ahead,' said Fernbeck.

Before they could take in the clearing in the distance, the enemy emerged from both sides ahead of them – a group of nine Black Knights, rushing straight at them.

In an instant, a knife flew from Dane's gauntlet, lodging in the throat of one of their attackers, killing him instantly. In the next movement, he drew his sword, swinging at his next foe.

Hawthorne reacted in the same manner as Dane; his knife striking truly – reducing the enemy to seven.

All were taking the fight to their opponents; undaunted by the fact they were outnumbered. Full of fury, the Brindabeare Knights gave no quarter, driving into the enemy, forcing them to retreat.

Dane had Thunder boring into the right flank of his assailant's horse, swinging across his body, cramping his foe; forcing him to defend. Dane swung again and again; forehand, backhand, leaning forward in the saddle as he pressed his advantage. His latest blow dislodged the Black Knight's sword; the next finished him.

A moment later he heard a slash next to him.

Stunned, he whirled to see Will had cut down a Black Knight who had been about to strike him from his left, where he was defenseless. With a quick nod, both launched into new opponents.

Dane let out all his pent-up fury.

Vanessa's kidnappers!

They've put her in the City of Lost Souls!

They're not going to get away with it!

Swinging at another opponent, Dane landed a barrage of blows, unseating him with a roar that echoed above the sounds of the battle.

Looking for his next opponent, a loud screeching noise distracted him.

Blaze swooped into his vision from behind him, dropping lower and lower in the sky, heading towards what appeared to be a large lake he hadn't noticed until now.

Understanding, he felt a burst of hope surge through him.

And then, in the next instant, with a loud squawk, Blaze shot forward like an arrow and disappeared.

Chapter 19
THE CITY OF LOST SOULS

Vanessa looked around.

Dazed and confused, nothing made sense.

Where was the water?

She'd been walking with the wolves towards the lake … they were going to drown her … but …

She wasn't in the water. There was no water.

What happened?

One moment she was at the water's edge, and in the next …?

She stood on hard, dry land, exactly where the lake should have been. And yet, the lake and surrounding mountains were gone.Instead of mountains, there were caves everywhere, with openings about ten feet tall, as far as she could see. They were made, not from rock, but some kind of sandy soil? They looked like they were somehow, new – as though they had just been made.

How could it be?

It seemed to be co-joined somehow, part of one large continuous … thing, like a maze of some kind. Looking around, the entire landscape appeared to be changing. As her eyes returned to a spot she'd looked at only moments before, it now seemed, different – the cave openings; the light shining on the outer surfaces. One moment smooth and shiny, yet, now starting to look rough and dirty in places.

Turning around, she expected to see Raegan and the Black Knights laughing at her.

They were nowhere to be seen.

To her shock, the land behind her looked the same as what lay ahead. Nothing but an endless system of caves and rock surfaces.

How could that possibly be?

It was as though she'd walked into a totally different time and place – a completely different *land*, to where she had been moments ago.

Turning slowly on the spot, she seemed to have emerged into the middle of this new land.

The wolves?

Gone.

Disappeared without trace.

The bindings lay on the ground at her feet.

She appeared to be alone.

She saw nothing waiting to attack her. Apart from herself and the wolves, who had to be somewhere, there appeared to be no other signs of life in this place.

She heard no sound, except …

Startled for a moment; now ingrained in her mind, it suddenly felt as though it had always been there. A horrible, constant, high-pitched noise.

A sound unlike any she'd heard before – a relentless, scraping sound, like a piece of steel scratching stone; only at a higher pitch – a piercing, screeching, constant scrape.

Raising her hands to her face, she stuck them in her ears, trying to block it out.

Nothing.

If anything, the harder she squeezed her hands to muffle the noise, the louder, and shriller it became.

'Stop,' she groaned. '*Stop!*'

Swaying and stumbling blindly against the sound; combined with the toll of the day's earlier exertions; her legs finally gave up, forcing her to slump to the ground.

Staring at the sky, she closed her eyes for a few moments, breathing rapidly, trying to gather herself and understand everything happening around her; fighting the piercing noise all the while. It wasn't to be drowning after all.

Her mind had filled itself with the reality of what she thought awaited her. She'd screamed against all her fears of drowning during the walk towards the lake; steeling herself to hold her breath for as long as she could, knowing it would be a matter of time before she collapsed against the wall of water that would surround her, choking and squirming as she fruitlessly struggled to get to the surface ...

Nothing else had been in her mind in those last moments.

But it hadn't happened. Suddenly, those thoughts, that terrible reality, that horrible fate, meant nothing.

It gave her no comfort; it meant something worse lay in store.

This new place had been what Raegan had planned from the moment she'd been captured. What had he called it – *The City of Lost Souls?*

Sitting up, she felt the soreness in her legs. Daring to remove her hands from her face, she rubbed her aching muscles.

Forcing herself to stand, raising her hands to her ears once more, she looked around again. There was no doubt – the landscape *had* changed. Looking to her left, to the same spot she'd first noticed, what had been a cave opening had now sealed itself.

'My eyes are *not* playing tricks on me,' she found herself saying, despite the impossibility of what they were showing her.

'*That noise!*' she said out loud, jamming her hands further into her ears. Lumbering forward, she walked around the clearing in front of her. Caves were everywhere, each about twenty feet from the next. Some were a few yards away; others twenty, forty, fifty and more; stretching far into the distance.

The entrances led into darkness. Even in the broadest daylight, she saw nothing to give a clue as to what might lay within.

Although the caves were all separate from each other, she couldn't help but think that, somehow, they were all connected.

The wolves were nowhere to be seen. Were they lying in wait in the caves? Were there dozens, maybe hundreds of them?

Was this Raegan's cruel plan – stay outside and cope with the noise, until it became so unbearable it forced her to choose one of these caves and whatever lay inside it?

If it wasn't wolves, what else could there be?

The wolves that brought her here were larger, more fearsome than any she'd seen before. Were they just a sampling of what might be waiting?

'*I won't do it!*' she screamed.

But the noise ... the incessant ... unrelenting noise.

If only it would stop!

Walk! she told herself.

If I walk, I might find a place where it's not so loud; where I can tolerate it, while I think about what to do.

Walking to her right, she headed towards a cave about fifty yards away; stopping and removing her hands from her ears every ten steps or so.

Reaching the first cave, nothing had changed – the same incessant scraping noise persisted.

Looking around, she saw the same seemingly co-joined cave system in all directions. Turning in a circle, she continued to see the same changing effect on the caves and the outer walls.

There had been no sight or sound of predators along the way.

Moving further to her right, she targeted another cave; this one about twenty yards away.

No change – the sound, the frequency, the same as before.

She tried one more to her right; this one about thirty yards away. Again, it made no difference to the volume or tone of the sound.Moving to her left this time, she picked out a cave entrance about thirty yards ahead.

The sound persisted.

She kept going. Left and right; forward and back; unaware how long she'd been walking before she stopped, giving up hope of finding relief from the noise.

It kept boring into her mind, penetrating every thought, every movement; as though it lived right there in the back of her brain; as though it was part of her – a part of her that tore at the very fabric of her being, in a place inside her mind, where, no matter what she tried to do, she couldn't get rid of it.

'Stop!' she cried out. '*Stop! It has to stop! I can't stand it!*'

The reality of her predicament washed over her – the longer she stayed outside, the longer she had to put up with the noise.

Did she risk entering a cave, despite what lay within?

Thinking it through again, she weighed up the alternatives.

It was a horrible, evil plan – to have to choose between the lesser of two fates.

Squeezing her hands harder and harder into her ears, she cried out in pain at the pressure, yet she noticed no change in the incessant scraping sound.

Looking at the endless maze of caves and walls surrounding her, she made up her mind.

I'll just try one.

Just a few steps.

Perhaps there's nothing there?

Walking slowly now, she approached the cave immediately in front of her.

The darkness within remained. She could neither see, nor hear, anything of what might be waiting inside.

Hesitating, she turned away, heading to another cave on her left, about twenty yards ahead.

Nothing at this entrance gave her a hint of what lay within.

Again, she turned away, running a few steps, before slowing to a walk, letting her anxiety settle a moment; once more weighing up whether it was better to remain outside and cope with the noise.

After a few minutes, the incessant scraping overtook her fear of the caves again, and she looked desperately for a friendly opening, one that gave the slightest hint there wasn't something fearsome waiting to trap her once she set foot inside; one that would help convince her it was the right decision to enter.

She moved to her right, approaching a cave about ten yards away.

It looked no different to the others – the opening smooth, almost perfectly rounded, about ten feet tall. Nothing near the entrance gave an indication that anything had recently, if ever, been there.

In a final effort to convince herself, she lowered her hands, removing whatever small buffering they offered against the noise.

With the full force of the scraping sound piercing through her mind, she walked into the cave, plunging into darkness.

'Sire, I'm afraid I have found no further trace of the Gargaun wolves,' said Lord Frederick.

The King nodded.

'She's in the city?' he asked quietly.

'I cannot say for sure,' Lord Frederick replied. 'I have been unable to find any trace of the city either. Knowing Raegan as I do; it is most likely she would be in the city by now.'

The King slowly shook his head.

'My daughter,' he said quietly. 'My *daughter*.'

Looking pleadingly, desperately, at Lord Frederick and Salsbury, he spoke slowly, struggling to get his next words out.

'She ... was ... innocent, in all of this. I may be the ruler of this land, she may be the Princess; but when it's all said and done; when you take all the titles away; I am, I will *always* be, her father – her *father!* Her only offence was to be my daughter. I should have *never* let this happen. I should have protected her. It's all my fault. *I* should have gone to Feryndale. Then she would be here – safe.'

'Sire, it is we who have failed,' said Lord Frederick.

The King stared straight ahead, lost in thought.

'Has the regiment reached the ranges?'

'General Silvers informs me they will be there by morning,' said Lord Frederick. 'The group that crossed the Osa River are there; searching as we speak.'

'Very well. Perhaps a shred of hope remains.'

Carruthers appeared at the antechamber's entrance.

'What is it?' asked the King.

Breathless, Carruthers handed over a piece of parchment.

Reading it quickly, the King lowered his head, letting the parchment drop to the floor.

'Sire?' said Lord Frederick, picking up the note.

'It's from Governor Mortensen,' said the King in a quiet, trembling voice; tears running down his cheeks. 'He says my daughter is in the city, and demands I surrender all title and claim to the throne.'

After a few steps, the cave turned sharply to the right. Adjusting her eyes, Vanessa could only see a couple of feet in front of her. The walls, roof and floor were smooth, almost shiny, all the way around. The entire inner surface appeared to be made of the same sandy-dirt material.

Thinking better of it for a moment, she turned to make her way back out. Only, she couldn't.

Disorientated, she turned again.

Where was the entrance?

It should have been right here.

Panicking, she looked down into the cave again.

Sure enough, she could see the way ahead, as she remembered. Visible for a couple of feet, then darkness. So that meant the entrance had to be ...

Turning again, she found a solid wall.

What?

What? ... wait ... how ...?

The entrance is gone!

As though it had disappeared completely.

In front of her lay the unknown emptiness of whatever might be hiding there. And yet behind her, from where she had come only moments ago, there was nothing but a wall.

She walked up to it, uncertainly, touching it gently with her hand.

It was solid.

Tearing at it with her hands, she screamed.

'Let me out! *Let me out!'*

After a few moments of scratching and scraping, she turned away, looking fearfully once more at the way ahead.

Nothing had reacted to her screams – no creatures had emerged from within, trapping her against the wall that should have been the entrance, from which she would now not be able to escape.

The scraping noise continued, pounding in her mind, the decrease in volume only enough that she didn't have her hands to her ears; offering the slightest respite from what she'd experienced outside. It would only be a matter of time before the silence of the cave; or, from what she could see now, the *tunnel,* would magnify the noise again, making it as insufferable as it had been before.

She had no choice now – she could only go straight ahead.

Walking slowly and cautiously, she looked for any sign or sound of anything lurking within. For as far as she could see, the dimensions of the entire tunnel were the same. Able to stand comfortably, the roof rose above her, the walls stretching about a foot to either side.

After a minute or two, she stopped.

Something didn't feel right.

In the same way she thought her eyes deceived her when she was outside, the tunnels appeared to be shifting. It felt as though there was something inside with her; something she couldn't see – yet she felt it just the same.

Turning to look behind her; to her shock, she found a wall.

How could that be?

She'd been walking a couple of minutes – where was the tunnel behind her – the tunnel she had just been walking along, that had led her to this exact spot?

If it wasn't there, how could she have possibly gotten here?

Trying to understand, her mind became a jumble of thoughts; and combined with the incessant scraping sound in the back of her mind, she couldn't stand it a moment longer.

Turning on the spot, swaying and dizzy with the madness of it all, she stumbled, crashing into the walls, lurching from one side to the other, one hand groping ahead, as though she were blindfolded and blundering around in the dark, avoiding hidden objects that weren't there.

'*Aaaarrrgh!*' she screamed again and again.

With nowhere else to go, she continued her path through the tunnel. It seemed endless, turning left, then right, then right again. Another series of turns; left, right, left, left, right, left, right, right. Any time her staggering and stumbling turned her back the way she had come, she found herself against a wall.

On and on it went, pushing her further and further through the tunnel. Stumbling and staggering; falling; picking herself up in a mad panic; stumbling forward, falling again. Blocking one ear, then the other; screaming in vain against the incessant scraping inside her mind; crying desperately; willing it all to stop.

There appeared no end in sight, until she found herself stumbling hopelessly through an opening, falling face first onto the ground. Hands over both ears, she lay there, breathing heavily, tears streaming down her cheeks and dripping on the ground, dirt sticking to her face. She writhed around uncontrollably, rolling over and over, screaming in vain for the noise to stop.

'Stop! Stop! Stop!'

How long she'd been in the cave; tunnel – whatever it was, she had no idea. Her mind wandered in and out of itself. The sun was fading. She closed her eyes. In the next moment, she rolled over, and the sun blared down on her. Blinking her eyes again, she saw a pitch-black sky.

Forcing herself to her feet, she turned around; staggering in all directions, looking through glazed, hazy eyes, as she sought to make some – any sense of where she was.

In and out of tunnels, some for a short-time; others seemingly forever, the only constant – the never-ending, relentless sound – pounding and pounding, utterly merciless.

She couldn't remember one moment from the next.

How much time had passed?

An hour?

A day?

Was it the same day, the next day, or *days* later?

Walking in a daze, she'd find herself bumping into walls at cave entrances; completely unaware; bouncing along the wall, until falling inside and landing in a heap; before standing and stumbling mindlessly through the darkness in front of her.

Stumbling from yet another cave, she tripped, falling heavily and banging the back of her head on the ground.

'*Aaarrrgh!*' she screamed, the force of the impact blacking out her vision for a moment.

'*No more!*' she screamed again and again. '*No more!*'

With the pounding in her ears drowning out the sound of her screams, she screamed louder still. It made no difference; the louder she screamed, the worse the noise in her ears became. Breathing heavily, hands to her face, her face in the ground, kicking her legs uncontrollably, she screamed one last time; before she found she could scream no more.

Her legs stopped moving; and for the moment, she lay still.

Somewhere, among the despair, the utter hopelessness of it all; despite the pounding in her ears – from a long way away; for the first time, she heard a new sound forcing its way into her mind.

A screeching noise, high above.

Coming closer; it seemed to be circling.

Turning her face to the sky, she searched for the source.

She could hear it, but ...

There!

Large, black, gliding towards her.

Straight towards her!

Squawking, the eagle circled lower and lower, closer and closer.

Turning away, Vanessa screamed, curling into a ball, covering her face.

This was it – her end had come at last – eagle fodder.

The great bird landed softly a few feet away.

With a gentle screech it started walking towards her.

Bracing herself, she waited, whimpering softly.

The eagle came closer, now emitting a gentle, almost reverent sound as it neared. Daring to turn towards it, she saw the eagle next to her. It wasn't attacking; it walked slowly and carefully; as though it were trying to see something.

Something roused deep within her consciousness.

She looked again.

She knew … she knew who it was.

Tumbling through the far reaches of her memory, she struggled to find the word, her voice barely more than a whisper.

'B-Blaze?'

The eagle came closer. In the next moment, she felt it nipping at her arm, tugging at something. Turning to see, she saw a loose piece of clothing in its beak. It had ripped to the point where it hung by a couple of threads – a few inches long, with a small piece of ribbon attached to it.

A couple more tugs tore it completely.

Vanessa lay still, watching as Blaze started walking away.

'No,' she said softly. 'Please. Don't go.'

Opening her wings, a moment later, Blaze took to the sky.

Vanessa raised a feeble hand in the direction of Blaze's flight.

'No,' she said, her voice almost a whisper.

As she lay there, watching Blaze rise higher and higher until she disappeared from view, her mind returned to the horrors she'd been dealing with since entering the city; the scraping noise in her head pounding as loudly and incessantly as ever.

Too numb to notice, she didn't see or hear the lone figure approaching.

Chapter 20

THROUGH THE PORTAL

With the battle raging around him, Dane had no time to understand what he'd just seen.

Another Black Knight attacked from his right.

As Dane turned to face him, he saw a look of recognition cross his adversary's face.

'Well, well,' said the leader, swiping Dane's blow away with ease. 'If it isn't Dane Thorburn.'

Swinging again, Dane had no idea why his assailant recognised him; but, as accustomed as he'd become to fighting against the stronger Black Knights, none were more difficult than the one in front of him.

'We meet again,' said the leader.

With no clue what his opponent was talking about, Dane slashed harder, anger rising at the fact his moves were having no effect; that his opponent was talking to him as though they were having nothing more than a casual fireside conversation.

Swinging across Dane's body, the leader's sword found a small gap between armour and skin; enough that Dane felt a surge of pain.

'So valiant, yet so overmatched,' said the leader.

Dane swung down and across, swiping across the leader's face.

The leader leaned back in his saddle.

Dane's blow met nothing but air.

'Just like before,' said the leader, swinging back towards Dane.

Dane blocked the blow at the last moment; before it would have torn right through him.

'You were fortunate the last time,' said the leader. 'I should have killed you before you disappeared over that cliff.'

In that instant Dane realised – the attack at the campsite – the one who charged him, who'd toyed with him before he fell. And here he was again, one of those who had brought Vanessa here, to the City of Lost Souls.

'I'll take great pleasure in this,' said the leader, raising his sword and swinging at Dane. 'She's in the city – probably dead; and you'll be next.'

Dane heard the words echo in his mind ... in the city ... probably dead.

'*No!*' he screamed; a new strength coursing through his veins, his mind locked in steely determination.

His next blows had a rapidity, a venom, a raw energy the leader had not expected.

Raining blows left and right, up and down in quick succession, Dane struck again and again. The leader staggered in the saddle, suddenly struggling to fend him off.

Dane swung harder and harder.

Another barrage of blows landed, one cutting into the leader's arm, another nearly dislodging the sword from his hand.

Dane saw fear on his opponent's face for the first time.

With an increasing roar, he swung harder and harder, faster and faster.

'*Aaarrgh!*' he screamed.

The next blow cut through skin near the shoulder.

With an anguished scream, the leader feebly raised his sword to block the next blow.

Swinging left, then right, Dane closed in, and with a final blow, the leader fell from his saddle. A moment later, nothing remained except an empty suit of armour.

Whirling Thunder around, Dane saw no enemy remaining. Will and Hawthorne were circling nearby; making sure there were no more.

'Are you hurt?' asked Will.

Apart from a small cut on his inside arm, Dane found himself in good order.

'Just a scratch,' he replied.

'Kerringvale and Fernbeck were killed,' said Hawthorne.

Dane nodded, taking in the entire scene before him.

Dismounting, he retrieved a couple of knives, restoring them to his gauntlets.

'We need to understand why they were here,' said Hawthorne.

'I know exactly why they were here,' said Dane, swinging himself back into his saddle. 'The Princess is somewhere down there.'

Following his gaze, Will and Hawthorne looked back at him, puzzled.

'The lake?' asked Will.

'Yes,' said Dane.

'That's not possible,' said Hawthorne.

'Yes, it is,' said Dane. 'Blaze circled here. While we were fighting. Then she disappeared, right down there.'

'What do you mean?' asked Will.

'She flew straight at the lake, the way she does when she knows where Vanessa is; straight, hard, and direct; the way Angus trained her. And she disappeared.'

Will and Hawthorne looked at each other.

'I don't see how that's possible,' said Hawthorne.

'It explains why they were here,' said Dane. 'And why we were attacked. They're guarding the entrance to the City of Lost Souls.'

'But it's a lake,' said Will.

'I know what I saw,' said Dane. 'Blaze disappeared right over it.'

'We need to search the area and see if we find anything,' said Hawthorne. 'There may be other clues about what may be here; and there may be more Black Knights around. Given there are only three of us, I can only hope not.'

Dane and Will nodded.

'We should stay in sight of each other,' said Hawthorne.

In the next moment, seemingly out of nowhere, Blaze emerged into their line of sight, above the lake; exactly where Dane had seen her disappear.

Will and Hawthorne blinked in disbelief, struggling to understand.

With a squawk, Blaze shot towards them.

Dismounting, Dane ran towards her, holding out his arm.

Zeroing in on her landing point, Blaze squawked again, fanning her wings, reaching her talons forward, gracefully coming to rest.

Walking back towards the others, Dane noticed something in her beak. Reaching with his other hand, he took it from her, studying it carefully as Blaze fluttered to a nearby tree.

'Look!' he said, waving it before the others.

Dismounting, Will and Hawthorne hurried over.

'From Vanessa's dress!' said Dane, full of excitement and hope.

Will and Hawthorne took the material in turn.

'You're right,' said Will. 'How?'

'She's found her!' said Dane. 'She's found her!'

'Where?' asked Will.

'You saw it!' said Dane. 'You saw her! Right over the lake! The entrance to the City of Lost Souls is somewhere down there!'

'Over the lake, or *in* the lake?' said Hawthorne. 'How do we find it?'

'I don't know,' said Dane, letting Blaze flutter to a nearby tree. 'But it's somewhere down there.'

Climbing into his saddle; Dane, Will and Hawthorne walked towards the lake.

'I suggest one of us,' said Hawthorne. 'We have no idea what may be in there.'

'I'll go,' said Will.

'Very well,' said Hawthorne. 'Don't go above your horse's flanks. If the footing is unsure, exit immediately.'

Dane watched Will make his way into the lake.

Sword drawn, Will took one step, then another, uncertain what to expect. Dane strained his eyes, looking for any sign of the entrance.

Nothing happened.

After about twenty yards, he saw Will level out.

Nothing. As he continued walking the lake, the only disturbance rippling the surface came from Will. No opening emerged; no entrance revealed itself.

Another couple of minutes, and realising he'd probably gone further than where he'd seen Blaze appear; Will turned in an arc, making his way back to shore.

'Nothing,' he said. 'It's sandy and flat; completely clear. Not a living thing in it. Nothing to show where the entrance might be.'

'It has to be there!' said Dane. 'If Blaze disappeared and came back, it has to be there!'

Will shrugged.

'Maybe we should all look,' he said. 'We'll cover more ground. I saw nothing to suggest we'll be attacked. I don't see any risk.'

'Commander?' Dane asked.

Hawthorne nodded.

Taking different points of entry, with swords drawn, the three knights entered the lake.

Dane found it just as Will described.

Making his way forward, he looked desperately for anything that might help them; his senses locking on every sight, every sound, every breath of wind.

As time went on, his eyes became more frantic.

It must be here – it just *has* to be here.

Nothing.

He saw Will and Hawthorne making their way towards the shore. Slamming his fist in the water in frustration, he followed them.

With every step towards the shore, his anger and frustration rose.

So close, and yet so far.

The entrance is here – we just can't find it!

'It has to be here!' he said, throwing his sword in the sand in frustration.

Dismounting, he scooped it up, slamming it into its sheath.

'It has to be here!'

'I know,' said Will. 'But we covered the whole area and didn't find it.'

'It has to be here!' Dane yelled again. 'It has to be here!'

'I saw tracks near the shore,' said Hawthorne. 'They were probably the tracks Fernbeck and Witheridge found. There are some torches there too.'

'That proves it,' said Dane, pacing desperately. 'The entrance has to be here!'

'I'm not suggesting you're wrong,' said Hawthorne, 'but I don't know how we find it.'

'Well, I'm not about to give up,' said Dane. 'I don't care if I have to search day and night!'

'Maybe there's more than one entrance,' said Will. 'By air, it may be over the lake. Entering on foot, it may be somewhere else.'

'Well thought,' said Hawthorne. 'You and Thorburn search the foreshore. I'll look around here. Split up, and make sure you stay in sight of each other. We don't know what we may find, or where we might find it.'

Dane moved to his left; Will to the right.

Dane saw the tracks and torches where Vanessa and the Black Knights had approached the lake. Nothing around them in any direction gave a hint to what he was looking for.

Along the foreshore, he found no joy. Everywhere he looked, the sand lay flat and smooth. The only prints were Thunder's.

He saw Will on the other side of the lake.

Had he seen anything?

The entrance must be here – somewhere.

After a few minutes, he heard Hawthorne's whistle, calling them back.

Looking into the distance as far as he could see, it all looked the same. Not a single sign to show any disturbance or hint of what may be the entrance they were looking for.

Dane took Thunder further away from the shore, searching along a different line of sight. The land sloped slightly upward in the natural shape of the lakebed. Apart from that, there was nothing different along this path to the previous one.

Meeting up with the others, he shook his head.

'Nothing,' he said with disgust.

'Me too,' said Will.

'I didn't find anything,' said Hawthorne.

'We have to keep looking,' said Dane.

'But we don't know what we're looking for,' said Will. 'We've looked in the lake; we've looked along the shore. Nothing.'

'We're missing something,' said Dane. 'I don't know what it is, but it has to be here. Blaze doesn't just disappear and reappear with a piece of clothing. The entrance has to be here.'

'Perhaps it's not the entrance at all,' said Hawthorne. 'We don't know where the clothing was found. It may have been on the ground, drifting on its own. We may be in the wrong place entirely. The entrance to the city may be miles from here.'

'Commander,' Dane replied, gathering all his self-control. 'You don't know Blaze as well as I do. The way she flies, the way she acts. She *found* the Princess. I have no doubt.'

'Without further proof, I don't think we can linger.'

'Send her to Lord Frederick,' said Will. 'If we can get Lord Frederick here, he may be able to make sense of it.'

'It will take too long,' said Dane. 'Think of the distance she has to travel.'

'Then I don't know what we do,' said Will.

Dane thought a moment, searching for an answer.

Blaze disappeared over the lake …

Blaze reappeared over the lake …

Blaze found the entrance to the city …

Blaze knew …

Blaze!

'I have an idea,' he said.

Will and Hawthorne watched Dane dismount and walk to where Blaze was perched. Holding out his arm, Blaze stepped onto it.

'I'll go to the lake with Blaze,' he said. 'She may be able to show me the exact point she disappeared.'

Will and Hawthorne looked doubtful.

'It won't take long,' said Dane. 'A few minutes at the most.'

Hawthorne nodded.

Walking Blaze towards the lake, Dane raised her to eye-level.

'*Vanessa*,' he said, showing her the piece of clothing.

Blaze gave a gentle squawk.

Dane lowered his arm, thrusting it skyward in the next instant.

Blaze took flight, shooting straight towards the lake. With a loud squawk, she disappeared.

Waiting near the shore, Dane watched the empty sky, hoping against hope he was right.

Will joined him.

'Did you see that?' said Dane.

'Yes,' said Will, 'but we searched that very place, and found nothing.'

'I know, but if she brings back another piece of clothing …'

'I don't want to say it,' said Will, 'but do you think, maybe, even if she finds something, that doesn't mean ... it doesn't mean she's ...'

'Don't,' said Dane. 'She's alive. Vanessa's alive.'

'I don't want to think it either,' said Will. 'But we don't know. We can't say for sure.'

'I don't want to consider it,' said Dane. 'We're going to find her. Somehow, we'll find her. We're close. I can feel it. I don't know why or how; but I can feel it. She's here. Somewhere – wherever Blaze has gone. We just need to find out how to get there.'

Neither said anything for a few moments, lost in their own thoughts.

'How long was she gone?' asked Will.

'I really don't remember,' said Dane. 'It happened towards the end of the battle. I saw her for an instant; then she disappeared. We all saw her when she came back. I can't say how long it took.'

Hawthorne joined them.

'When she disappeared?' he said. 'How long did it take for her to return?'

'I don't know,' Dane replied.

In the next moment he saw Blaze emerge out of the sky.

'But now we'll see!' he said, running towards the lake.

Just as before, Blaze landed on his arm, another piece of clothing in her beak. Before he could react, Dane felt Blaze digging into him, squawking incessantly.

In the next moment, he felt her pulling on him; as though she was leading him towards the lake. Dane had never seen Blaze so agitated. On instinct, he started walking; but it had little effect. Blaze continued digging into his arm, squawking all the while.

Letting her lead, Dane walked forward.

A few steps more, and he felt the air change. A coldness passed over him, and for an instant the sun blinded him.

Watching on, Will and Hawthorne gasped as they saw Dane disappear before their eyes.

Dazed for a moment, Dane's eyes came back into focus.

Caves and rock faces were everywhere, as far as he could see.

The lake had disappeared. It should have been right in front of him.

Blaze continued squawking, and in the next moment, launched herself into the sky.

Dane started piecing together what had happened.

Blaze has led me through the entrance - I'm in the City of Lost Souls!

The cold air; the blinding sun, had been the entry – the cross-over point.

The City of Lost Souls lay in the same landspace as the lake and the surrounding area; only it wasn't there. Well; it was there – it just existed in a different place, a different time, a different – *something* - that allowed each to co-exist in harmony with and in ignorance of the other.

Behind him, he saw nothing of Will, Hawthorne, or the land of the Gargaun Ranges from which he'd come. All he could see were the caves and rock faces that existed in this new land.

I'm here.

I'm finally here.

Circling above, he heard Blaze, squawking and squawking.

'*Vanessa!*' he shouted to her.

Blaze shot forward.

Sword drawn; Dane ran after her; one eye on Blaze; the other on whatever might confront him.

Blaze flew in large circles, allowing Dane to keep pace with her.

Scanning the area around him as he ran, he had the strange feeling he'd interrupted something – as though his presence had stopped everything mid-stream.

It wasn't the sound of Blaze's squawking, the only thing he could hear, that unsettled him – it was the caves and rock mounds all around him.

Some entrances were as he'd expect, completely open and round; but others looked as though they were in various stages of being – closed? Some were being filled in from the top; others from the ground, some from the left, others from the right; and others still, in combinations of all.

Looking again, some of the rock-surfaces appeared to have what looked like small openings emerging.

The whole area, indeed the entire city as far as he could see, seemed to be in some stage of continual construction or evolution; and while he could see movement in the distance, everything directly in front and around him appeared as though it had suddenly stopped moving.

What, why, or how; Dane had no idea.

Running on, expecting to be attacked at any moment, he couldn't understand how he'd made it this far without hearing the terrible sound Lord Frederick had spoken of – he heard nothing other than Blaze squawking above him.

Following her to his right, he saw movement cease in the caves ahead as he approached. Looking over his shoulder, caves and rock faces that moments ago lay still were suddenly moving again.

It had to be some kind of trap.

Were exiled wizards lurking around?

Were Gargaun wolves waiting around the next corner?

What have I come into?

I have to find Vanessa and get her out of here. Now!

Glancing to the sky, he saw Blaze getting further ahead of him. The lay of the land meant he couldn't follow a direct path. He had to move from left to right, ducking around the caves and rock mounds in front of him. Looking back every few strides slowed him down, but did he risk ignoring something that might be waiting to pounce?

The way ahead cut sharply to the left, before straightening out a little. After what seemed several minutes, Blaze appeared to change course, heading in an arc leading in another direction.

What's happening? We're backtracking!

Has she lost the trail?

Is Vanessa in a different place from where she'd found her?

Has she been captured?

Is she really here?

What had initially been elation at the prospect of a quick rescue had been overtaken by the frustration he now felt. Wiping sweat from his face in the mid-afternoon sun; he realised if he didn't find her by sunset, he'd have to shelter somewhere, and face whatever might be waiting in the night.

Rounding a corner, he thought he saw movement out of the corner of his eye. Looking up, Blaze hadn't slowed or changed course.

Do I follow her?

Trusting his instincts, he pushed the other thought from his mind as Blaze continued squawking overhead. The ground was rough, hard and bare, and apart from slight undulations along the way, nothing had changed since he arrived.

Apart from an occasional tuft of grass, it was a wasteland of sandy-soil caves and rock mounds.

The sun was now to his right; so they were definitely moving in the opposite direction. Had he covered this ground before? With the way the caves were changing, it was impossible to know.

Grunting in frustration, he looked desperately into the sky.

'Come on, Blaze!' he said out loud. 'Where is she?'

Something flashed at the edge of his vision as he passed a cluster of caves. He'd seen it for an instant, but he was sure of it this time.

What do I do?

Glancing over his shoulder, his mind lingered for a few seconds and he lost his footing; stumbling on some loose stones in front of him. Cursing, he regathered himself, forcing his eyes forward.

'Where is she, Blaze?!' he yelled overhead.

Whether she heard him or not, Blaze continued circling overhead, squawking the entire time. Banking a little to the left, she guided him to a cluster of caves sheltered in the afternoon shade.

The way ahead looked the same as before; all movement in the caves ahead stopped as he approached, resuming again shortly after he passed.

Following the path to his left, a flash of light blinded his vision for a moment; so sudden and bright he staggered a couple of steps and stopped running, so he wouldn't stumble and fall. Shaking his head and squinting the light away, he looked skyward once more.

In the next moment, he felt something long and thin wrapping itself around his ankles. With a sudden, sharp tug, Dane's feet were swept from under him, he crashed to the ground, and everything went dark.

Chapter 21
MEDWIN'S COTERIE

D ane woke to a throbbing pain in the back of his head.

Next, a sound – high-pitched, piercing, constant. He'd never heard anything like it before. Cringing, trying to move his hands to his face, he knew what it was – the deadly sound of the City of Lost Souls.

With his next thought, it felt as if it had been there for-ever, embedded in the back of his mind; thumping and pulsing like a heartbeat – each beat another scrape, another piercing scrape.

He found himself sitting; his legs in front of him, his hands bound around a wooden stake behind his back. He could feel something on top of them; uneven, and though he could move it a little, it continued to weigh down on him.

Unable to use his hands, moving his head from side to side was all he could do to try and fight against the noise – which meant he could do nothing.

Squinting his eyes shut, leaning back, bumping his head on the stake, he tried in vain to force the sound from his mind.

Voices drifted into his mind, from the right of where he was sitting.

'I'm telling you, Medwin,' said the first, a woman's voice. 'It's a risk having them here.'

'Be quiet,' said the second – a man. 'Unless you want to end up like her over there.'

The first voice muttered something Dane wasn't able to hear.

Opening his eyes, he saw the first slivers of dawn light on the horizon. The city and caves ahead were nothing but dull, black blobs.

'We will see what power they have,' said Medwin. 'Fresh as they are, they're bound to have something left, and we'll use it while we can.'

'And if they use it against us?' said the woman.

'We have the rituals,' said Medwin. 'Be you worried one be of fire, Anala?'

Dane heard the woman spit in reply.

'I've bested others before,' she replied. 'I be ready if they are.'

Turning his head slightly, he found the source of the voices a few feet away, standing in tattered, thread-bare clothes. Their bodies were caked in dirt and grime, their hair tangled and knotted. Taller and more intimidating than his counterpart, Medwin was clearly the one in charge.

Dane knew who they were: *prisoners* – exiled wizards of the City of Lost Souls.

By the look of them, they were ancient – as old as the beginning of time.

How long have they been here?

How have they survived the scraping sound?

Do they still have their power – something that counteracts it?

Will they use their power on me?

Do they know Raegan's spell of death?

He shuddered at the last thought, breaking out in a sweat.

Looking around, he could see they were in a clearing of sorts, under a shelter of vines and foliage hanging about seven feet off the ground, connected to the surrounding rock mounds, the entire area about a thirty-foot square.

The remains of a fire lay smouldering to his left; a couple of feet beyond lay four dusty bed mats of the same roof material, and finally, a scattering of what looked to be half-made pots made of rock and other pieces of stone and rubble.

He felt movement behind him.

Sudden, as though jolted awake, it straightened, leaning against the stake that separated them.

He felt movement on top of his hands.

Despite the throbbing pulse in his mind, he knew it instantly – someone was tied behind him, their hands on top of his own.

It thrashed around, swinging its head, bumping itself against the stake.

'*Let me go!*' it cried.

Dane sat bolt upright.

Despite the incessant noise in his head, he felt a surge of adrenaline.

Vanessa!

She's here!

She yelled again.

'*Let me go! Let me go!*'

Their captors did nothing, seemingly oblivious to her screams. Their conversation over, the two separated; Anala fussing about near the entrance to the shelter, Medwin walking towards them.

'Well, well,' he said, as Vanessa continued thrashing about and yelling. 'They wake at last.'

Leaning out of Dane's line of sight, Medwin said, 'Well, my lady; what a pleasure it is to meet you.'

Vanessa screamed.

'Let me go! Let me go!'

'Don't touch her!' Dane yelled. *'Don't you dare!'*

'And what of it if he does?' said Anala, walking towards him.

Crouching in front of him, her eyes wide with relish, Dane stared into her haggard, half-toothless face; her putrid, rasping breath smothering him.

'What of it?' she asked again.

'Don't touch her!' he said, trying not look to at her and straining against the throbbing sound in his head at the same time.

Standing behind Anala now, Medwin stared down at him.

'I'll be giving the instructions around here,' he said.

Turning away, he walked to the front of the shelter, gazing into the distance.

Anala walked behind Dane.

Vanessa screamed again.

'It makes no difference to me,' he heard her say. 'You can scream and yell all day, for the little good it will do. But, all the same, such a pretty face ...'

Dane heard the slap, feeling its force as Vanessa's head swung violently to its left.

'No!' he yelled.

Against the piercing sound in his mind, his body surged with anger.

Vanessa was here – *right here* – and he could do nothing to help her.

Had she heard his voice?

Did she recognise it?

Struggling against his bindings, he writhed and pulled for all he was worth.

'And you'll be sitting still, too,' Anala snarled, leaning towards him, 'unless you be wanting to suffer the same.'

Walking to the edge of the shelter, fidgeting among some things until she found what she'd been looking for, she returned, brandishing his sword.

'Don't think I won't be running you through with it,' she said, waving it at him, before turning and striding away.

'Sandon and Daven return!' said Medwin.

Looking towards the entrance of the shelter, Dane saw two men approaching. One wore a vine, coiled in loops around his chest.

The one who captured me.

'Did you find it?' asked Medwin.

'No,' said the first. 'I say it's long gone.'

'Well, perhaps not as long as you think,' said Medwin, looking towards his prisoners. 'We were just making our acquaintances with our guests.'

Looking to Anala, he said, 'bring her.'

Throwing Dane's sword on the ground, Anala shuffled to where Vanessa sat behind him.

'You'll be standing now,' Dane heard her say. 'And don't you be trying anything. Sobbing you may be, you'll not be the first who's tried to fool us that way.'

He felt Vanessa shift behind him, her body rising and her hands lifting.

'*Let me go!*' she said, struggling against the strong hand gripping her arm as she walked past Dane.

Seeing her for the first time, he saw her clothes were tattered and torn, her face and hair full of dirt and grime. Worst of all, he saw only misery and defeat in her eyes, not a sliver of her usual spark; as though she'd lost all hope. Her head twitched from side to side, no doubt struggling against the sound pulsing in his own mind.

He looked at her desperately, hoping for a hint of recognition. He couldn't tell if she noticed he was even there, much less whether she recognised him.

With her hands bound, she stood helplessly before Medwin and Sandon.

'What do you know of it?' asked Medwin.

Vanessa said nothing, jerking from side to side, pain and despair on her face.

'What do you know of it? Medwin asked more forcefully.

'*Let me go!*' she said. '*Let me go!*'

'Not until we know what you are,' said Medwin. 'Then we'll consider it.'

Trying hard to listen, Dane wondered what Medwin was talking about.

'If we don't like what we hear,' said Medwin, gesturing to his left as he spoke his next words, 'you'll end up like Valonia over there.'

Glancing to his right, Dane rocked back, sitting straighter against the stake.

A pile of bones, clearly the remains of a skeleton, lay in a corner of the shelter.

'She's only good for the marrow now,' said Medwin. 'Be time we had something fresh.'

Dane shuddered.

'I'll ask you one more time,' said Medwin. 'What do you know of it?'

Dane locked his eyes on Vanessa, begging her to say something, anything to quell the growing anger in Medwin's voice.

'Begging your pardon, Medwin,' said Anala. 'She's not been cleansed of the scream.'

Medwin grunted his agreement.

Looking towards Dane for a moment, he said, 'I don't believe it be hers in any case.'

Turning to Sandon, he asked, 'You say he be the one following it?'

Sandon nodded.

'Bring him,' said Medwin.

Sandon approached Dane, grabbing him by the top of the shoulder and hauling him to his feet. Glancing at the stake he'd been tied to, Dane let Sandon lead him to Vanessa and the others.

Standing opposite, Dane looked directly into Vanessa's eyes for the first time; hoping, *pleading* for a sign of recognition. She didn't react, continuing to squirm and swivel her head against the inner noise they were both fighting.

'You,' said Medwin. 'What be your strength? Controlling the eagle as you do, you must be Air-strong?'

Dane had no clue what Medwin was talking about.

What 'strength'?

Air-strong?

'You're not as close to the scream as she,' said Medwin, motioning to Vanessa, 'so I know you hear me. Don't try my patience. Before you be brought here, what be your strength?'

Before I be ...

Despite his struggle to think clearly, he understood.

They think we're wizards!

'I won't ask again,' said Medwin. 'What be your strength?'

'Air,' said Dane, agreeing with him.

Medwin nodded thoughtfully.

'Hers?' he said, nodding to Vanessa.

'Earth,' Dane replied.

Watching the four in turn, he saw them considering his responses.

'Well, well,' said Medwin, 'Air, indeed.'

All four wizards were nodding.

'We complete the coterie at last,' said Medwin.

Dane saw his face change from anger to lustful greed.

'Yes,' he said with hunger in his voice, walking around, talking to himself as much as anyone. 'Yes, indeed. Masterlord, Earthlord, Waterlord, Firelord and finally Airlord – we complete the coterie and restore our power. *At last!*'

Anala, Sandon and Daven stared after him.

'How do I know you be telling the truth?' said Medwin, standing in front of Dane, looking at him from head to toe. 'Dressed as you are?'

Medwin glanced towards the entrance of the shelter for a moment.

'And how you be getting in here with weapons?'

Following Medwin's gaze, Dane saw both his swords among a pile of other things near the entrance to the shelter. He hadn't realised his small sword had also been taken.

He knew he didn't have long to answer.

'Well?' said Medwin, growing impatient.

'I disguised myself,' said Dane, concentrating as hard as he could, trying to sound calm.

'I armed myself and changed my appearance. Everyone thought I was in common clothes. I changed back when we came through the portal.'

Medwin took a step back, considering.

'Something one of our kind would do,' he said with a smile. 'The eagle? We not seen one in all our time. It be yours?'

'Yes,' said Dane.

Medwin nodded thoughtfully, looking at Dane through new, respectful eyes.

'You be a crafty wizard to do all this,' he said.

'She's just as clever as me,' said Dane, nodding to Vanessa. 'They sent her first. We became separated and lost sight of each other.'

'And lost her by a long way,' said Medwin, 'based on where you be found. Where be the eagle now?'

'I don't know,' said Dane.

'You can call it?'

Dane nodded.

'Very well,' said Medwin. 'We be seeing if you speak true in time. And we be needing to keep you safe until you're cleansed of the screaming.'

Dane had no idea what Medwin meant, the only comfort being, at least for the moment, his explanations had bought him some time. Turning to Vanessa, Medwin said, 'I don't see much use for you, not unless you can best Sandon.'

'*She's with me!*' said Dane. '*She's with me!*'

Ignoring him, Medwin turned to Sandon.

'What say you?'

Dane felt Sandon stand taller next to him.

'If it be your wish,' said Sandon, 'so it shall be.'

'Very well!' said Medwin in a loud, clear voice. *'So it shall be!'*

To Dane, he said, *'So it shall be!'*

He said it to Anala, Daven and Vanessa in turn.

Daven said nothing.

Anala nodded.

'So it shall be,' she said quietly.

Vanessa gave no sign she'd heard anything Medwin had said, seemingly oblivious to it all.

'At sunrise,' Medwin said to Sandon, Daven, Anala, Vanessa and Dane in turn.

The three wizards nodded in turn.

Anala gently tapped Medwin on the arm.

'The screaming, Medwin,' she said when he turned to face her. 'She has to be cleansed of the screaming.'

'Don't be bothering me about that now, Anala,' said Medwin. 'On this day, we complete the coterie at last. *At last!'*

'But ...'

'She'll know what she has to do soon enough,' said Medwin, standing directly in front of Vanessa.

Anala nodded meekly, dropping her shoulders and lowering her head.

Vanessa continued to stand there, wincing in pain, jerking her head from side to side, seemingly oblivious to everyone and everything around her.

'She's with me!' said Dane, desperately trying to sort out what was going on, finding it harder and harder to concentrate.

With his back to him, Medwin said nothing.

'If she can best Sandon,' said Anala, 'she be with you still.'

'What do you mean?' asked Dane.

'You'll see soon enough.'

Sandon turned towards the shelter, leading Dane back to the stake, guiding his hands around it and pushing him to the ground; tethered as before.

'While you have the screaming,' said Sandon, 'we need to keep you safe.'

Looking desperately into Vanessa's eyes as Anala led her past, he saw nothing but a blank stare.

'It won't be fair,' Anala muttered as she lowered Vanessa behind Dane. 'Not with the screaming still inside her. It won't be fair.'

Dane felt Vanessa's hands come to rest on top of his, her back sliding against the stake as she plopped to the ground.

'*Vanessa!*' he whispered, once Anala walked away. '*Vanessa! I'll find a way to get us out of here!*'

No response.

Watching his captors once more, he saw Medwin stalking around, muttering to himself. He still had the same lustful look on his face.

He thinks I'm an Airlord.

Why does that make him so happy? So excited?

'Anala,' said Medwin. 'Anala!'

She didn't respond, continuing to walk aimlessly, muttering to herself.

Dane wondered why she was ignoring him. Whenever Medwin spoke, she'd immediately obeyed, not wanting to incur his wrath.

Grabbing her roughly by the shoulder, her head snapping around, Medwin said, 'clear the things away!'

Anala nodded submissively.

'Begging your pardon,' she said. 'Begging your pardon.'

She shuffled away, pottering around and picking up pots and other rubble.

Confused, Dane looked to Daven, wandering outside the shelter, before turning his attention to Sandon, who he saw doing a series of movements, twisting his arms and legs.

Like a flash, it dawned on him.

A fight!

He means to set Sandon against her!

It would be hopeless; utterly hopeless – Vanessa wouldn't last longer than the time it took for Sandon to strike her.

Despite his aged and tattered appearance, Sandon looked to have some strength and finesse about him. He certainly knew how to use the vine that lay on the ground beside him.

Vanessa appeared to be little more than a babbling mess, tortured both by the constant scraping they were despairing against and whatever else Raegan had done to her.

It would be over in moments.

'No!' Dane yelled. '*You can't do this! You can't do this!*'

He didn't care what they did to him; if they slapped or stabbed him – he wasn't going to let Vanessa die this way.

He yelled again, waiting for one of them to react.

They had their backs turned, going about their business. It seemed as though they hadn't heard him.

They hadn't heard him ...

Trying desperately to separate his thoughts from the scraping, he dug to the depths of his mind ...

The screaming ... until we cleanse you from the screaming ...

Scanning the shelter, he looked for the closest captor, locking his eyes on Medwin as he walked past. From where he sat, he couldn't tell. He had to get one of them directly in front of him.

Watching each in turn, he waited for one to glance in his direction.

'Anala!' he yelled when she shuffled around nearby.

At first he thought she'd ignored him, then, a moment later, she toddled over, standing in front of him.

'You wish speak with me, young wizard?' she said.

'Anala,' he said again. 'Please. Tell me. *A fight?* Sandon and the wizard lady?'

Anala hesitated, her eyes flicking from side with a mixture of fear and uncertainty.

'*Please,*' said Dane.

Anala crouched beside him, busying herself with her hands.

'Yes, young wizard,' she said. 'When a new comes our way, we sort out the stronger in each element. The survivor stays. The defeated ...'

Her voice trailed away, and she sat completely still, frozen in thought. Glancing at the side of her withered face, Dane saw what he needed to see.

Anala seemed lost, in a trance.

'Our power?' said Dane.

'Yes, young wizard,' she said with a nod. 'You've felt it already, bound and restrained as you are. But a day or two it lasts, then it's gone. We live a wizard's lifetime in here, but no power. Part of our punishment.'

'And the screaming?'

Anala continued staring straight ahead.

'Some never cleanse,' she said quietly, staring into the distance. 'Seen it with my own eyes, many times. It becomes too much.'

With what he was enduring, Dane knew exactly why some chose to end their suffering.

'Those that come here, we cleanse them of all traces of it. On this day, we will do the same for you.'

Following her nod towards a part of the shelter he hadn't seen, Dane noticed a long thin vine, with what looked like a sharpened point attached to the end.

'It's done quick,' said Anala, touching her hand to the side of her face. 'All the better. Sandon has a remedy to stop the bleeding and ease the pain.'

'The coterie,' said Dane. 'Why is Medwin so excited about it?'

'He speaks of a ritual,' said Anala. 'Needing a Lord from each element and a Masterlord to initiate it. We've not had an Airlord until now. He believes it will restore our power.'

With a glance towards Medwin, she appeared to return from her thoughts.

'Best you be quiet now,' she said, shuffling away.

Thinking through what he'd heard, Dane tried to work out what to do.

'Vanessa!' he said desperately, twisting his head towards her, hoping their captors weren't watching. '*Look at me!*'

No response.

'*I don't know if you can hear me, but I'm going to find a way out of here!*'

Again, his words were met with silence.

Medwin appeared before him, Anala at his side.

'The time has come,' he said, repeating the words when Anala looked at him knowingly. 'Bring her.'

Walking behind Dane once more, he felt Vanessa lean against the stake as Anala grabbed her by the arm.

'*No!*' Dane yelled at Medwin. '*No!*'

Looking down at him, Medwin said, 'you'll be silent. Or I might reconsider your place in the coterie.'

Dane felt Vanessa move against him, shimmying up the stake.

As before, she offered no hint of recognition, not even a fleeting glance as Anala walked her towards the front of the shelter.

Medwin walked to the end of an area perhaps twenty feet square, leading out to the caves and rock surfaces beyond, looking back towards the shelter. Daven stood beside him. Both had eager, hungry looks on their faces.

Sandon stood halfway along the right edge of the square, relaxed, alert, and ready to begin.

Anala walked Vanessa to the other side, directly opposite her opponent. Dane sat tied to the stake, pushing through the madness within, willing her to show some sign, some understanding of what was about to happen while he tried to work out what to do.

'According to the Master,' Medwin began, placing his hand on his chest, 'we come today, to bear witness to the right of earth. To decide which of her servants she deems worthy to bear her name. By her will, and her will alone, so it shall be.'

Dane couldn't bear to watch, straining himself against his bindings.

'Witness today, are those of fire, water, and air,' said Medwin, nodding to Anala, Daven and Dane in turn.

'Let all witness, yet none interfere.'

Taking a step back, Medwin bowed.

Daven did the same.

Removing a rock with a sharpened edge from within her clothes, Anala cut through Vanessa's bonds, taking a step back and bowing as she did so.

Dane watched as Vanessa stood there, staring as she brought her hands in front of her, studying them as though seeing them for the first time.

Sandon bowed, moving into a crouch as he did so, ready to pounce. With all the attention on the ensuing ritual, Dane knew he only had a few moments.

Pushing himself backward, he forced his body off the ground, sliding himself up the length of the stake.

Moving to a half-standing position, he felt his hands slip free. At the same time, Sandon took his first step forward.

Vanessa remained rooted to the spot, continuing to look dazedly at her hands. Lowering himself to the ground, Dane moved his hands forward, under his legs, folding his knees towards his chest.

Outside the shelter, Sandon took another step forward.

Dane stretched his arms in front him, under his feet.

With a quick, crab-like movement, Sandon shuffled several paces to his left, his fingertips touching the ground, watching and waiting a moment, before returning to his original position. Stepping one foot at a time through the gap between his hands, Dane brought his hands in front of himself.

Outside, Sandon took a final step back.

Leaping to his feet, Dane ran to his sword, lying unnoticed at the foot of the entry. He raced out in the same moment Sandon ran towards Vanessa.

Sandon made it halfway across the square, before, with a two-handed swipe, Dane struck, dropping him on the spot.

Racing to Vanessa, with a swift shove he sent her stumbling away from the arena, where she tottered for several steps before tripping and falling to the ground.

Anala stood motionless, her mouth half open.

Ignoring her, Dane ran to Medwin, who barely had time to brace himself before Dane cut into him. With an extra moment to react, Daven threw himself at Dane, knocking them both to the ground.

Dane's sword fell from his grip.

Laying on top of Dane, hands around his throat, Daven squeezed hard, trying to get to a sitting position, where he'd have greater leverage. If he succeeded, he'd strangle Dane to death.

Feeling the air pressing in his throat, combined with the scraping in his ears, Dane felt himself starting to black out.

With all the energy he could gather, he kicked his legs, twisting his body at the same time. Daven was thrown sideways, the two separating for a moment.

Crawling on all fours, gathering himself to his knees, Dane raised his hands and with a side-arm swipe, clubbed Daven in the side of the head, striking him at the top of the jaw, directly under his ear. Daven's body went limp, allowing Dane time to swivel to his feet and retrieve his sword. With a quick stroke, it came slamming down.

Turning to Vanessa, he saw her on the ground; motionless except for a gentle rocking as she moved from side to side, her hands clamped against her ears.

Anala remained unmoved, her eyes and body still.

In the next moment, Dane felt himself thrown sideways, as Medwin, blood flowing from his wound, cannoned into him, knocking his sword loose once more.

Winded for a moment, Dane rolled over, gathering himself and rising to his feet. He had to get to Vanessa before Medwin and Anala did.

Medwin struggled to his feet, breathing heavily, his crazed eyes locked on Dane.

'You ... you ...'

Bleeding heavily, Dane saw Medwin wasn't the threat.

His problem now was ...

Before he could react, he heard a loud *CRACK!* as a rock with a sharpened edge lodged itself in the back of Medwin's skull.

Medwin's lifeless body dropped to the ground in front of him. Anala stood where Medwin had been, a strange, wonderous look on her face.

She looked at the prone figure in front of her, then to her hands. Finally, raising her eyes to meet him, she looked at Dane; his mouth wide, staring back at her, wide-eyed with shock.

They stood looking at each other, frozen for a moment; seemingly unable to get past the enormity of what Anala had done.

'When I first came here,' she said slowly, 'I was with my beloved, Bardo. Fire and water, we were opposites who together did unspeakable things.

'We came upon Medwin, and he had Avena with him. He convinced Bardo that if we joined them and waited for an Airlord, he'd be able to restore our power, allowing us to be great once more. He said we'd go back to Nadensa and wreak revenge on those that put us here.

'He showed us how to cleanse the screaming, and once we learned to mouth-read, all was well enough.

'Then Daven came; and Medwin told of another ritual – where two of the same would battle; so that when the coterie was complete, it would be as strong as could be.'

'Bardo...' she said, shaking her head, a tear trickling down her ancient, dirt-encrusted cheek. 'I don't know what Medwin did, but Bardo was weak. I could see it in his eyes, like he was ill on something.

'I told Medwin it wasn't fair, but he wouldn't listen. He thought Bardo and I, together, were a threat, and I knew he wanted Daven to win.

'I could do nothing but stand and watch ... while Daven killed my Bardo ...'

Understanding the grief in her words, despite being the evil creature she was, at that moment, Dane pitied the woman in front of him. Retrieving her rock, Anala cut his bindings, freeing his hands at last.

'Thank you,' he said, walking over and retrieving his sword.

'You best be going,' she replied, nodding behind him.

Turning to see what Anala was looking at, he saw Vanessa disappearing into a cave, the entrance sealing behind her.

Chapter 22
TUNNELS AND ROCKS

'**N**o!' Dane yelled, rushing to the hard, sealed opening he'd seen Vanessa walk through moments before.

Pounding with his fists, he did nothing more than scrape himself. Clawing at it with his sword did nothing to the rock surface either.

'No!' he yelled again.

'It's no use young wizard,' said Anala.

Turning, he looked at her desperately, his face contorted with a mixture of pain and frustration.

'Where does it go?' he asked.

'I don't know,' Anala replied with a shrug. 'Never been able to tell. Been lost in the caves for days, sometimes weeks at a time. Once a cave claims you, there be no other way than to follow it until it opens.'

'I have to find her!' said Dane. 'I have to find her!'

Anala nodded.

'For her sake, best she be found soon. Before the screaming claims her.'

With his own thoughts fighting against the scraping, Dane wondered how long Vanessa had been here; how much longer she'd endured it.

'Can you help me?' he asked desperately.

Anala shook her head.

'I'll not be going into the caves ever again. And I have enough food to last me weeks, maybe months.'

Dane shuddered as Anala looked hungrily at the bodies around her.

With a final nod, he raced into the morning sun.

Wandering aimlessly along the tunnel, Vanessa didn't know how long she would last.

Nothing mattered any more.

Clamping her hands to her ears made no difference, and yet she couldn't help but keep them there.

Bumping against the walls as she moved along, shuffling from side to side, her mind filled with a jumble of thoughts.

Who were the old people?

I was tied up, then they let me go.

And Dane was there?

No – it can't be.

Just a dream.

But I fell and hit my head.

Everything brightened, the sun shining around her. The walls were gone, as though they'd suddenly disappeared.

Looking up, she saw blue sky.

Stumbling around, she turned back in the direction she'd come.

Where's the cave?

Tapping lightly on the wall, she felt the hard rock against her hand.

Turning again, she saw an opening ahead.

The cave – let me into the cave.
Walking to the opening, she hit the rock.
What?
Turning again, she stumbled away.
She saw another cave to her left.
No, that's gone too.
To her right, at a run this time.
Now her shoulder hurt; a dull, throbbing pain.
What happened?
All the caves are disappearing!
The old people are playing a trick on me.
Are they going to catch me again?
Wait – there's one over there.
At a run this time, throwing herself at the entrance, she tripped, glancing off the wall, hitting the ground with a thud, and her vision faded to black.

After running for about half an hour with no success, Dane stopped in a clearing, out of the sun, catching his breath.

He'd been hesitant at first, not wanting to raise attention, but before he knew it, he found himself calling, *screaming* Vanessa's name. He didn't know why – because he no longer feared coming across exiled wizards, his increased desperation, or his mind failing in its battle against the scraping – once he realised he was doing it, he couldn't stop.

Now, wiping the sweat from his face, he looked around, desperate for something, anything that might help him. No matter which way he looked, everything was the same.

Did he try a cave?

Anala's words rang in his ears – *'been lost in the caves for days, sometimes weeks at a time.'*

No – he couldn't afford that. He had to stay outside, no matter the cost. Out here, he could change course if he saw something, if he heard something.

If only I had some eyes in the sky.

Wait ...

Walking out from the shade, into broad daylight, he looked skyward.

Nothing.

Starting to run, he whistled into the air.

Shaking the dust from her hair, Vanessa stood up.

Where am I?

How did I get here?

A cave?

Trying to make sense of it, she started walking, the scraping as constant and ceaseless as ever.

Images flashed into her mind.

An old man ...

And a woman ...

Another, and another, and ...

And ...

Dane ...?

Stumbling on, she knew the last thought couldn't be true – she hadn't seen Dane since ... since ...

It didn't matter.

Nothing mattered in this place – it was nothing but tunnels and rocks.

Tunnels and rocks, rocks and tunnels, tunnels and rocks – never-ending, just like the scraping.

The scraping – *the scraping.*

Why won't it stop?

Please!

Just for a moment – please! Let it stop!

Light ahead, and she found herself in a clearing.

Looking around, she saw nothing but tunnels and rocks.

The heat struck her; hot, humid and heavy.

It was pointless.

Forward, back, left, right, near, far …

Wherever she went, wherever she found herself, there was no rest, no respite from the scraping, not even for a moment.

The cave yawned open in front of her.

Well, at least I'll be out of the sun …

He'd been running a few minutes when he heard it.

Quiet and distant at first, fighting against the scraping sound, getting louder as it came closer.

Now, as he looked to the sky, he saw her enter his field of vision.

Standing with his arm out, he waited as Blaze, squawking overhead, circled in a sweeping, downward arc, before landing on his gauntlet.

'I'm glad to see you,' he said.

Blaze squawked, as if she understood.

Dane couldn't help but marvel at her for a moment, standing proudly on his wrist, squawking as she waited. He didn't know how much time had passed, but it felt good to hear something other than the scraping.

The scraping ...

It was ... it was ...

Gone?

Gone!

Concentrating, listening in wonder and disbelief, he waited to hear it in the back of his mind, where it would surely be; where it had been – where it had always been.

But ... nothing ...

Nothing – all he could hear were the sounds of his own breathing and Blaze squawking.

But, how?

Wait ...

Standing still for a moment, he let his eyes wander, then turned on the spot, before standing still again.

How?

Not only had the scraping gone, everything around him had stopped moving.

Like ... before?

Before?

Before I was captured!

His mind suddenly clear, he put it together.

Blaze – when she's near, there's no scraping, no movement.

Why?

For the moment, it didn't matter. As long as he could see and hear Blaze, he heard no scraping, and more importantly, he could think clearly.

'I have to keep you close,' he said.

Blaze nipped his arm gently.

'Yes,' he said, 'Vanessa – we have to find her!'

With an upward thrust of his hand, Blaze launched into the air.

Once she reached her circling level, she started banking to the left.

Dane followed, determined to stay close and keep the scraping sound out of his mind.

She found her twice – can she find her again?

She could be anywhere – trapped in a cave. If that were true, the cause would be lost.

Somehow, *somehow*, he was going to find her.

If it takes me to my last breath, I will find her.

Making his way around the caves in front of him, he had to move away from the direct path he wanted to follow. It took him to the right for a few minutes before he could find a way back. Now his mind had cleared, he remembered the frustrations he'd felt having to do the same when he first entered the city. There were no landmarks to identify where he was, where he was going, or where he'd been.

It was a huge maze of rock mounds and caves, with no end.

He thought of the wizards – they knew their way around – he and Vanessa had both been captured and taken to the shelter, and they'd ducked in and out around the caves when they were hunting him – so there had to be some way to navigate, to know where they were, how to find their way back.

You can work it out when you've been here for centuries!

Cursing to himself, he pushed on, the path twisting back.

He looked at Blaze, and saw her banking to her right, a wide, sweeping, arc, turning back the way they had come.

'No!' he yelled.

This had happened the last time, too.

He couldn't afford to be running around in circles.

I was so close!

Why did she run off?

Eyes on Blaze, wondering if she really could find Vanessa, or whether she was just as lost as he was, he didn't realise he'd wandered from the path.

The light around him suddenly went dark, and when Blaze disappeared from his line of sight, he stopped for a moment, confused. Turning on the spot, he saw a tiny slice of blue sky and sun, before all the light blacked out.

Blinking for a moment, leaning against the wall, he tried to understand. The scraping filled his mind, as loud and intense as before.

But ... what ...?

Another piercing, unbearable scrape.

Stumbling blindly, he bumped against the wall on the other side of the cave.

Cave?

No ... tunnel.

From what he could see in the semi-darkness surrounding him, the way ahead looked like an endless, twisting tunnel.

The noise!

With an effort, he sheathed his sword; wondering why he held it with this terrible, ear-splitting sound pounding in his mind.

Jamming his hands against his ears, it continued to pulse, slightly less in volume, but pounding just the same.

Following the tunnel, jogging, then running as fast he could, bouncing from side to side as it turned left and right, he looked desperately for a flicker of light that would show he was near the end.

He couldn't afford to be stuck in a cave – he had to get out as quickly as he could.

The scraping in his head raged on, and he knew the longer he stayed in the cave, the more it would entrench itself and take control of his mind.

The tunnel continued, straightening for a stretch, before twisting to the right again. Willing himself to run faster, he felt his adrenaline raging against the scraping, against the cave, against the City of Lost Souls, against the fact he'd lost Vanessa – against everything that appeared to be conspiring against him.

'You're not going to defeat me!' he screamed. 'Do you hear me?! You're not going to beat me!'

Pressing his hands harder against his ears, rounding a bend in the tunnel, he ran faster still, yelling the whole way. With all the anger and rage boiling inside him, he ran blindly into the light ahead, stumbling as he burst into the open air.

It took him a few steps to gather himself, and he slowed to a walk, and finally a stop, where he stood, hands on his knees, breathing heavily.

How far had he travelled through that tunnel?

As always, everything in the surrounding landscape looked exactly the same.

Looking up, he saw clouds rolling in from the west, swallowing the sun. In the few moments he'd had before the sun disappeared, as best he could remember, it had been more in front of him than before – so, west – the tunnel had taken him to the west.

He could still hear the scraping, so where was …

In the next instant he heard a squawk in the distance.

At the same time, the scraping started to go quiet.

Whistling again, he walked away from the rock-mound in front of him, held out his arm and waited.

A minute later, Blaze was on his arm, and the scraping had disappeared once more.

'Sorry,' said Dane, stroking the back of her head gently, 'I wandered into a cave.'

Blaze continued squawking as she had before.

'She's here somewhere. We have to keep trying.'

Launching her into the air again, Dane drew his sword and walked forward, breaking into a run once Blaze reached her cruising height.

Vanessa could see light ahead.

Walking numbly towards it, she felt the sharp breeze and the water forcing its way into the entrance, pelting against her.

Rain?

Why not? It's about the only thing that hasn't happened.

With her hands already clamped to her ears, she turned her head to keep the rain off her face. It made little difference, as the force of the wind and rain seemed to push her back into the wall behind her, quickly drenching her.

Leaning into the wall, she found herself more and more exposed to the weather.

Helpless, with only a thread of understanding, she saw the entrance becoming smaller and smaller as it sealed itself.

The cave was pushing her into the rain!

As the realisation registered in the depths of her mind, tears started running down her face. With the rain washing them away, she didn't even know she was crying.

Leaning on the surface of the newly sealed cave, she looked into the distance and saw another to her left. Making her way towards it, the intensity of the wind and rain increased. Her clothes and hair stuck to her body, the cold making her shiver.

The wall of the cave pushed its way forward, sealing itself before she could get inside. Looking around, she saw all the cave entrances sealing themselves.

She shouldn't have expected any less in a place like this.

'No!' she screamed in vain.

Walking in a dream, face to the sky, she closed her eyes and took her hands away from her ears, holding them out to her sides, palms up. The rain continued pounding against her body, the scraping continued throbbing in her mind, her whole sense of self lost.

Twirling on the spot, she felt the last slivers of hope ebbing away. Turning again, she tripped, twisting her ankle, and found herself on the ground. With a final cry of pain, she curled in a ball, continuing to shiver as the City of Lost Souls claimed her.

Let it end ...

Just let it end ...

Time wore on, and Dane had no idea whether he'd covered the area in front of him once, twice, three times, ten times ... or whether he was seeing it for the first time. Blaze had circled to the left and right; it seemed she had taken him forward and backward several times. It had all become a blur, the mind-numbingly endless running through the city, with no hint, no sign that he was any closer to finding Vanessa than he had been when he'd left the wizard's shelter hours before.

The rain came, sudden and heavy, making the journey more treacherous as the paths became wet and slippery. From what he could see, if he didn't know better, the caves were sealing them-selves against the rain.

Is that even possible - another cruel reality of The City of Lost Souls?

Is Vanessa in a cave?

Will she be stranded, sealed inside, until the rain stopped?

Will she be sealed in the cave forever?

Pushing the thoughts from his mind, at the same time becoming more and more desperate, he looked at Blaze, circling ahead of him.

Will the rain make it harder to search?

Nothing he thought about gave him the slightest hope, comfort or clue he was any closer to finding her.

Blaze wouldn't find her if she was in a cave. She could be in the cave directly in front him, to his right, his left, the cave he'd just passed, and there was no way to know. Nor would he know where the exit might be - it could be miles in any direction.

Running on, he rounded a corner and in the distance he saw the first landmark he knew. The wizard's shelter way about a hundred yards ahead.

'No!'

All the searching he'd done to this point, the hours that had passed since he'd left, and he found himself back where he started. The shelter appeared to be empty. He saw no sign of Anala, and the stake he and Vanessa had been tied to stood unused in the centre.

He didn't want to show himself. While he'd left simply enough, how would Anala react if he came back?

Can she see Blaze?

Does she know I'm nearby?

She has my small sword – is she lying in wait around the next corner?

His senses heightened, he slowed a little, making sure to look behind as he rounded corners and entered into open areas.

Looking desperately at Blaze, she veered in a wide arc to his left, taking him away from the shelter. He found himself breathing a sigh of relief, and after a few minutes, he'd lost sight of it completely.

Blaze took him further to his left, and as he made his way around the caves and rock mounds, he found himself running directly into the rain. The ground was soaked now, a trail of dirty, muddy water running along the ground.

As he watched Blaze again, she arced back towards him, before turning away, in a smaller, tighter circle, heading towards him once more, squawking all the while.

In an instant, he knew.

She's hovering!

Squinting into the rain, he looked into the distance.

To his far left, he saw an open area, larger and more exposed than most.

Looking again, he saw something out of place; something that didn't belong among all the caves and rock faces.

A mound of muddy dirt and grime; clothes tattered and torn; curled in a ball with her hands to her face, lying still in the pouring rain.

Chapter 23

THE EAGLE AND THE WOLF

'*Vanessa!*'

Running through the driving rain with every ounce of his energy, Dane covered the ground between them in no time at all.

'*Vanessa!*' he said, dropping his sword and crouching beside her. '*Vanessa!*'

No response.

Leaning in, he heard nothing. Her body felt cold and she didn't appear to be breathing,

'*Vanessa!*' he said again. '*Vanessa! Please! Please be alive!*'

He heard a low, guttural growl behind him.

Turning towards it, he saw a Gargaun wolf enter the clearing.

No!

Not now.

Please, please, go away.

The wolf came closer. Seemingly oblivious to the rain, it walked in a circle around them, sizing up its meal. Its growl grew louder, clearly angry someone had swooped on its prey.

What could he do?

He had to get out of here, and Vanessa hadn't moved since he'd found her.

He'd have to carry her, which would make a run slow and cumbersome, an easy target for the powerful beast circling them.

He wouldn't get far – he'd be able to cover a short distance, enough ground to get to a …

Looking around, he saw openings emerging in the rocks.

The closest lay about thirty feet to his right.

Carefully, he reached around and sheathed his sword.

With one eye on the wolf and the other on the cave opening in front of him, he waited. He'd wait until the wolf was as far away as possible, then take his chance.

Crouching and reaching his arms around Vanessa's limp body, he heard another growl to his left.

Another wolf entered the clearing.

Then another, and another.

The first had been sent to scout their prey, and, sensing an escape, the others had emerged to assist.

In quick time, a pack of six surrounded him, moving as one, an even gap between each – cutting off his escape.

His only way out would be to risk running through them.

The growling grew louder.

He had no choice – no matter what he did, they were going to attack. As the certainty dawned on him, Dane felt his mind go quiet, his heartbeat slow, all trace of fear evaporating.

Slowly standing, Vanessa in his arms, leaning her head to his chest, he locked his eyes on the cave.

The wolves' growling turned into a growl-bark; first one, then the next, and the next, until the sound filled the clearing.

They stopped circling, turning directly towards him.

Leaning forward, Dane ran towards the cave.

As one, the wolves sprang after him.

One ran straight at him, directly in front of the cave.

Unarmed and burdened with Vanessa in his arms, he did the only thing he could.

With a well-timed kick, he struck the wolf nearside, at the top of its neck. It yelped and fell away.

Stumbling for a moment, Dane gathered himself, eyes only for the cave. He felt teeth at his heels, one set latching on for a moment, before letting go.

Diving into the cave, he threw Vanessa forward in the same movement, where she rolled over and lay motionless. Jumping up and turning in the same motion, he drew a knife from his legging, ready to face the wolf, or wolves that followed him into the cave. With the entrance closing, one made a desperate lunge towards him.

As it came leaping through the opening at what would have been chest-high, Dane crouched, thrusting the knife upwards in the same motion. The blow struck truly, and as the wolf's now lifeless body fell on him, he in turn tumbled over Vanessa as he rolled on the ground.

To his relief, the entrance had closed completely, separating them from the other wolves.

Never did he think he'd be glad to find himself stuck in a cave, and as he felt the scraping sound in his mind possessing his thoughts once more, he wondered if he'd made the right choice.

Replacing the knife, he gently kicked the wolf, making sure he'd killed it.

Crouching over Vanessa, he placed an arm under her neck, lifting her to a sitting position, his knee supporting her back.

'Vanessa,' he said desperately against the scraping in his mind. 'Vanessa. Please.'

With little light in the cave, he couldn't see her face clearly, and, as had happened earlier, he felt no reaction from her.

Panic filled his mind.

Am I too late?

Is she dead?

No!

Please! Don't let her be dead.

In a response combining both fear and blind determination, he lifted Vanessa off the ground and started walking through the cave. He didn't know why he was doing it, but it felt better to be doing something, that it would help if he could get her into the open air where he'd be able to see her properly.

As fast as he could, he made his way along the passageway, turning left and right as the cave wound its way ahead.

She's all right.

She's all right.

She's going to be all right.

Bumping around corners he ran on.

She's going to be all right.

I'll just get her outside and she'll be all right.

His adrenaline running high, the scraping sound piercing his mind, he rushed on, his feelings of panic releasing more energy into his muscles as he searched for the opening.

Rounding a corner, an ear-piercing scream filled the cave.

For a moment he didn't know what he'd heard, thinking it to be the scraping sound working its way further into his mind.

It screamed again, and a third time.

'Let me go! Let me go!'

Dane looked down.

'Let me go! Let me go!'

The screams were coming from his chest.

What?

What!

With his mind fighting against the scraping sound, it would have taken longer to piece together, if not for the fact he felt a sudden, violent movement in his arms, as Vanessa struggled frantically.

'Let me go!' she said again.

Dane felt a surge of relief run through him.

'Vanessa!' he said, as he rounded a bend. 'It's me! Dane!'

Vanessa continued thrashing in his arms, forcing Dane to slow down a little to make sure he didn't drop her.

'Vanessa!' he said again. 'It's me!'

Vanessa pounded her fists against his chest.

'Put me down! Let me go!'

Dane couldn't understand why she was struggling.

'We just need to get outside!' he yelled.

Vanessa continued to struggle, punching with her hands and kicking her legs desperately.

Dane tightened his grip.

'Vanessa!' he yelled. *'Stop!* It's me – Dane! Just let me get us outside!'

His words had no effect.

'Let me go! Let me go!'

Struggling on, Dane rounded another bend, and felt a surge of relief as he saw light ahead.

'We're almost there!' he said, running on, Vanessa screaming and squirming in his arms.

The opening emerged ahead, and Dane ran into the small clearing. Vanessa continued thrashing and yelling as Dane gently lowered her to the ground. Free from his clutches at last, she stood, walking only a couple of paces before falling over, writhing in pain.

Dane let her sit for a moment.

Sobbing, Vanessa raised her hands to her ears.

'No,' she said. 'No.'

'Vanessa,' said Dane gently.

'*Let me go!*' she said. '*Let me go!*'

Dane kneeled in front of her.

'Vanessa,' he said. 'It's me.'

She looked at him with a crazed, distant look on her face.

'*Leave me alone!*' she said. '*Let me go and leave me alone!*'

Dane didn't know what to do – he'd found her at last, yet she didn't know who he was. More to the point; from both the look on her face and her state of mind, he doubted whether she knew anything at all – not just who he was, but who *she* was.

The scraping sound pierced his mind again.

That's it!

Turning away for a moment, he directed his attention to the sky. The rain had slowed to a drizzle, and traces of blue sky were starting to show overhead. Searching for Blaze, he let out his whistle call.

A few moments later, he heard the squawk, then saw her in the sky to his right, heading towards him.

Once she perched on his arm, his mind clear of the scraping sound once more, Dane let her flutter to the ground, and walked towards Vanessa.

Crouching beside her; at first she hesitated; drawing back, then relaxing.

'Blaze,' she said quietly.

'Yes,' said Dane. 'Blaze brought me here.'

Vanessa tilted her head towards Dane, as though seeing him for the first time.

'Vanessa,' he said. 'It's me.'

He saw her eyes searching his; nervous, unsure, uncertain.

Dane gently reached his hands to hers.

'*No!*' she said, fighting against him, shaking herself from side to side.

Dane let go.

'What's wrong?'

'*Noise!*' she said strongly. '*Noise!*'

Dane gently touched her hands again.

'There's no noise,' he said gently. 'Just Blaze.'

'Blaze,' Vanessa said, watching the eagle squawking in front of her.

'Yes,' said Dane gently, wiping her hair from her eyes. 'Blaze found you and brought me here.'

Vanessa looked at Dane again, seeing but not really seeing.

'It's me,' said Dane, smiling softly.

Vanessa stared blankly for a few moments, recognition slowly registering on her face.

'Dane?'

'Yes,' he said with a nod.

'*Dane!*' she said, leaning into him.

Dane held her close.

Relief swept over both of them.

Neither spoke for a minute or two.

Releasing her gently, Dane took one hand, then the other, bringing them to her side.

'There's no sound,' he said. 'Only Blaze.'

Looking fearful for a few moments; struggling against Dane's gentle, but firm grip, Vanessa allowed him to draw her hands to her side.

'It's only Blaze,' said Dane.

Looking longingly into his eyes, Vanessa breathed a heavy sigh.

'No scraping,' she said. *'No sound!'*

Dane nodded.

Collapsing into him again, hugging him tightly, she started sobbing.

'It's over,' said Dane, patting her gently. 'It's over.'

Letting all the fear, dread and agony from her ordeal drain through her tears, Vanessa hugged Dane tighter and tighter, relief washing through her in wave after wave.

'Dane,' she said finally.

Dane let go, helping her to her feet.

'It was horrible,' Vanessa said softly. 'The noise ... the caves ... horrible.'

Shuddering at the memories, she hugged him again.

'There's so much I don't remember,' she said.

Dane nodded knowingly.

'It's over,' he said.

Vanessa looked into his eyes.

Strong.

Fearless.

Safe.

She smiled.

'Thank you,' she said.

'You knew I'd come,' said Dane.

Vanessa smiled again, looking at her tattered clothes for a moment.

'I must look a mess.'

'Never better,' said Dane. 'Never better.'

'Blaze found me?'

Dane nodded, and after a gentle whistle, Blaze took to the air.

'She found the entrance and led me through it. I was captured - you, we were both captured.'

Vanessa looked at him, stunned.

'You don't remember?' said Dane.

Vanessa shook her head.

'I don't know how long I've been here. There are gaps - things I don't remember.'

Dane pointed at the sealed rock to his left.

'Do you remember kicking and screaming while I carried you through that cave?'

Vanessa hesitated.

'I ... don't really remember much until the noise stopped.'

Dane nodded.

'It's Blaze,' he said. 'For whatever reason, her squawking counters the scraping. I found it almost impossible to think with that noise. You've been here longer; it would have been a lot harder for you.'

Vanessa shuddered at the memory.

'It's over,' said Dane, gently rubbing her arm. 'We need to get out of here.'

Looking skyward, he saw Blaze circling ahead of them.

'Blaze knows where the entrance is. I'm sure she'll find it again.'

Vanessa stumbled; grabbing hold of Dane to stop herself falling.

'I – I don't think I can walk,' she said.

'It's no matter,' said Dane, reaching down and lifting her off the ground.

Following Blaze towards the entrance, elation and adrenaline surging through him, Vanessa felt as light as a feather in his arms.

Relieved her ordeal was over, Vanessa hugged herself to Dane; resting her head on his chest, feeling his strength as he carried her.

Dane watched Blaze circle higher, moving away from them, squawking all the while. Following her path with his eyes, he saw her rising higher and higher, tilt slightly, and dive towards the ground. Eyes wide, he wondered what in the name of the Gods she was doing.

Blaze rose again.

Dane hesitated, trying to understand. She would only do that if …

Then he saw them.

First one, then another, another and another. In short order, a pack of four Gargaun wolves emerged into the clearing ahead.

'Dane,' said Vanessa fearfully.

Letting her down gently, Dane rested her against a rock-face.

Stepping forward a few paces, he drew his sword.

The wolves started fanning out, blocking the way ahead.

Blaze continued diving at them.

Dane stood a few feet in front of Vanessa. The wolves were a few feet away; teeth bared, growling at him.

For the moment, it was a stand off.

Neither moved; each sizing up the other, wondering what would happen next.

Weighing his options, Dane knew they were in trouble.

He might get one, perhaps two; depending on how they chose to attack. He couldn't charge them – that would leave Vanessa defenseless against however many eluded him.

The caves weren't a solution this time. There were no openings close enough to run to, and with everything around them still once more, they would stay as they were, offering no refuge.

Standing his ground was the only choice.

The wolves seemed to sense it too, knowing it would only be a matter of time before they'd overwhelm him.

Blaze struck, diving harder and lower than before, striking one of the wolves heavily across the scruff of its neck. Rising in the next moment, her strength lifted the wolf completely off the ground for an instant, before she let go.

Stunned at its predicament, the wolf howled in pain, before slinking away. Seizing the moment, Dane strode forward, swinging his sword in long, swishing strokes, covering as much space in front of him as he could.

The remaining wolves retreated, uncertain what to do.

Dane took a step back, gathering himself, not wanting to increase the space between himself and Vanessa.

The wolves advanced once more.

Blaze dived again.

The wolves were ready this time.

As she closed in, the nearest wolf rose on its hind legs, jumping towards her, snapping its teeth.

Pulling out of her dive, Blaze rose back into the air.

Dane swished his sword again, stepping forward as he'd done before.

The wolves retreated a couple of steps.

Dane noticed one of the wolves dominating the others; clearly the alpha leader. Standing taller and stronger than the others, with a lighter coat, he saw something strange in the way it looked back at him.

Gripping his sword tighter, he lunged forward again.

The process repeated several times: Dane strode forward; the wolves retreated; Dane stepped back; the wolves advanced once more. He hadn't been able to get close enough to strike any of them. Each time he moved forward, they remained tantalisingly out of reach.

He knew he would tire at some point.

The wolves advanced again; the leader more adventurous this time, sensing the end. Stepping forward, Dane swished his sword with more vigor, the tip giving the slightest vibration as it grazed the teeth of the lead wolf.

Enraged, the lead wolf barked angrily, pawing the ground, staring at him with a hot, violent intensity.

Raising his sword, ready to swipe again; a thought crossed his mind. In mid-swipe, his sword fell to the ground.

The lead wolf appeared to smile in satisfaction, knowing it had its prey captured.

With a *swoosh!* a knife from Dane's legging lodged itself firmly in the neck of the lead wolf; a moment later, another planted itself high in the front leg of the wolf to his right.

With howls of pain, both wolves rocked back. The one to his right; crippled by the knife in its leg, slumped to the ground. To Dane's surprise, the lead wolf raised itself onto its hind legs, staggering a couple of steps, before dropping onto all fours and stumbling away, out of sight behind a rock face.

At the sounds of its two maimed friends, the remaining wolf hesitated. Retrieving his sword, Dane chased it a few strides, yelling and screaming. Switching to survival mode, the wolf took flight, running away, dodging a low-swooping Blaze all the while.

'Are you all right?' Dane asked, making his way to Vanessa and slumping against the rock-face.

'Yes,' said Vanessa, the relief clear on her face.

Sheathing his sword, Dane heard the first wolf a few feet away, whimpering in pain. He saw it lying helplessly on the ground; its breathing heavy and laboured, his knife deeply embedded in its leg. Walking over, he looked for a moment, before bending down and wrenching the knife out.

'Let that be a lesson to you,' he said, wiping the knife and walking back to Vanessa.

She stood gingerly.

'Come on,' said Dane, picking her up again. 'Let's get out of here.'

Wrapping her arms around Dane once more, Vanessa leaned in close and said softly, 'thank you for saving me.'

Dane smiled, his body tingling with pride.

'I had to,' he said. 'I can't tease Mother on my own.'

Vanessa giggled, squeezing herself tightly against him.

'Did you see the other one?' said Dane. 'The leader of the pack?'

'Not really,' said Vanessa.

'No matter. I don't think we're going to see any more of them.'

As they walked, Dane told Vanessa about their encounter with the exiled wizards.

Vanessa listened, her face a mixture of surprise and disbelief.

'And when you disappeared into the cave, I thought I'd lost you again,' said Dane.

'That's ... incredible,' Vanessa replied.

'You don't remember any of it?'

Vanessa shook her head.

'Towards the end, I don't really remember anything.'

Her voice dropping to little more than a whisper, she said, 'The scraping was so intense, I didn't want to go on. I just wanted to ...'

'You're safe now,' said Dane, saving her from reliving the reality of what she'd been about to say.

Vanessa hugged him again.

Neither spoke for a minute or two; the sound of their squawking eagle filling the silence, before Blaze started hovering above them.

'She wants to land,' said Vanessa.

'I think we can manage,' said Dane.

Letting Vanessa down; standing so she could lean against him, Dane held out his arm. Blaze landed for a moment, before perching on his left shoulder.

'I'm not sure what she's doing,' said Dane. 'It's like she's leading us. She did the same to get me here.'

Cradling Vanessa in his arms once more, they made their way towards the entrance. Nothing they could see gave any hint as to where it may be. Blaze sat comfortably, squawking all the while.

Dane felt Vanessa flinch for a moment, looking around uncertainly, before settling against him once more.

'Are you all right?' he asked.

'Yes,' Vanessa replied, looking around nervously. 'Just ... sore.'

On reaching a flatter, more open area of the landscape, Dane felt the same sensations as before – the momentary blindness of the sun, the cold air washing through him.

In the next instant the sandy surrounds of the lake were under his feet, and he found himself walking towards Will and Hawthorne; who, with looks of stunned disbelief on their faces, were running towards him.

Chapter 24
FINAL ENCOUNTERS

'Princess!' said Hawthorne. 'Are you injured? Are you all right?'

'Where did you go?' asked Will. 'How did you find her? How did you get back?'

Taking in their new surroundings, neither Dane nor Vanessa spoke for a few moments.

Blaze took flight, perching in a nearby tree.

'Are you all right?' Hawthorne asked again.

'Yes,' Vanessa replied.

Setting Vanessa down near the horses, Dane found a water-skin and handed it to her.

'Thank you,' she said.

Kneeling at her feet, Dane started gently rubbing the lower leg she'd been favouring.

'Where does it hurt?' he asked.

Vanessa gasped, kicking out in reflex against the pain, striking Dane in the face.

'Well,' said Dane, rubbing himself where he'd been struck. 'I'd say we've found where it hurts.'

Vanessa smiled, before taking another thirsty drink.

'We shouldn't linger,' said Hawthorne. 'We don't know what else, or who else may be here, or on its way here. Let's be on our way.'

Ruffling Thunder's mane playfully as he untethered him, Dane looked him over from front to back. Seeing no cuts or scratches, he checked his saddle and equipment.

'We were ready to leave,' said Will, sorting through his things. 'Commander Hawthorne wanted to find the regiment and get word back to Brindabeare and Lord Frederick. It took all my powers of persuasion to convince him to stay.'

'For a time, I didn't think we were going to make it back,' said Dane, checking his gauntlets. 'I've used most of my knives, and my small sword was taken.'

Will pointed to a pile of weapons from vanquished colleagues and enemy piled nearby. They would take what they could carry, leaving the rest.

Fully equipped once more, Dane made his way to a spare horse, checking to make sure it would be suitable for Vanessa.

In the next moment, several things happened simultaneously.

With a flash of white light, and a *BANG!* Lord Frederick appeared. At the same time, the ground started shaking around them; the force so sudden and violent, Dane, Will and Hawthorne stumbled, struggling to stay on their feet.

Blue sky disappeared; replaced by dark black clouds, roiling in anger, ready to unleash a torrent of rain. A wind picked up, gathering to gale-force in a matter of moments.

A large tree uprooted, flying through the air, striking Hawthorne in the back so hard the force threw him forward a clear ten feet, before crashing to the ground; the impact so hard and heavy it crushed his armour from front to back.

In front of them, the lake frothed violently; hot, bubbling water replacing what had been a smooth, peaceful surface a moment before.

Horses reared in fright.

Vanessa screamed.

Stumbling his way to Vanessa, Dane covered her with his body, protecting her from any flying debris. The looked at each other, panic on their faces as they watched the mayhem around them.

Lord Frederick raised his hands, spreading them in an arc. As he did so, a silvery-white dome appeared; spreading around Dane, Vanessa, Will, Blaze and the horses; encasing them.

The ground continued shaking; the earth around them quaking and turning over, trees uprooting and disappearing, as they were crushed, splintered and buried beneath the dirt and rocks raining down.

The lake bubbled higher and higher; hotter and hotter; before, with an almighty surge, the entire body of water shot skyward, an endless stream of scalding water erupting from the lakebed.

Dane glanced at Vanessa and Will, and saw they were equally stunned at what they were seeing.

Watching the lake, Lord Frederick stood still, seemingly calm amidst all the chaos around them.

On and on it went; violent, unceasing, endless.

Making his way to Lord Frederick, Dane hesitated, not wanting to cause a distraction.

Lord Frederick glanced towards Dane, a gentle smile on his face.

'What?' Dane asked.

'One moment,' said Lord Frederick.

Turning to the lake and spreading his arms, Lord Frederick brought his hands in an arc towards the top of his head, opening the dome around them.

At the same time, Dane felt everything weakening – the shaking of the ground, the force of the wind, the colour of the sky, the water shooting out of the lake.

Everything calmed down; softer and softer, before, after another minute or two, it stopped entirely.

'Is everyone all right?' asked Lord Frederick.

'I think Commander Hawthorne is dead,' said Dane.

Lord Frederick glanced to where Hawthorne had fallen.

'I'm afraid so,' he said.

Dane and Will lowered their heads.

'He didn't deserve that,' said Will.

'It's unfortunate,' said Lord Frederick. 'It hit so quickly.'

Everyone spoke at once.

'What was that?' asked Dane.

'How did you find us?' asked Vanessa

'What just happened?' asked Will.

Lord Frederick raised his hand.

'In a moment,' he said, looking to Vanessa. 'First, I must say what a joy it is to see you.'

Kneeling next to Vanessa, taking her hand in his, Lord Frederick asked her gently, 'are you well?'

Vanessa nodded, hugging him.

'Yes,' she replied. 'I'm exhausted; my foot aches, but I'm fine.'

Reaching down, Lord Frederick touched her just above the ankle; a faint glow emitting from his fingers. Vanessa felt her body warm at the touch, as the healing energy absorbed itself into the area of her discomfort.

'Better?'

Vanessa nodded. 'Better.'

'I see you've drained a waterskin,' said Lord Frederick.

With a wave of his hand, it was full again.

'I've added an elixir. It will help.'

Vanessa drank gratefully, and like air releasing from a balloon, she felt the stresses in her mind and body ebbing away.

'Lord Frederick,' said Dane. 'What happened?'

'A disturbance in the balance of the Ruling Elements of Nature,' Lord Frederick replied.

Confused looks greeted his answer.

'What do you mean?' asked Dane.

'It happens from time to time,' said Lord Frederick. 'With the ever-changing state of nature, sometimes the elements find themselves out of balance, and an event like we've just seen seeks to restore it.'

Dane looked at the land around him.

Things lay everywhere, completely out of place. Trees were half-buried in the earth, poking out at strange angles; others had been crushed to nothing. Chunks of rock had been thrown down from the mountains, littering the ground and the lake.

Little water remained in the lake itself; a dark, sticky layer of mud and grime, bubbling and sizzling from the heat it had generated.

'What about the City of Lost Souls?' asked Dane. 'Could this disturbance have affected it too? Maybe even destroyed it?'

'I'm afraid I don't know,' said Lord Frederick. 'Why do you ask?'

'The entrance is right down there,' said Dane, pointing towards the lake.

'We will need time to consider it,' said Lord Frederick. 'At the moment I'm most interested to know how you managed to find the Princess.'

Dane recounted his story, from the time Blaze led him into the city, their encounter with Medwin and the wizards, to their final encounter with the Gargaun wolves.

Lord Frederick listened intently, asking questions about the otterlings and exiled wizards in turn.

'That is an amazing sequence of events,' he said when Dane finished. 'Since the beginning of time, there has been no record of anyone escaping the City of Lost Souls.'

'With that scraping sound, I'm not surprised,' said Dane.

Vanessa nodded her agreement.

'Not to mention how hard it is to find the entrance,' said Will.

'Indeed,' said Lord Frederick, glancing at Vanessa as he spoke. 'I've been here many times since we heard you were being sent here, including this very place as recently as a few days ago; searching for the entrance, and found nothing.'

To Dane, he said, 'not only did you go into the city – you came back.'

'I'll never understand how these parallel existences happen,' said Dane. 'One moment I was walking towards the lake, and the next, I was in a totally different place.'

'It's one of the most advanced instances of the workings of the Elements of Nature in the history of the land,' said Lord Frederick. 'Very few ever knew how it worked; all the better to keep its secrets.'

'A pack of wolves took me through the entrance,' said Vanessa. 'Raegan controlled them, but he didn't go into the city.'

'Until now,' said Lord Frederick, 'the Gargaun wolves were the only known way of entering the city.'

'How did Raegan control them?' asked Will. 'And how could he know all he did, without being able to enter and exit? He must have found a way.'

'Yes and no,' said Lord Frederick.

'What do you mean?' said Dane.

'One of the skills some, but not all wizards can acquire, once they establish their dominant element, is to be able to transform into an animal of that element,' said Lord Frederick.

'Let me guess,' said Vanessa. 'The animal of a Firelord is a wolf.'

'Among others, yes,' said Lord Frederick. 'Until your capture, I'd never had reason to consider whether Raegan could transform. It explains everything.'

'He transforms into a Gargaun wolf and enters the city,' said Will. 'And then transforms back into himself?'

'No,' said Lord Frederick. 'With all the known attributes of the city, and not wanting to risk losing his power, Raegan would transform outside the city; enter; and transform again on exit.'

Dane's eyes went wide.

'What's the matter?' asked Vanessa.

'The pack of wolves that tried to stop us,' said Dane.

'Yes?' said Lord Frederick.

'Remember,' said Dane, excitement gathering in his voice, 'when I told you one of them looked like the leader of the pack?'

'Yes,' said Vanessa uncertainly.

'Well, it's true. One was the alpha leader, and when I remember it now, it looked different, and it didn't act like the others.'

'Does that mean anything?' asked Will.

'It means two things,' said Dane, piecing it all together, speaking faster and faster. 'It explains why they tried to stop us – because the alpha leader controlled the others. And, when I wounded it, it stood on its hind legs for a couple of steps, like … a man!'

Vanessa gasped.

Will's mouth dropped open.

'Say that again,' said Lord Frederick gently.

'It stood on its hind legs *like a man!*' said Dane.

'Did it die?' asked Will.

'I don't know!' said Dane, cursing himself. 'It staggered away, and I lost sight of it. I hurt it badly; but I don't know if I killed it.'

'But we all know a wizard can only die in battle from the wound of a wizard's sword,' said Will.

'But if he's a wolf,' said Dane, 'is he still a wizard?'

Dane, Vanessa and Will looked at Lord Frederick.

'I'm afraid I don't know,' he said. 'It's something I've never had to contemplate.'

'Even if Dane didn't kill it,' said Vanessa, 'if there was a disturbance in the city, that destroyed it, then surely he ... it ... died in there?'

No one said a word for a moment; thinking through all they'd heard; daring to wonder – was Raegan dead?

With a clear day dawning around them, the journey to Brindabeare began.

'I'll be glad to get out of here,' said Dane, as they left the lake and all the destruction behind them.

Vanessa and Will nodded their agreement.

Lord Frederick smiled, his eyes on the path ahead.

The sun was cresting the ranges when they heard them.

Hooves – thundering towards them.

Dismounting, Lord Frederick vanished in a flash of light.

Peeling into the shadows; Dane, Vanessa and Will waited.

A few moments later, Lord Frederick returned.

'The remainder of the regiment has arrived,' he said.

Emerging from their shelter; Dane leading Lord Frederick's horse, they joined him on the path.

Dane and Will hadn't seen their colleagues since crossing the Osa River.

Rounding a corner ahead of them, the regiment came into view. At the sight of their Princess, led by Hindmarsh, a cheer erupted as they closed ranks around them.

Stopping in front of them; a wide smile on his face, Hindmarsh fully absorbed the sight of Vanessa before him; bedraggled and tired; and yet, beneath the dirt and grime, he saw the underlying strength and majesty, mixed with the tenderness and humility they all loved.

'Princess!' he said. 'We're so glad you're safe!'

Vanessa smiled.

'Thank you. Thank you all, for risking so much to find me.'

'We would do it again, without hesitation!' Hindmarsh replied, raising his fist in the air.

With another cheer, the entire regiment mimicked their Commander.

Looking to Dane and Will, Hindmarsh asked, 'the others?'

Dane shook his head.

'Very well,' said Hindmarsh. 'They will be properly recognised on our return to Brindabeare.'

'Commander,' said Lord Frederick. 'You have sufficient supplies for the journey?'

'We'll manage,' Hindmarsh replied.

'Very well,' said Lord Frederick. 'I think it best we send no word until we cross the Penton River. That will allow us to travel without being intercepted by friend or foe.'

'Agreed,' said Hindmarsh.

A sound to his left distracted him. Turning towards it, looking past the regiment, he heard it again; closer now.

Dane, Will, Hindmarsh and some of the regiment heard it too.

'We're surrounded!' said Lord Frederick, mounting his horse and turning on the spot.

A wave of enemy knights swept into their path, emerging from within the ranges.

On instinct, Dane, Will and Lord Frederick closed in around Vanessa.

As one, swords drawn, the regiment turned to face their foe, fanning out in an arc with Vanessa and her protectors in the middle of the group. Dane saw Hezabar colours on the chests of the enemy. If none had been lost after he and Will crossed the Osa River, the regiment remained at least a hundred strong. The opposition force looked to be larger.

Moving as a smooth, coordinated unit, the regiment were unfazed; standing their ground, waiting to meet their attackers. With an arm's length between each man, they covered every point of their protective circle around Vanessa.

Covering the ground quickly, the enemy reached the strike point, about ten yards from the regiment, when Lord Frederick reacted.

A sizzling light fired into a space from where the enemy were coming from, blinding the immediate area for the moment.

At the same time, the regiment charged forward; Dane, Vanessa, Will and Lord Frederick following the light shining from Lord Frederick's hand.

It worked exactly as planned.

The light punched a hole in the enemy line, allowing Vanessa and her protectors to cut straight through, past the fighting, making good their escape.

In the time it would take for the light to fade, they'd be clear of the battle.

The regiment would fight as though they were protecting Vanessa from the enemy; maintaining their protective circle, keeping their foes from breaking through and realising their prize had fled. Dane, Vanessa, Will and Lord Frederick rode on, using the ranges for cover.

After a clear ten minutes, Lord Frederick slowed to a stop, turning and facing back towards the fighting.

'Well done to all,' he said.

'We had to expect it,' said Dane. 'Ever since we've been here, there have been enemy forces everywhere.'

'If they were waiting for us, we're lucky they didn't find us last night,' said Will.

'Not really,' said Lord Frederick.

'What do you mean?' said Dane.

'Everything you have just seen has happened as Commander Hindmarsh and I planned.'

Vanessa gasped.

'What?' she said. 'How?'

'Word spread throughout the land we'd sent forces here. There is no doubt Raegan and his allies knew of it. I was sure Raegan would have something waiting for us when we left – with or without you.

'Last evening, after I established the proper protection around you, I left the campsite and found the regiment. I met with Commander Hindmarsh and told him what he needed to do.

'The revelry, the shouting and cheering, was a deliberate effort to draw out the enemy.

'I detected traces of them before we started our journey this morning, so I knew the plan was sound. I wanted to be sure when we reunited with the regiment we drew out the entire enemy force.'

'What do we do now?' asked Dane.

'We ride on; wait at day's end to see what has become of the regiment and make a decision on how we proceed.'

'There was no sign of Raegan,' said Dane hopefully. 'Perhaps he really is dead.'

'We can't be sure of that,' said Lord Frederick. 'He would not be concerned whether his forces won; only that they inflicted as much damage as possible. He had no reason to be a part of it.'

'I hope he is dead,' said Dane. 'I curse that I didn't kill that wolf.'

'You were in no position to know,' said Lord Frederick.

Dane looked unconvinced.

'It may all be an illusion,' said Vanessa soothingly. 'I'm not saying you were wrong; but what you saw may not have been what you thought. We're guessing and hoping.'

'All the same ...'

'All the same nothing,' said Vanessa, taking his hand. 'Your aim wasn't to find and kill Raegan. You showed compassion to the other wolf. You would have helped that wolf, not killed it.'

Dane's eyes went wide.

'No!' said Vanessa. 'Don't let yourself down by feeling guilty about something you were in no position to understand.'

'Very well,' said Dane, letting out a deep breath, 'I guess you're right.'

'Everything you did was incredibly brave. I wouldn't be here if it wasn't for you.'

'She's right,' said Lord Frederick.

Will nodded.

'Everyone will hear of this,' he said. 'You'll go down in the Annals as the one who saved the Princess from the City of Lost Souls.'

'Both of us,' said Dane. 'We did it together.'

'Governor Mortensen, on behalf of Lord Raegan, commands you surrender unconditionally to Lord Raegan's authority as ruler of Valentaland. Any defiance will be seen as an act of treason, and you, and all who follow you, will be treated accordingly.'

'*How dare you!*' screamed Medhurst.

'*You do not speak to the King in such a manner!*' yelled Fairbrother.

The King said nothing.

The envoy continued.

'Your daughter is dead, killed by the forces within the City of Lost Souls.'

The King remained silent.

'I am asked to take your response to Governor Mortensen and Lord Raegan,' said the envoy. 'What do you wish me to tell them?'

Silent for a few moments, the King stood, stepping from the dais, walking slowly to where the envoy was standing.

Eye to eye with the envoy, the King said, 'tell Governor Mortensen, and Raegan, I will avenge my daughter to my dying breath.'

'There were minimal losses,' said Hindmarsh. 'Once we were on level terms, they started to panic. We broke their line in several places and they became disorganised. In the end, those that remained fled. We saw no benefit in pursuing them.'

Lord Frederick nodded.

Dane, Vanessa and Will listened intently.

'What will they do now?' Dane ventured to ask.

'That is not our immediate concern,' said Hindmarsh. 'We need to concentrate on getting the Princess back to Brindabeare.'

'You're not concerned about being attacked again?' asked Dane.

'I doubt it will happen,' said Hindmarsh.

'As do I,' said Lord Frederick. 'Given they were soundly defeated, it will take some time before word reaches Raegan about what happened here.'

'Actually, it was the one thing in all of this I was concerned about,' said Hindmarsh.

'Go on,' said Lord Frederick.

'Why didn't Raegan appear? Once we broke their lines, I expected him to appear at any moment and strike us down. You and the Princess would have escaped as planned, but I was nervous about the prospect of facing Raegan, just the same.'

'Who is to know what his plans are?' said Lord Frederick.

Hindmarsh contemplated the question for a moment, then nodded.

'You were right to be thinking of it, Commander,' said Lord Frederick.

In line with their plan, Lord Frederick and the regiment stayed their course on the journey back to Brindabeare. Keeping to the east of the Alvion Hills, they approached none of the settlements along the way.

Although Vanessa hadn't seen many of these places for several years; after some gentle persuasion from Lord Frederick, she agreed not to call on any of them.

'Each will want to celebrate your return, and keep you as long as they can,' Lord Frederick had said. 'It could take months to get back to Brindabeare.'

Dane and Will had plenty of time to recount all that happened since they separated from the regiment at the Osa River. When the subject of Raegan's whereabouts came up, neither hinted at what may have happened in the city.

Not wanting to risk another encounter with the sarkoe at the Osa River, the regiment took the Penton River route.

'Send Blaze to the castle,' Lord Frederick said to Dane later that evening. 'Let them know where we are.'

'Very well,' said Dane, his mind suddenly lost in thought.

'Yes?' said Lord Frederick, seeing the look on Dane's face.

'You won't take Vanessa yourself?' asked Dane. 'Can't you disappear and take her with you?'

'If circumstances called for it, I would,' said Lord Frederick. 'But we're in no danger, and it's not appropriate for me to whisk her away. You and Will saved her; so it will be you, Will, and the regiment who lead her into the city.'

The city erupted with joy.

'She's alive!'

'They found her!'

'She's safe!'

'She's coming home!'

'The gods be praised!'

People danced in the streets, frolicking and laughing.

'Hooray for Lord Frederick!'

'Hooray for the Princess!'

'You haven't seen him?' asked Governor Mortensen.

'No. We fought in the ranges as instructed, and he was not with us.'

'We do not question Lord Raegan's actions,' said Mortensen.

'I lost many men, and the girl escaped. He said she would die in the city.'

'We will speak of this no more,' said Mortensen. 'We await Lord Raegan's return, and we will carry out his orders, whatever they may be.'

Approaching the Great Forest, Dane, Vanessa and Will caught sight of the city for the first time, rising in the distance ahead.

'Look!' said Dane.

Vanessa beamed back at him.

'There were many times I thought I'd never see it again,' she replied.

Apart from her tattered clothes, Dane saw little indicating what she'd been through. The fullness of her energy and vitality had returned, her demeanor and the way she conducted herself restored. If anything, he thought she now had an even deeper sense of appreciation for everything and everyone around her.

'We weren't going to come back without you,' said Dane.

'Absolutely,' said Will. 'And once they see us, you can be sure the whole city will want to come out to welcome you.'

'I'm sure there's a particular maid who will be more interested to see you,' said Vanessa.

Will blushed.

Dane and Vanessa smiled to each other at his apparent discomfort.

Riding up to them, Lord Frederick said, 'I will go ahead and make sure the proper steps are taken for your arrival. The Great Forest will be manned with patrols to escort you the rest of the way.'

'Very well,' said Vanessa, her mind soaring with the anticipation of finally being within the city walls again.

'It won't be long now,' said Dane.

Approaching the main gatehouse, Dane, Vanessa and Will could already hear the sounds on the other side of the walls.

Handing over the papers, Hindmarsh announced their arrival. With knowing smiles, the guards moved aside, allowing the gate to open and the party to enter.

A deafening roar greeted them; the noise louder than any they'd ever heard. Emerging into the city proper, they were met by a sea of smiling faces, several rows deep, on both side of the road. Cheering, clapping, yelling uncontrollably; the crowd surged forward, all eager for a glance of Vanessa. The knights stationed along the road struggled to keep the crowd back.

'Princess!' people yelled. 'Princess! Here! Over here!'

Flanked by Dane and Will, Vanessa waved excitedly; just as happy to see all of them.

The crowd pushed closer.

Hindmarsh whistled.

Fanning out to help the other knights, the regiment started gently easing the crowd to the sides of the road.

Dane kept a watchful eye on everything around him. It was a momentous occasion, and he understood the people wanted to express their joy to Vanessa; celebrate with her, letting her know how much they adored her.

Despite that, it was occasions such as these ...

He saw it an instant before it happened.

Unseen by everyone in the mass of the crowd, four men broke through the cover of the guards; two from each side of the road; ducking under horses, running straight towards them.

At first they looked to be ordinary men, dressed in common street clothes, although the hoods hanging low over their faces were not quite normal. As Dane caught a better view of them, he saw traces of armour under their clothes – black armour, and under the hoods he saw their faces were black.

This was no common threat – *Black Knights!*

Reacting in an instant, a knife-sizzled side-arm from his gauntlet, he struck one in the throat dropping him in the middle of the road, where his body disappeared.

To his right, Will and Hindmarsh took care of two more.

The last one lunged towards Vanessa.

Turning Thunder hard, Dane slammed into Vanessa's horse; the force jolting her sideways; turning her away from the attack.

Leaping from his saddle in the next moment; knocking the Black Knight to the ground and stabbing him with his spare knife, Dane ended the threat then and there.

Stunned for a moment; unsure what had happened, Vanessa continued waving to the crowd as she watched Dane climb back into his saddle.

'What are you doing?' she asked. 'What happened?'

Dane, Will and Hindmarsh closed tightly around her.

'Four Black Knights just tried to kill you!' Dane said under his breath.

Vanessa's eyes widened with shock.

'Inside the city?'

'Inside the city,' said Dane.

'But how?'

'Something we'll have to work out later.'

'But that means ...'

'I know what it means,' said Dane. 'We have traitors inside the city.'

Vanessa gasped.

'Not many saw it,' said Dane. 'Keep waving. Act like nothing happened.'

With an uncertain look on her face, Vanessa did as she was told.

'*Commander!*' Dane hissed. '*We have to get to the castle!*'

'We're almost there,' said Hindmarsh. 'Stay tight, and keep your eyes peeled.'

Wending their way to the castle, willing the time it took to get there to speed up, Dane kept a hand on his sword the entire way.

Finally, the castle gatehouse stood before them.

Entering the main courtyard, a full honour guard awaited them.

The King, Queen, Lord Frederick, Marilena, Harold Salsbury, Patrice Whiltshire, Medhurst, Fairbrother, Lindstrom, General

Silvers, and the entire castle staff were there; flanked by Royal Knights.

Dismounting and handing Thunder to a guard, Dane held out his hand, helping Vanessa out of her saddle.

Will, Hindmarsh and the rest of the regiment dismounted.

Lord Frederick nodded to Hindmarsh, who spoke briefly to Dane and Will. Leading Vanessa forward, with Will behind them; Dane approached the King.

'Sire. I am Royal Knight Dane Thorburn. Together with Royal Knight Will Hevenshire, I present your daughter, Princess Vanessa Meriwether.'

To either side of Vanessa, Dane and Will went down on one knee. Glancing at those in front of him, Dane saw the smiling faces of the councillors and staff; the tears of joy running down the cheeks of Marilena and the Queen; the stoic pride of Lord Frederick and General Silvers, and the look of extreme gratitude on the face of the King.

Vanessa curtsied; a wide smile breaking on her face, tears in her eyes.

'Father,' she said.

Stepping forward, the King took his daughter's hands in his.

'*Vanessa*,' he said, his voice breaking, wrapping her in a hug. '*Welcome home!*'

ACKNOWLEDGEMENTS

First and foremost, I owe everything to Caroline for all her love, support and encouragement. Lots of love and thanks to Melissa and Michael for believing in me and supporting me over the evolution of the story.

Thanks to Kit and her team at MAA for helping me improve the story and giving me the confidence to keep going. Thank you to William and the team at Inspiring Publishers for bringing the book to life.

Finally, a big thank you to my readers and everyone who has given me an encouraging word along the way. Without you, none of this would have been possible.

To find out more about Matt and his books visit his website: www.mattgalanos.com